Second Week In November

An Amelia Bay Mystery

Kathleen Joyce

Don't wait until next September to pick up a copy of this book. It is a great read anytime of the year. *First of September* is the first installment of the Clare Harrigan Cozy Mystery Series. Clare Harrigan is thrilled when her childhood friend, Addie Halls moves back to Amelia Bay. When Addie dies in what the police are calling an accident, Clare knows it's up to her to step in and find out what happened to her friend. What she finds are more secrets than she bargained for and it leaves her wondering if she ever really knew Addie as well as she thought she did.

A Cozy Experience: Online Cozy Mystery Book Club

Cynthia Hilston, Author, Goodreads Reviewer
Lorna versus Laura and Hannah's Rainbow: Every Color Beautiful
You know that cozy feeling of holding a warm beverage, wrapped in a blanket, and curling up with a good book by the fire? That's Kathleen Joyce's cozy mystery…with a murder or two in the mix. This cozy mystery puts you right in the heart of beautiful Northwest America. The characters are charming and come to life off the page. The writing is superb and draws the reader in. The description of the place and the food make me wish I was there. The story will keep you guessing whodunnit.

Kelly Griffiths, Author, Award Winning Short Story Writer
Trespass
Kathleen Joyce has truly perfected the cozy style: an enchanting world where even trouble, adventure, and mystery are glazed with gentleness and warmth. Kathleen's command of character and setting leaves me smiling and wanting more and more of the world she creates.

B. Lee Wilson, Writer/Anthropologist
Congress Whispers, Reservation Nations Endure
I so enjoyed Kathleen Joyce's new murder mystery, *First of September*. It transported me into a circle of longtime friends as their lives rolled with the gentle breezes, and threatening storms, of shared childhood memories. Her detailed descriptions of multi-faceted characters drew me into this story of one dynamic woman's search for justice.

Mary Halverson Schofield, Author
River of Champions and Henry Boucha: Star of the North
A perfect cozy mystery to get lost in anywhere, anytime... The setting in the Pacific Northwest is brought beautifully into focus by the author, and is almost a character in the book. The author weaves in a wonderful set of folks with which to paint her story. You can't help but rooting for Clare as she navigates through her own life, and the murder she knows has been committed. Twists and turns, of course, which make it fun, mysterious and a marvelously good read.

Five Star Reviews from Readers on Amazon

I loved this book and can't wait for the next!
I enjoyed every bit of getting to know Clare and her girlfriends. They remind me so much of my own group of best girlfriends. The picture painted of the Pacific Northwest was immersive and I could picture and get the feeling of life in Amelia Bay. I want to go eat in the pub and take a walk through town!

First time reading this author. Can't wait till next book. For a girl from OH she knows a lot about Amelia Bay.

Really enjoyed this book filled with charming and real characters. The story and mystery is a great read. I look forward to reading more (hint hint) and going back into this town and living among the characters.

If you love cozy mysteries with wit, charm and well-developed entertaining characters, then this is an immensely enjoyable read. It kept me in suspense until the end and I look forward to more from this talented author!

I thought the novel was great. It held my interest right up until the end. Normally pretty good at solving mysteries, I missed the mark initially on this one. It was easy to picture Amelia Bay due to the detailed descriptions. Felt like I was there. Definitely a good read.

I really enjoyed this book. I couldn't put it down. The friendship that these ladies had reminds me of my girlfriends and I could connect easily with the characters. I highly recommend this book. You won't be disappointed.

Do yourself a favor...slow down, take an afternoon to curl up and read 1st of September!! You will have given yourself a special treat!

I am totally enjoying this mystery and look forward to the continuing series. Thank you, Miss Joyce, I love it.

A nice cozy mystery. The author's description of food in the story will leave your mouth watering and the mystery will leave you guessing right up to the very enjoyable,

Peach Tree Mysteries

This is a work of fiction. The characters and happenings in this book are fictitious. Any similarity to incidents or real persons, living or dead, is coincidental.

The town of Amelia Bay is fictitious and was created in the author's imagination.

Second Week in November

First Edition April 2018

Follow Clare Harrigan Mysteries on Facebook
Kathleen Joyce, Author, Clare Harrigan Mysteries

Other titles by this author

First of September

For my husband, Bob, he has
supported me & my dreams.
Encouraged me.
Loved me.
Thank you isn't enough
but they are words
that come from
deep in my heart
and soul.

Acknowledgements

Sometimes you are blessed with being in the right place at the right time. Such as it was with me when I found my writers' group family. I thank them for the positive and insightful critiques which have served to make me a better writer and have helped me write better books. Betty Wilson, Kelly Griffiths, Cynthia Hilston, Nancy Beach, Alexia Patrick, Paul Pater, Scott Heidrich, John Arnold, Richard Mann, and our fearless leader, Scot Allyn. I will always be grateful for their support.

And special thanks to my dear friends who have read for me, discussed the finer points of syntax, and offered valuable advice, Mary, Cyndi, Wendy, and my daughter, Dawn. Thank you!

To my characters, I put them on the page, breathe life into them, and they create twists and turns that continue to delight and surprise me!

Last, but most importantly, thank you to my readers. I hope this book delights and surprises you too!

Crime Solving Girlfriends

Clare Harrigan
Bev Hawkins
Sophie Quinn
Libby Bailes

Clare's family

Grace and Mike Harrigan (Parents)
Dana & Pete Harrigan (Brother & his wife)
Finn Harrigan (Younger brother)
Hedda Harrigan (Sister)
Stan Parrish (Clare's Ex-Husband)
Mac Parrish (Son)
Carolyn Chadwick (Police Officer & Mac's fiancée)
Emma Parrish (Daughter)
Cole (Finn's son)

Other Characters

Jack Hawkins (Bev's father)
Ollie Moran (Head Chef at the Pub)
Glen Wynter (Author & Friend of Pete)
Eddy (The Handyman)
Henry Bradshaw (Retiring Chief of Police)
Jake Fleming (Acting Chief of Police)
Rocky Rockman (Assistant to chief)
Chris Reed (Police Officer & Carolyn's Partner)
Brenda & Burl Woodman (The Evening Star)
True Bergman (The Evening Star)
Becca & Josiah Bergman (The Evening Star)
Leah Foster (The Evening Star)
John (The man with the gun)
Everest Johansson (Cole's Mother)
Mia Jackson (Cole's Nanny)
Anna Jackson (Mia's mother)
Bee & Brad Sikes in Corte d'Alene

Chapter 1

November 5, 2007

"Clare, take a look at those people. Who are they?" Clare followed her younger brother's curious gaze out the window of their father's pub. Her eyes settled on a small group of people. Five men and one woman. The shaved heads of the men glistened in the sun, and gusts of wind whipped their thin robes and bedraggled beards. Four of them gestured in the direction of Harrigan's Irish Pub. A fifth man stood and glared. The woman shivered as she huddled in the doorway of a coffee shop across the street. She tugged at a white veil that shrouded most of her face.

"Are they some religious cult? She looks like a nun…or what, I don't know. What the hell…" He stretched his lanky frame across the table to get a better look.

"That's exactly what they are. They call themselves The Evening Star, but I've never seen them in Amelia Bay before. There's a compound somewhere along the Hood Canal on the Olympic Peninsula. Look at the backs of their robes. They're embroidered with emblems of the sun and a star. I wonder what it means? They sure as shootin' seem upset about something on this side of the street."

Clare felt a sadness wash over her for the woman. The dampness of winter in the Pacific Northwest cut to the bone. She watched as Bibi, the owner of the coffee shop, opened the door and motioned her to come inside. The woman shook her head and shifted away.

"Hmm." Finn's curiosity satisfied, he moved his gaze to the waitress who brought their lunch to the table. He had the attention span of a teenager viewing a documentary on the territorial habits of the platypus. Clare watched her brother give the waitress a lingering look as she set their lunch plates down. When it came to young and pretty, his attention span significantly increased.

Finn had come home for the holidays. Clare felt something was amiss, but he had not yet fessed up, and told her why he was here for such a long time. Normally he whipped in and out for a few days over the holidays, usually with the latest *femme du jour* in tow. He preferred to spend most of his time in Los Angeles or some exotic locale with the beautiful and glamorous people of Hollywood. Making movies held Finn's attention, and he was dynamic at producing box office hits. Yet here he was, the second week of November, with Thanksgiving a stone's throw away, and Christmas just around the corner. Him being here for about six weeks was…unquestionably odd.

"You're new here, what's your name?" Finn's eyes slid to the waitress' hand—a ring third finger left hand. Finn drew the line at married women. He learned a hard lesson at the tender age of seventeen, when an irate husband came after him intent on doing great bodily harm to Finn's most private and sacred parts. He escaped injury through the intervention of their father and vowed never to cross that particular line again. Finn claimed he didn't know she was married and twenty-five. Clare wasn't so sure, but the dressing down their father gave him kept him on a straight and narrow. He was a man who simply loved women—all women of all shapes, sizes, and age. And they adored his fresh-faced good looks. Their mother's friends had twittered and fluttered around him like a flock of happy birds from the time he was a babe in arms.

The pretty waitress smiled. "Yup, I was hired this morning.

My name's Lynn. Bev Hawkins recommended me. I used to work with her at the Amelia Bay Hotel. Bev's a friend of yours, right? And your father, Mr. Harrigan, owns the pub?" she asked, looking at Clare as she placed their plates on the table. Clare nodded. "Anyway, when I came in to apply this morning Bev's dad hired me on the spot. One of the regular waitresses, Bets I think, was a no show today. My lucky day."

Lynn was a tiny girl with a shining cap of dark hair that framed her face. Large brown eyes peered out from behind the slim rectangular frames of her glasses. The glasses suited her strong square jawline.

"I'll be right back to refill your coffee," Lynn said. "Is there anything else you need?"

"No, just the coffee. Thanks." Clare looked at the expression on Finn's boyish face. "What's the matter, Finn? You look puzzled about something." She cocked her head to one side and stared at him across the scarred table. Their father had kept a few of the original tables and wooden booths in the bar area from earlier days. He said they reminded him of how far he had come.

"It's nothing, Clare. I'm fine." She continued to look at him. He was bothered about something, but thoughts of Finn's discomfort flew out of her mind when the heavy wooden doors to the pub crashed open and slammed against the walls. Lynn screamed and dropped the glass coffee carafe she was carrying. Clare watched it explode into tiny shards of glass and spew out its scalding liquid.

A blast of cold air followed the swirling mass of blue and white robes as the members of The Evening Star filled the pub. The men fanned out through the dining room with the exception of one who stood in the bar area. The woman hesitated, then walked through the door and pressed herself against the wall to the left of the doors. Clare's heart pounded. Every one of the patrons' eyes filled with fear as the scene unfolded before them. The glowing warmth from the old stone fireplace, the murmur of pleasant conversation, the soft laughter, and gentle sounds of people enjoying good food with good friends in a pleasant atmosphere had vanished.

Jack Hawkins placed both hands on the bar and swung himself over. He landed nimbly in front of the solitary man who stood by the bar. Clare marveled at the dexterity he displayed, considering Jack was in his late sixties.

"Let's calm down here, sport. You're disturbing my guests." He pulled himself up to his full height of six feet three inches. Jack towered over the man.

Another robed man stepped behind the first man. He was larger and gave Jack a menacing look. Both men stared at him—defiance burned in their eyes.

"Don't call me *sport*. I am the leader of The Evening Star. We are God's chosen ones. His arm swept toward the dining room. "People who come to a place such as this, a place that serves liquor and caters to sinners, deserve to feel anguish." He turned back and glared into Jack's dark eyes. "They and you should feel shame!" His voice boomed and reverberated off the walls. The other three men began to crisscross the room and scowl at the diners as they wove their way in and out of the tables.

"Okay. *Sir*. I'd like you to leave…right now." Jack sensed real trouble and shot a quick look at Finn and gave him a barely discernable nod. Finn reached in his pocket and pulled out his cell phone. One of the robed men stepped up to the table and glowered at Finn.

"That is a tool of the devil." His voice quivered as he stared at Finn's phone.

"Look pal, if you don't want to deal with the cops, I suggest you take your band of merry men and leave this establishment." Finn stood up and slid his phone over to Clare without taking his eyes off the man. "Clare, call the police while I help Jack escort these gentlemen outside."

The man in front of Jack spoke in a threatening tone. "I want my daughter. I want her out of this Satin's den." His voice started low and swelled. "Elizabeth, come out here right now! You're coming home with us."

Jack responded, "There's no one working here by the name of Elizabeth."

The spokesman of the group turned with terrifying fierceness to the woman who had come in with them. She pushed herself further back against the wall, as if wishing she could squeeze through the cracks in the paneling and disappear. "Wife, you told me this was the place," he said, as he strode over to her. The blur of blue-robed men stopped their circling of the room and stared at their leader.

The frightened woman's hands involuntarily reached up to shield her face.

"Bets, she goes by the name Bets." She looked down—fearful to meet the man's eyes. Clare could hear a tremor in her voice, then she noticed an ugly bruise on the woman's cheek when her veil slipped back.

Clare's fingers flubbed the numbers for the police station three times, before getting it right. It was a number she knew by heart, because of the terrible murders she had been involved with only two months ago. She realized too late she should have dialed 911.

"Please, please send someone to Harrigan's Pub on Main Street," she said. "We have a disturbance here and need some help. *Hurry. Please.*" She listened for a moment. "Harrigan, Clare Harrigan," she told the woman whose voice she didn't recognize. "My father owns the pub. Yes, on Main Street. Thank you." She placed Finn's phone on the table, she was mystified because she knew everyone who worked at the station, but the woman she spoke to didn't know her either.

Chef Ollie Moran came out of the kitchen clutching a billy club, one of a couple leftover from days gone by when the pub had been a raucous place. Finn held up his hand to stop him at the door. Ollie nodded and stepped back into the kitchen. Clare hoped he was not going back to the storeroom where her father kept a gun.

"Bets didn't show up for work today. I have no idea where she is. Now I'm asking you again to leave. The police are on their way," Jack said, as the man turned away from his wife and walked back to him. Finn edged over to Jack and stood next to him. The men of The Evening Star fell in line behind their leader.

"I have no fear of police," he said in a booming voice. "The Lord is the only One. His judgement you should fear." He poked his finger close to Jack's chest, but was wise enough not to touch him. "I am on His side. I do His work."

"Y'all don't have no need to fear the police, sir. Less maybe you broke some law here about." Chief Bradshaw maneuvered his considerable bulk through the door with several uniformed officers behind him. "Let's just step on outside and let these nice people finish their lunch."

The policemen moved in behind the group, and tried to guide them to the doors. They stood firm until, with a final penetrating look around the room, their leader began to move toward the door. With a rough shake, he pulled away from the guiding hand the chief had placed on his back. Clare could feel the tension drop as the doors closed behind them.

"Folks, I'm real sorry for what just happened here. Everyone's lunch is on the house. I'll get the staff out here to refill your drinks and bring you some fresh, hot food," Jack stepped behind the bar and flipped a switch on the stereo. The melodious strains of Kenny G filled the room and people visibly relaxed. Chatter slowly resumed as the diners started to discuss what they had witnessed. Clare stooped down to pick up the glass fragments on the floor and Finn grabbed a towel from behind the bar to soak up the coffee mess. Eddy, the handyman and all round good guy, walked out of the kitchen with a broom and mop. Clare felt protective of him. He smiled and shooed her away. He was back to his old self after the brush with death the poor man suffered a couple of months ago. It could have been her or her friend, Bev, in the car that night, and they might not have been as lucky.

"Jack, where's Bets?" Clare asked as she walked up to him and Finn with a napkin full of bits of glass.

Jack didn't answer her, but instead bent over in front of Lynn. When he straightened up, he said, "There's a bathroom off the office, Lynn. You'll need to go to the clinic to make sure there's no pieces of glass imbedded in your legs. I don't see any, and the cuts don't look too deep, but the burns need attention."

Clare looked down and saw blood on Lynn's legs where shards of glass had sliced her skin when the carafe shattered. Nasty blisters were already beginning to form from the hot coffee.

Jack walked her back to the kitchen and called to Ollie to soak some towels in cold water and wrap them around Lynn's legs, being careful to check for bits of glass.

Bets had been working at the pub since last summer. Clare knew her to be a sweet, attractive young woman who was taking a break between finishing her master's degree and starting her doctorate. Clare pictured her innocent face with its sprinkling of freckles framed by a soft cloud of strawberry-blond hair. She worked hard and charmed everyone she met. Clare had served with her a few times whenever extra help was needed at the pub.

Jack raised his eyebrows at Finn, as he took the napkin from Clare's hand and tossed it into the trash can next to the bar. Finn responded with a shrug and said, "Come on, Clare, let's finish our lunch." Clare looked back and forth between them, then turned to walk over to the table when Chief Bradshaw came back through the door. He was followed by an attractive man Clare didn't recognize.

"They're gone, Jack. Least for now anyways," Chief Bradshaw said. "What's the story with the girl he was lookin' for?"

Jack explained about Bets not showing up for work, and how long she had worked at the pub—about four or five months.

"Where does she live, Jack?"

"Down by the marina in one of those new apartments. I'll check in the office for whatever information we have for her. I didn't want to tell them where she lived. I'm pretty surprised, Bets never mentioned family to me. But I guess now that I've seen the family…I understand why."

"Okay, I'll have my people check out her place. Make sure she's okay. Let me introduce you to this fella first. This here's the man who is takin' my place when I retire at the end of the year. All the final papers aren't finished yet, but I don't see no problems with this fine fella." The chief stepped back and put his arm around the shoulder of the man standing next to him. "Meet Jake Fleming, the Acting Chief of Police of Amelia Bay. Hell, I've got so much vacation time built up, I'm headin' outta here tomorrow and won't be back till my retirement party after Christmas.

Clare stood listening for a moment to the good ole Texas boy, who had been a member of the Amelia Bay Police Department for decades. She checked to make sure Eddy had the clean-up under control and didn't need any help before she sat down. She shifted her gaze to Jake Fleming.

"Close your mouth, Clare. Remember Mom always tells us it's rude to stare." Finn followed her to the booth and signaled for a waitress to bring fresh coffee. "He's a great looking guy." He paused and looked the man over. "Rugged, not too good looking or smooth. Yeah, he looks like someone central casting would send over. A little short, though, wouldn't you say?"

"He is *not* too short. He's normal. Not everyone has to be a giant like you and the rest of the family, Finn." Why did she feel defensive of this guy?

"Those all-American good looks—clean-cut. He looks athletic too. Probably just about the right size for you, little one."

Clare had always been patted-on-the-head by the rest the family because she had to stretch to reach five-feet-two inches. She wasn't the youngest in the family, but her sister and two brothers treated her that way. Clare took after their Irish father, Mike Harrigan. She had his loopy auburn curls and emerald green eyes, while the others had inherited the long legs and blond hair of their Scandinavian mother, Grace. Their mother's fair, creamy skin was a gift they were all blessed with.

"Don't be silly. I'm surprised, that's all. I heard the new chief was single. I never expected him to be so young. I thought he'd look more like Bradshaw," Clare said, taking a bite of her grilled cheese sandwich. Jake Fleming had caught her stare and smiled. She nodded and smiled back as best she could with a mouthful of food.

"Bradshaw's been here around twenty-plus years. Maybe he looked like…" They looked at each other and laughed. "Uh…no." The retiring chief looked like an ex-prizefighter who stayed too long in the ring, opened a bakery, ate all his mistakes and then some.

"Single, you say? Hell, if I wasn't straight, I'd fall for him myself. Of course, maybe he's looking but not for a woman."

"Finn, the man is an officer of the law, *and* divorced. I believe, I also heard he had a son," Clare said, with a slight edge to her voice.

"Clare, you lead a sheltered life. Most of the guys in LA who look like him are gay. Some of them have even been married, hell…are still married *and* have kids."

"Well, this isn't LA, and the people here are not actors you hire for your movies." She had just taken another bite of her sandwich when Chief Bradshaw approached their table with Jake Fleming.

"This here young lady is somebody you gotta watch out for, Jake. She's been known to go meddlin' in police work." Bradshaw chuckled. "Clare, Finn, I'd like you to meet Jake Fleming. He's the Acting Chief of Police of Amelia Bay. But if all goes well, this fine man will take over my job. Can't think of a reason why not." Both men stood next to the table looking down at Clare as she chewed and tried to swallow her sandwich. She took a quick sip of coffee and swallowed as gracefully as possible—gracefulness never being her strong suit.

"I did not *meddle* in your case, Chief. I first had to convince you that you even had a case, or a murder would have gone unsolved." Clare wiped her hands on her napkin and reached out to shake Jake Fleming's hand as Chief Bradshaw cleared his throat and sputtered a bit. "Clare Harrigan, and this is my brother Finn Harrigan. It's nice to put a face to a name. The town's been buzzing about you. I understand you're from Portland." A fleeting look flashed across his face. Pain or something else? It was gone in an instant, and replaced by a smile.

"Yep. I retired last January after twenty years on the force down there, but you can only do so much fishing," Jake said. "I guess news sure travels fast around here."

"That's the way all small towns are."

"The fishing here's great, and it's usually a quiet town. Too quiet for my taste," Finn said.

"Their daddy owns this here place." The chief jumped into the conversation. "Won it in a poker game back in the fifties. Isn't that right, Finn?"

"Yes, sir, that's a true story. Of course, it's changed and expanded considerably over the years. Please, join us." Finn motioned to the empty seats next to himself and Clare.

"Nah, but thanks anyway. We promised those strange folks we'd try to track down that young lady. Make sure she's okay."

Clare noticed Finn looked down and become very interested in his sandwich.

"Who were those people, Chief?"

"The old fella says he's her daddy. The Woodman guy. The younger one who was standin' behind him claims to be her fiancé."

Finn's head snapped up. "Fiancé?" Clare looked at him. He dropped his eyes back down and picked up his sandwich.

"Yep. The lady I'm assumin' is her mama."

"What about the others? They tried to frighten the people here in the dining room by rushing around the tables and glaring at everyone. They sure made me nervous."

"One of the fellas said his name was Elder Josiah Bergman. His son, True Bergman, was the one who claimed to be the betrothed."

"Did you see the bruise on the woman's cheek, Chief? She was very meek, like a woman whose husband is violent. He didn't even call her by name, just *wife*. Maybe Bets doesn't want to be found. Not by them anyway. Bets isn't a child. She's old enough to legally down a beer, cast a vote, and make her own choices in life."

"I don't go lookin' for problems, Clare. Plenty seem to find their way to me without my searchin' for 'em." There was a finality in his voice. "If y'all hear from Bets, tell her to give me a call. We'll see you folks later."

"It was great to meet you both," Jake said. "Hope to see you again…soon." His eyes lingered on Clare for a moment, then he turned to follow the chief. They stopped by the bar on the way out, and Jack handed the chief a card with what must have been the information about Bets.

Clare waited until they were out of earshot then turned to Finn who had finished his sandwich. "I'm sensing something a little off kilter here, Finn. Each time Bets' name is mentioned you pull your head in like a turtle. What's going on?"

"Nothing. Leave it alone. I've got to go home and help Mom get some boxes out of the barn. The chief's right, you just go looking for trouble." He stood and tossed his napkin on the table. "Will I see you later at the farm?"

Clare held him there with her eyes for a moment, then said, "Not tonight. I'm going home. I plan to curl up with a good book next to a cozy fire."

He turned and collided with Bev Hawkins in his rush to get away from Clare and her questions. "Sorry, Bev." And he was gone.

***

"What was that all about? Finn's usually so mellow."

"I don't know. He isn't confiding in me, but he's been acting very un-Finn-like since he got here."

"I'll grab some fresh coffee. You can tell me all about it and the bruhaha with the police cars out front." Bev gathered the plates on the table and took them to the kitchen. Clare watched the male diners, seated around the room, steal quick glances at Bev. She had a body women envied and men lusted after. Her tousled white-blond hair, luminous brown eyes and Marilyn Monroe looks turned heads wherever she went. Bev's father, Jack, managed the pub. Clare didn't know life without Bev any more than she knew life without her family. The women had been buddies from the playpen days. Today Bev was dressed in a fringed western jacket, jeans, and white ruffled blouse. Clare looked down at her own slim denim skirt and yellow turtleneck sweater. At least today she didn't have any clay stains on her clothing from her passion and livelihood—pottery. Always a plus, she thought.

Clare looked up and noticed a man sitting at the far end of the bar while she waited for Bev to come back. He didn't look like a tourist, and she couldn't recall seeing him around town. He stood and pushed a few bills across the bar top, then headed out the door. His overdeveloped muscles strained the fabric of his jacket, and there was a conspicuous bulge tucked in the back of his waistband.

Clare slid out of the booth and walked over to Jack. "Who was the guy at the end of the bar? I noticed he might have a gun tucked in the waistband of his pants?"

"Yeah, I noticed. Says his name's John. Been coming in for the last several days. Told me he was from Portland—born and raised. Lived there his whole life and was considering a move here for work. But that dog don't hunt with me."

"Why?"

"I saw him get out of his car the first day he came in here. It's a rental. Okay. So maybe he didn't want to drive his own car. Whatever. But when I asked him one day if he wanted another drink, he told me two was his limit, but he wouldn't say no to a cup of coffee…regular."

Clare gave him a quizzical look. "I don't understand, Jack. What did he mean by that?"

"My experience is folks who order coffee regular are from New York. It means with cream and sugar. I picked up some trace accents in his speech too. I looked in the window of his car after that. Saw a packet from a car rental agency at SeaTac."

"Interesting. You don't drive up from Portland to the airport to rent a car and leave yours there."

"I respect people's privacy, Clare, but when someone packing a gun lies to me..." Jack shrugged. "I want to protect the folks I care about and our town. Besides, cop is written all over him. He's got a limp. Maybe he's private. I don't know. I'm keeping an eye on him."

"Thanks, Jack. We'll both keep an eye on him." Clare turned and saw Bev carrying a tray with a carafe of coffee, a pitcher of milk and cups. Clare and all of her friends had worked as waitresses in the pub over the years, and knew their way around. She walked over to the booth.

"Okay. Tell me what went on today." She placed the tray on the table and unloaded the coffee paraphernalia, along with a platter piled with the apple-cinnamon donuts Ollie always made in the fall.

Clare glanced at the three cups, "Who's joining us?"

"Libby'll be here in a few minutes. I saw her earlier. She's finishing her errands."

As if on cue, Libby breezed through the door. Her golden-brown hair brushed the shoulders of her navy-blue blazer with matching wool skirt. A simple gold cross hung down the front of her white turtleneck sweater. The picture of the perfect wife and mother. *And* a true and loyal friend.

"Hey, what's up with the police cars that were parked out front? It's a little early in the day for someone to be snockered and creating a ruckus." She walked up to the booth and placed her purse on the bench seat.

"Clare is just about to tell us. Sit." Bev filled their mugs with steamy coffee. The aroma floated around the table and the spicy scent of cinnamon tempted each of them to pick up a donut.

"Hmm... I wish Ollie would make these all year long." Clare explained the scene that transpired with The Evening Star group and the bruise on the woman's face. "I really don't know anything about them, but Finn certainly acted strange at the mention of Bets' name and, when your friend, Lynn, mentioned she was a no-show today, Bev. Well..."

"Odd. I saw Lynn in the back with bandages on her legs. My dad is taking her to clinic to check her out." Bev stirred milk and sugar into her coffee, blew on the golden brew before taking a sip and a bite of her donut. "Bets is a cutie pie. Isn't she taking some time off before going back to school for her doctorate degree? I am sure she'll turn up."

"Yep. She looks like she's sixteen, not twenty-six, and I think my little brother may be involved with her," Clare said. "I also think he expected to see her here today, *and* he didn't like it when I asked about her."

"Hmm…? I wonder what his deal is, and didn't we decide it wasn't that she looked so young, but that we were just getting older?"

"Forty-six is the new thirty, or so I've heard, *and* choose to believe," Clare said.

"Why is Finn staying here so long? Usually he's here and gone in a few days."

"He claims all his projects are wrapped up and nothing new is in the works until after the first of the year. I'm not sure I buy it."

Libby, who had been quiet, spoke up. "I know a little about The Evening Star. Last summer Tom and I took our boys up to Sophie's house for a week of crabbing, fishing and relaxing."

Libby and Tom had five boys—three when Clare, Bev, and another dear friend, Gina Vitale, had their children—then she popped two more out years later. Now she referred to them as her big guys and little guys. Career-driven journalist Sophie Quinn, the fifth friend of their group, had remained unmarried and childless.

"Sophie and I saw some of them when we were shopping in Port Angeles. She explained she wanted to write a series of articles on various cults. The Evening Star would be one of the cults she planned to profile. She also told me she met a woman who left the group, and according to Sophie, the woman barely escaped with her life." Libby shivered at the inconceivable thought. Her husband and boys adored her. The very idea a woman was not cherished frightened her, although she knew this was not the case for many women. Clare and Bev understood husbands, make that ex-husbands—one for Clare and two for Bev—who didn't seem to have a problem hurting their wives. In Clare's case, it was emotional, and in Bev's case, it was physical abuse.

"They base their religion on astrology and Mayan beliefs. Something about a Feather Serpent and a bunch of mumbo jumbo I didn't grasp. You'll have to ask Sophie when she gets back from New York later this week. She isn't traveling again until after the first of the year, so we'll see a lot of her."

"Okay, enough about that. Tell me, Clare, who was that handsome guy with Chief Bradshaw?" Bev asked, with a gleam in her eye.

"The new Chief of Police, Jake Fleming. Well, Acting Chief of Police for now." Clare smiled.

Jack came over and tapped Bev on the shoulder. "Could you cover for me while I take Lynn to the clinic?"

"Duty calls." Bev stood up and leaned over the table. "Hmm…is our little Clare smitten?"

"I don't know about that, but just looking at him seems like an extravagant indulgence for the senses. Definitely eye candy."

Chapter 2

Clare paused at the edge of her driveway and gazed at the charming cottage her Irish grandmother left to her when she died. It had been originally built by an English ship captain. Clare's father and his brother, Pug, purchased the cottage from the captain when they brought their mother over from Ireland. A year after her divorce from Stan Parrish, Clare moved from a big house where they had raised their family, and where she caught Stan with a much younger woman— much, much younger woman. She gave the big house to her son, Mac, and his future bride, Caroline Chadwick, as a wedding gift. The wedding was planned for the middle of December. They would have a couple of weeks for a honeymoon and still have time to settle into their new life. Mac would be on Christmas break from his final year of law school. Caroline, an officer with the Amelia Bay police force, had saved her vacation. Clare wasn't sure what she would give her younger two, Emma and Sean, when they married. A house was a tough act to follow. She hoped Stan would pitch in and help. In a moment of *Thank-God-I'm-Alive* she had attached Stan's name to the gift. Even though the house was part of her divorce settlement, he had, after all, saved her life just a week before she presented the house to the soon-to-be-newlyweds.

The antique glass window panes of the cottage twinkled in the late afternoon light and beckoned Clare into the warm, welcoming interior. She loved coming home now. At times, she felt her grandmother's presence, usually in the kitchen and sometimes in the walkout basement where her pottery studio was located. She adored the tiny woman who could sing like an angel and taught Clare and her sister, Hedda, along with their two brothers, Finn and Pete, to dance the jig. So many beautiful memories filled the cottage, and Clare hoped to add even more.

Clare drove around the back and was surprised to see her brother Pete's little red sports car parked on the grass next to the garage. Finn slumped in one of the lawn chairs and stared out toward the bay. He jumped up when he heard her drive in and crossed the distance in three long strides. He glanced through the window and said, "Let me help you with those bags."

"What are you doing here, and where's your car?" He looked vulnerable standing there, his soft blond curls flopped on his forehead, like a little boy who had been caught holding a baseball glove, while the ball rested inside the house in a pile of broken glass.

"I guess I need to talk to someone. Pete's out of town, and I can't burden Mom and Dad with this. I know you've been through a lot lately, but...what the hell…I don't know where to turn. I need to talk to someone I can trust."

"I'm always here for you, Finn, and you can always count on me." Clare looked at him with a gentle smile. "Let's get this stuff inside. I have plenty for both of us. I never know who might drop in, and here you are! Plus, I'm starved. We can talk and fix dinner."

Finn stopped on the steps leading up to the deck and pushed hard on a loose stair tread with his foot. "Clare, you have to replace this step." They carried her groceries into the house and set them on the counter. Maggie, Clare's golden retriever, did a few pirouettes around the kitchen, then darted outside. Maggie had been dropped off at her parents' house when she was a young pup. Clare instantly fell in love with the skinny, hungry, mud-covered ball of fur. It was mutual.

"I know. The whole deck needs a redo. I'll asked Eddy to have a look at it. I was hoping to wait until spring, but with all the people coming in and out during the wedding, I should have it reinforced in places. I can replace the entire deck later." Clare sighed. "It's always something when you own a house. Will you get the grill going? Watch out for the railing on the side—it's wobbly too. I'll put the groceries away and start dinner."

Clare set the table, popped the potatoes into the oven, and mixed a marinate for the steaks. She was tossing the salad when Finn and Maggie came inside. She reached in the refrigerator and pulled out a bowl filled with the stew she made every other day for her pampered pooch, then heated it in the microwave to take the chill off before filling Maggie's bowl.

Finn rubbed his hands together. "Man, it's getting chilly out there."

"Pour a couple of glasses of wine, and we'll sit in the living room by the fire. We have some time before we have to put the steaks on." She handed him a tray loaded with some munchies. "I picked up some cheese and smoked salmon when I was at Pike Place Market last week. I do love going to Seattle but love coming back to Amelia Bay even more."

Finn took the tray and asked, "You already have a fire going too? You're a whirlwind."

"No. I laid it this morning. The matches are in the little box on the side table. I'll be right in after I put the salad in the frig to chill then, I'll zip upstairs and change clothes."

After Clare changed into a comfy pair of grey sweats and a soft yellow tee shirt. She found Finn pacing the living room when she came back downstairs. He paused to study some the books on her shelves.

"There are so many good books that I'd like to make into movies." He picked up a spy novel and leafed through it. "This author, Wynter, lives around here I think."

Clare shrugged and plunked down on one of the club chairs next to the fireplace. She reached over to the tray and piled two crackers with cheese and smoked salmon. She handed one to Finn, then leaned back in a comfy club chair with her legs tucked underneath her.

"Okay Finn, what's going on?" she asked, taking a bite of the delicious mixture on the buttery cracker.

His eyes darted away from her steady gaze. He sat down. "I don't know where to start."

"Start with today—with Bets."

His body went tense, but he tried to appear casual and relaxed—his arms rested on his thighs as he twirled his glass between his palms. With a sigh, he began. "I've been dating her, Bets that is, since I got back here. She's not like the other women I date. She's smart, for one thing, and funny. The women I'm usually with only care about their looks, and what I can do to further their acting careers. But I never, never take advantage of that. If a woman wants a part in one of my movies, she reads for it. If the talent is there, and she has the right look for the part, I give her the job. I'm not like the lousy crumbs in Hollywood that force women to have sex to get a part." He shrugged. "What the hell...I was raised better than that, but if they flirt with me… Hey, you know me, I do love women.

"Finn, you are shallow."

"You're right," he said with a boyish grin. "But at least I have enough depth to know I'm shallow." He got serious. "Grace and Mike raised all of us to respect people until they give a reason not to."

"Most women would find you attractive even if you weren't a big-time Hollywood producer. Mom's friends flitter around you like hummingbirds at a honeysuckle vine."

Finn smiled. "I do enjoy the company of those ladies."

"Let's move this story along. So far you haven't told me much of anything I haven't already figured out."

"What the hell… Bets spent most of the night with me last night. I heard her phone ring. I remember glancing at the clock, and it was around two thirty. I drifted back to sleep after we had a brief conversation, and I told her I'd see her at the pub. You know I'm a heavy sleeper. I didn't hear a thing after that." He finished his wine and poured another glass.

Clare waited. She knew there was much more to come. So far she didn't see anything wrong with what he told her.

"After I left you at the pub, I went up to the farm and helped Mom get her fall decorations out of the barn, then I drove over to Bets' apartment." He paused and sighed. "There was crime scene tape all around and cop cars everywhere."

"Oh my God, is she…?"

"I don't know. I spotted Caroline and asked what was going on. She said the chief had asked her and her partner, Chris, to check on the woman who lived in the apartment. They found blood leading from the parking lot to Bets' door. When no one answered the door, they assumed a crime had been committed." Finn took a gulp of his wine and grimaced. "Then that prickly bastard, Chris, came up and started asking me what I wanted to know for and why I was there. That kind of thing. Questions I didn't know how to answer. Then he told me to move along if I didn't have any business there."

"Chris is a nice guy. But he's all cop." Clare loved that about him *and* the way he looked after his partner—her future daughter-in-law. Not that Caroline could not take care of herself, she had attained her black belt in karate at the age of sixteen, and often taught the Marines at the Bangor Naval Submarine Base whenever their sensei was out of town. Clare hoped Caroline would quit the force once she and Mac were ready to start a family, and he finished law school. She was a big advocate of stay-at-home moms. Not very modern thinking by some folks' standards, but she maintained her beliefs. Although she did know a couple of stay-at-home-dads who were doing a great job raising their kids.

"I'm scared, Clare. Really scared something bad has happened to Bets, and I'll never get to see her again. Scared the cops will look at me if she's...you know…uh…hurt or…worse." He downed his wine and poured another glass.

"Slow down on the wine, partner."

"I've been staying at Pete's house while he and Dana are in Europe. My prints are all over Bets' place, and her prints are all over Pete's house. Clare, I really like her. What should I do?"

"Maybe, just maybe, you're not as shallow as I thought, Finn." Clare set her glass down and stood. She walked around the coffee table and perched on the edge of it in front of him. She reached for his hands. "Right now you are going to grill two magnificent steaks, and we'll eat a lovely dinner. Tomorrow morning I'll go with you to the station, and you can tell Chief Bradshaw you were dating her, and the last time you saw her was early this morning. It's much better if you fess up on your own."

Finn shook his head. “I don’t know, Clare.”

“Finn, this isn’t Hollywood. It’s not some movie script you’re working on. This is real life.” She stared into his eyes and in an attempt to calm him. “Come on, I’m starving. “She pulled him to his feet. “Everything will work out.”

“Yeah, like the blood you found a couple months ago?”

Clare flinched. “That was different. Now go put the steaks on the grill. Bets will show up in the morning with a perfectly good explanation of what happened.” She hoped she sounded more confident than she felt. Clare opened a small gateleg table and brought two chairs in from the dining room so they could eat by the fire in the cozy living room.

Over dinner, Clare asked Finn if he had known about Bets’ family and told him what Libby said about their religious cult.

“I don’t think she ever talked about her family. Just about her degrees and that she went to college in Oregon. She was taking a break to save some money so she didn’t have to work too much while writing the dissertation for her doctorate. She told me she had worked fulltime while getting her undergrad and masters. I guess there were some small scholarships along the way but definitely not a free ride.”

“What’s her field of study?” she asked, as she poured coffee for them both.

“Education. I questioned her a little, but she was…I guess private would be the word to describe her. Now I understand why.”

The ring of the phone interrupted their conversation. Clare let the machine answer it, but when she heard their mother’s voice, she picked up.

“Mom, I’m here.” Clare listened for a minute. “Finn’s here with me.” She stood stock still for a moment then said with a calmness in her voice she didn’t feel, “We’ll meet you at the clinic.”

Finn froze and stared at Clare.

“Dad hurt his leg helping Mom put up her decorations. He fell off the ladder. The EMTs think it might be broken.”

“That crazy old man. What the hell...”

***

Clare and Finn arrived at the clinic just as the ambulance pulled away from the doors. Their mother, Grace, pulled into the parking spot next to them, and they walked in together. Grace was normally like a willow—tall and slender with shining, silver-gray hair. Tonight, it was pinned up in a loose french twist with wisps of curls that floated around her face and tickled the back of her neck. An anxious look on Grace's normally serene face frightened Clare. Her mind went back to the night her father, Mike, had had his heart episode. The night of the attack, and now tonight, it looked as if the willow might snap.

"I always think it would be best if he went first. I'm not sure he could survive without me, but I'm not sure I could last too long without him." Grace fidgeted with a button on her jacket until she pulled it off. She stopped and looked at the button in her hand as if it held the answer to a question that eluded her.

"Mom, if it's a broken leg, he'll be fine." Clare took the button from her and slipped it in her pocket. She placed her arm around her mother's waist and guided her into the waiting room.

"They asked about his medical history. He could have had a heart attack and then fallen. I should have waited for you, Finn, and done the decorating tomorrow. Lord love a duck! Why did I let him climb the—?"

"Mom, please. Shoulda, woulda, coulda. What is, is. We'll deal with it," Clare said, trying to sound cheerful and confident. "He's going to be fine." She sent a prayer to the heavens.

Clare sat in silence and clutched her mother's hand. It was clammy and ice cold. This woman and the man behind the curtain were her rocks. She leaned her head against the wall and let her eyes drift around the room. The bottom half of the walls was painted a soft cream and the top half a sky blue. The soothing colors and bucolic landscapes that hung on the walls did little to ease the worry and frustration of those waiting for news of their loved ones. The glass in the only vending machine had been smashed. Packing tape across its broken glass sealed what might have been an explosion of fury—rage at the circumstances of life and death.

Clare checked the clock, only fifteen minutes had passed.

Finally, the nurse, Astrid Bell, came out. Her family and the Harrigans had known each other for years.

"Mrs. Harrigan," she said, placing her hand on Grace's shoulder, "you, Clare, and Finn can go in for a few minutes."

"Thank you, Astrid." Grace stood and smoothed her clothing, patted her hair, then walked with Finn toward the closed curtains. Clare hung back and looked at Astrid with raised eyebrows.

"They ran an EKG. It wasn't a heart attack. A simple fracture, although, that's hard enough on a man his age. His recovery time could be lengthy."

"Thank you." Clare blew out a breath, and her shoulders relaxed. "Please tell your sister, Cat, and your family hello."

"I will. You and those you love have had a rough go of it these last few months. Keep your chin up." She gave Clare a quick hug before she turned to answer the phone. As Clare slipped behind the curtain, she noticed a smile of relief on her mother's face.

The x-ray films were on the lighted viewing screen, and the doctor pointed to the x-ray of her father's leg. "It's a minor fracture—no real worries. In some cases, surgery is required. I would guess not in this case. It'll take about four weeks to heal, and I'm sure the orthopedic doc will recommend physical therapy." He patted Grace on the shoulder. "My guess is they won't put a plaster cast on right away. They'll want the swelling to go down before they proceed. Then he'll have a boot. Bones take longer to heal the older we get. But Mike has good strong bones—no osteoporosis."

Mike was on the table with a silly grin on his face. He had, obviously, been given something for the pain. Clare hated to see him like this. He was small in stature, but always seemed larger-than-life to those around him, and he was her hero.

"Clare, dear. They are going to take your father down to the hospital in Bremerton to further examine his leg. I'll ride along with him in the ambulance, you and Finn follow. Clare, you can drive my car so I will have a way to get home. You and Finn can drive back together."

Grace was back in control.

Chapter 3

Maggie bounded off the bed, barking, as Clare tried to wrest herself from a deep sleep. She rolled over and looked at the clock—only seven. She had set the alarm for seven-thirty when she finally got home at three that morning. Clare dropped an exhausted Finn off at the farm and drove the little sports car home.

Between Maggie's barks Clare heard someone knocking at the back door.

"Go away," she mumbled and snuggled deeper into the pillows and feather mattress. She pulled the covers over her head and drifted off to sleep. Clare felt what she thought was Maggie jump on the bed, but when the covers were pulled back, Libby and Bev peered at her. "Go away. I get another half-an-hour to sleep. Then I have to pick Finn up at nine o'clock. Long story. I'll explain later."

"How's your dad?" Libby ignored her request.

"He'll be fine," Clare grumbled and was asleep before Libby and Bev left the room.

An hour later Bev gently shook Clare's shoulder. "Wake up.

It's eight o'clock." She placed a cup of coffee on the bedside table and went into the bathroom to start the shower. When she came out, Clare was propped up on the pillows sipping her coffee. "Libby's got some breakfast going."

"Thanks for the coffee, Bev. You and Lib are so good to me. I'm starved. I need something to soothe this growling tiger in my stomach." Clare turned and slid her legs over the side of her four-poster bed. She didn't need to ask how they got in the cottage. They each had keys to the others' homes and knew the alarm codes, which they had all installed after the harrowing experiences they suffered two months ago. A tragedy none of the women would ever get over. But the grief process worked its way through each of them at its own pace. There would forever be a hollow place carved in their hearts for a friend whose life was lost all too soon.

Clare came out of the shower wrapped in a fluffy terry cloth bathrobe and noticed Bev had made her bed. She was blessed with the most wonderful friends. She stood for a moment and looked around the room—soft and feminine. She would sometimes laze away a rainy afternoon snuggled on the chaise that was nestled next to her little fireplace. Reading, napping, and sipping tea while cuddled under an afghan was heaven. The arched canopy over her bed held soft, creamy fabric that draped down the posts to her soft bed linens. She loved going to sleep and waking up in this dreamy room. Clare sighed with contentment and for a moment the tension washed away.

Clare chose her clothes with care, all the while telling herself it wasn't because she might see Jake Fleming at the police station. A quick phone call to check on her father's condition, and she followed the wonderful smell that floated up from the kitchen.

"My, my, don't you look nice today," Bev said, as she looked up from the newspaper she'd been reading. She tilted her head down and studied Clare over the top of her reading glasses. Clare was wearing a pair of wool camel-colored slacks and a matching sweater. She placed a hunter-green swing jacket over the back of a chair. Her long mane of auburn curls swirled around her shoulders. She took extra time to make up her eyes.

"Just where are you and Finn off to this morning?" Libby asked as she placed a plate on the table stacked with cinnamon french toast and a mound of plump blueberries. A pitcher of warm maple syrup stood next to it. The entire plate was dusted with powdered sugar. Simple pleasures.

"Thank you Lib and Bev. I'm happy to accept a little spoiling today after the day I had yesterday."

Clare dug in while she told them between mouthfuls about Finn's fears, and that they were going to the station to speak to Chief Bradshaw. She asked Libby to stay with her parents while she and Finn were gone.

"Did either of you hear anything about Bets or her disappearance?"

Bev checked her watch. "Nothing. Dad and I are going out at ten on horseback with some volunteers from our riding group to search the woods for her. God, forbid we find her there. Didn't you tell us Bradshaw was leaving today for vacation until his retirement party at the end of the year? Although I think it's a little early to start searching the woods. But I'll go along."

"Aha, now I know why you're all spiffed up. You're thinking you might run into Jake Fleming." Libby leaned against the counter laughing. "You are *so* transparent."

"Of course not! No, I just…well…maybe." Clare laughed with them.

***

Libby followed Clare up the driveway of Grace and Mike's home. She drove around the back of the old Victorian farmhouse with its wraparound porch and parked her van. Finn waited on the porch.

"Wow, you look nice today. What's the occasion?" he asked as Clare wiggled her way out of the low-slung car. "Oh ho, I get it—the new Chief of Police. You should have shown a little leg and some cleavage if you really want to catch his eye."

"*Just get in the damn car,* and let's go." Perhaps she should move to a big city and be anonymous. A place where everyone didn't know everyone else's business, she thought. A place where she wasn't so…transparent. But that is what she loved about Amelia Bay. So many folks caring for each other and helping each other in big and small ways.

The station was only a few minutes away, but dark clouds loomed overhead and threatened to spill at any moment. As Clare looked up, she hoped it was not an omen of things to come.

"Have you heard anything about Bets?"

"Sorry, Finn. We might hear good news at the station." She didn't mention Bev and her riding group going out to search.

Finn parked at the far end of the lot and reached for Clare's hand as they walked into the station. There was no one sitting at the desk in the reception area when they walked in. They passed through a large, open room holding a dozen or so desks with several officers seated at them. Clare looked over to the glass-enclosed office of Chief Bradshaw. She noticed a woman she didn't recognize standing next to the desk outside the chief's office. Hmm, Clare thought, who might this be? The nameplate on her desk read, *Rocky Rockman - Assistant to the Chief of Police.* This must have been the lady she spoke to on the phone yesterday when she reported the disturbance at the pub. Poor thing, she's built like a fireplug and just about as tall.

"Good morning, Ms. Rockman. I'm Clare Harrigan, and this is my brother Finn Harrigan. We'd like to see Chief Bradshaw. Is he in?" she asked, as she and Finn approached the tiny woman.

"No."

"Do you know when he'll be back?"

"He's gone on vacation until the end of the year. There's a new chief now, Chief Fleming," she said with an icy tone as she looked Clare and Finn up and down.

"Is he available? We'd be happy to speak to him," Finn said with his charming, boyish grin. A smile known to melt the hearts of many women young and old.

"He's busy. Make an appointment. You'll have to come back." The icy little fireplug refused to melt.

"This concerns Bets, the young woman who's missing." Clare tried a frontal, firm approach. "We need to speak to him immediately."

"What about her? You can tell me, and I'll relay the information to him. If he wants to talk to you, he will let me know."

"Ms. Rockman," Clare said, losing patience, "this is a small town. I don't know how they do things where you come from, but here…"

The fireplug puffed herself up with self-importance and was ready to toss her weight around when Jake Fleming walked out of his office. "What's going on out here? Clare, Finn, do you need to see me?" He smiled, as he patted his assistant on the shoulder and said, "It's all right, Rocky. I can see them now."

Clare glanced over and noticed Caroline had witnessed the entire exchange. She covered her mouth with her hand to hide her smirk, but her eyes were sparkling with humor. Clare herself stifled a grin. The fireplug sat back down at her desk and shot a venomous look at Clare. I'd like to see a Rottweiler lift his leg on that little fireplug, Clare thought. Who put the bee in this gal's bonnet, and why is she taking it out on us? This guy might not be worth the effort it would take to get through the impenetrable wall Ms. Rockman seemed to be throwing up around him.

"Please excuse Rocky, she's very protective of me since…" He let the sentence hang, and again a look of pain, or maybe even anger, flashed across his face before it was replaced with a forced smile.

It sparked Clare's interest. Since what? Hmm…? she asked herself. "I take it you brought Ms. Rockman from Portland, Chief Fleming?"

"Yes. Please call me Jake. Now, how may I help you today?" he asked when they were seated in the old wooden chairs facing the desk. The paneled walls of the office were covered with photos of Chief Bradshaw and the various awards and commendations he had received over the years. These would all be removed next month, the best of them hung in Chief Bradshaw's home study. The rest would be tossed in a box and forgotten. A life—a career—hanging on the walls. Clare wondered what the new chief would hang on these walls. Her thoughts were interrupted when Finn spoke.

"Have you found Bets?"

"Not yet. Why do you ask?"

Finn fidgeted for a moment, then said, "I was dating her and…well…may have been one of last people to see her before she disappeared."

"I see." Jake was all business as he moved a stack of folders on his desk looking for—what turned out to be—a notepad. He pulled it out from under the folders that teetered at the edge of the desk. Clare reached out to catch the pile before it hit the floor.

"Thank you, Clare." He rescued them from her hands. "I'm trying to familiarize myself with the workings of the station and the current caseload." He cleared his throat and asked Finn, "What time did you last see her?"

"Early yesterday morning—around two-thirty. She told me she had to go home and would see me at the pub later that day. Well…you know what happened at the pub." Nervousness crept into Finn's voice.

"Do you want to make an official statement at this time, or do you want to have a lawyer present when you do?"

"Why would I need a lawyer?" Finn looked back and forth between Clare and Jake. "I don't have anything to hide."

Clare realized she had been a fool to think talking to the police would be a simple matter. She knew if Bradshaw had been around, he would have listened to Finn without placing suspicion on him immediately. She stood up and turned to Finn. "We're leaving, and yes, as a matter of fact, we do want to have a lawyer present. Thank you for your time, *Acting* Chief Fleming."

"Wait a minute, Clare. What the hell... Look Fleming, I came here in good faith." The chief's impassive expression stopped Finn in his tracks. Cops must practice that look in mirrors. Finn sat for a moment, then shook his head and got up. He walked around the back of the chair and stopped. Finn did not turn to face the chief, but shrugged, and reached for Clare's arm.

"I will accept your statement in good faith, Mr. Harrigan, but until I know what happened to that young lady, I have to consider all possibilities. *And* gather all the information I can. *Formally*."

Clare and Finn ignored him and walked out the door.

"Hey! You can't just walk out of here," he called after them. "Small town people," he mumbled.

***

The rain pelted the windshield as they drove away from the station in the direction of Clare's cottage. The steady beat of the windshield wipers and water that whipped up from the tires were the only sounds.

Finally, Finn asked, "Why didn't you want me to talk to him?"

"He would have asked you a hundred different questions, in a hundred different ways until he thought he tripped you up. I was crazy to think we could go down there and be upfront. Well, I thought Bradshaw'd still be around."

"Maybe you're right, but my leaving might make him think I'm guilty of something."

"Finn, he's a big city cop, and we just made you his number one suspect. I'm really, really sorry, but I thought the sooner we got it out on the table, the better it would look for you. I have a feeling he'll be beating down your door very shortly—in an official capacity. At least he knows you came in voluntarily."

"Just great! What the hell..." Finn stared at the road, and they rode along in silence for a few more minutes. "Everything will be fine you said. Just talk to the nice policeman, Finn—my ass, Clare."

"I am sorry, Finn. Maybe we should have gone with a lawyer, but that would make him really think you had something to hide." Clare shook her head and blew out a breath. "What's the mood at the farm like?" Clare asked, changing the subject.

"Okay. Dad's still a little loopy on his pain meds." Frustration still tinged his voice. "He called Uncle Pug this morning and asked him to come over to help out."

"Why? He has a life in Ireland. We can manage."

"Dad said this is his busy time of the year, and what with the holidays, Mac and Caroline's wedding… He felt we needed him. Uncle Pug planned to come to the wedding next month anyway. It's just a little earlier. I'm going to the farm. I'll relieve Libby and try to grab a nap."

Clare sighed. A rest would do them both a world of good. She felt fuzzy-headed from lack of sleep. "Okay. I could do with a little sleep myself. Tell Mom I'll be there for dinner around six, if that's okay. We'll have to tell her about Bets sooner or later."

"Yeah, I'll tell her as soon as I get over there. *And* I need to come up with an attorney. With brother Pete in Europe, I guess…well…I'll call his office and see if I can find someone there who can help me."

"Good idea, Finn. Make sure the attorney is there when the cops come, and please call me when or if they show up." Clare, again, struggled her way out of the sports car. Getting in and out of her old Jeep Grand Wagoneer with its running boards was a lot easier.

She stood in the rain for a few moments as Finn's tires spun on the wet pavement, as they grappled for traction.

Chapter 4

Clare fed Maggie, changed her clothes and paced throughout the house—sleep eluded her. Ultimately she ended up in her basement studio and pulled out some clay. A few hours on the wheel should calm the apprehension she was feeling.

The cottage was built into the side of hill, with a walkout basement leading to a patio. Clare's yard gently sloped down to Amelia Bay. The basement had been the room her grandmother used for canning, quilting, and laundry. The outside wall had only one small window and a single door that led outside when she moved in. Neither allowed much view of the water. Clare had the entire wall removed and replaced with french doors that slid back into pockets on either side. Opposite the doors was a storage room she divided in thirds. One space was a damp room where she stored pieces of pottery still in need of work, and another was for finished pieces or bisque waiting to be glazed. The third section she used for normal storage. Her electric kiln was tucked away in the garage where she had installed an exhaust fan to pull the fumes out. It was not a good idea for someone to be in an enclosed area when the kiln was firing. She had yet to assemble her gas kiln outside. It was sitting behind the garage—a stack of bricks and blocks—waiting to be rebuilt. Clare was content with the setup as it was, and the thought of rebuilding the kiln didn't appeal to her. She liked the computerized automation of the electric kiln. She was no longer the purist she once was. There was a time when she dug her own clay. No more.

Clare grabbed a bag of red clay to start a set of redware dishes for Libby and Tom as a Christmas gift. The dishes were more popular in the Midwest and East, but Libby's entire house looked like it had been picked up from New England and placed in Amelia Bay. After a few hours of steady work, she felt relaxed as evening fell. There were fifteen dinner plates and cups sitting in the damp room where they could partially dry so she could trim them before firing. The extras were in case some cracked or broke in the firing process. She was starting on the bowls when she heard a tap on the sliding french doors.

"Knock, knock."

"Hey Sophie, what a nice surprise! I thought you weren't due back until the end of the week." Clare jumped up from her wheel. "I'd hug you, but, as you can see, I'm covered in wet clay."

Sophie Quinn stepped into Clare's studio and let loose with one of her deep throaty laughs. "What a mess you make!" Anyone around her couldn't help but join in. Sophie laughed at the drop of a hat, and fell in and out of love just as quickly. She had that big Greek, larger than life aura about her—an earthy quality that immediately put a person at ease. She wasn't pretty in the classic way of Libby. Her nose was too big and her mouth was wide with full lips and perfect white teeth. Sophie's short black hair softly framed her face and set off her snapping, dark brown eyes. Bev had always been the blond bombshell of the group of friends, while Clare and Gina Vitale were deemed incurably cute.

Clare looked down at her overalls that were covered in clay, and back up at her tall, broad-shouldered friend with laughter bubbling up inside of her. "I don't know why. My first instructor called me 'splatter girl' and gave me a wide berth. He told me I would get neater with time. He was wrong."

"I stopped by Bibi's Beans for coffee earlier, and got a full dose of gossip to go with it from Bibi's husband, Brady, but I'd like to hear what you know about this young woman who's missing."

Clare sighed. "Go upstairs and put on a pot of coffee. Libby left some fresh muffins. Let me clean this mess, take a quick shower, and I'll be right up."

Sophie reached in her bag and pulled out a bottle of red wine. "I think a glass of wine is more to my liking right now. I brought it back from France. I was doing some coverage on the unrest in the immigrant communities there. It's a sad state of affairs without a solution in sight." She sighed. "A charming diplomat I interviewed gifted me the bottle. And I can't think of a better companion to share it with than you."

"Thank you! There's cheese in the frig. Skip the muffins. Besides I'm starved. If you'll pull everything out… Oh, Libby made some jelly out of chardonnay grapes. It goes great with pepper jack cheese, and of course, fine wine."

Clare cleaned up and put the bowls she had finished in the damp room, then covered her work with thin plastic. She showered in the small combination bathroom and laundry room she had installed when she did the remodel. She grabbed a pair of sweatpants and long-sleeved T-shirt out of clothes dryer. Sophie, who had been out on the rickety deck off the kitchen having a cigarette, came in when Clare walked into the kitchen. The entire group had smoked like chimneys in high school and college, but gave it up when they started having families. Sophie was still hanging on. Clare loved the smell of the smoke, but resisted the urge to indulge herself.

"So what gives? Why are you back in town early?" Clare asked as she finished loading the cheese, crackers and the jelly onto a tray Sophie had set out. She carried the tray into the living room. Sophie followed with the wine and glasses.

"In answer to your question, after all that we went through two months ago I decided I wanted to be with my family and friends as much as possible." Sophie settled into a chair, kicked off her shoes, and stretched her long legs onto an ottoman.

"I miss her so much," Clare said, referring to their dear friend who had been murdered.

"Me too, kiddo, me too. It's an empty feeling knowing she won't be around to grab a bite with when I land in Seattle. She picked me up at the airport sometimes." They were both quiet for a moment—remembering. Sophie shook her head and changed the subject. "What's this about your dad breaking his leg?"

"Fell off a ladder, broke his leg and called Uncle Pug to come and help."

"It'll be nice to see Uncle Pug, but, your dad, he's going to be okay?"

"He'll be fine, but out of commission for a while."

"I heard about the young gal who's missing. I also, heard she was dating Finn."

"Brady must have really had his gossip machine in high gear." Clare crumbled newspapers and set kindling in the fireplace as she explained all that had transpired, starting with the invasion of blue robes in the pub to the scene at the police station. By the time she finished the story, the warmth of the blaze filled the room. She settled herself in one of faded chintz chairs that had belonged to her gran.

Sophie listened, then said, "You're right about Finn being the main suspect in her disappearance." She refilled their wine glasses and started talking about The Evening Star. "I know quite a bit about this group. I guess it was about a year ago. I saw a woman huddled on a bench in the park one morning. I could see by her body language she was tired and cold."

"Where?" Clare picked up a cracker and a slice of cheese, then settled back to listen to Sophie's story.

"In Sequim. I struck up a conversation with her, and she told me she'd been living on the streets for a couple of days. She'd managed to sneak away from The Evening Star compound where these folks live. Not an easy feat—they watch the women like hawks."

"What's her name?"

"Belinda," Sophie said. "I bought her a good meal and some clothes, then took her to a woman's shelter in Seattle after she told me her story. I wanted to get her as far away from the compound as possible. It seems she'd had enough of some in the group's abuse of woman and sadly, the children. Mainly from the leader, Burl Woodman. The guy you saw at the pub—Bets' father, I assume. He wasn't sexually abusive to the children, but physically and verbally. A very violent man. Linda was covered with bruises from a beating he'd given her for breaking a bowl while cleaning the kitchen."

"Did she file a police report?"

"She refused, but over the past year we've kept in touch and more information has come out."

"How's she doing now?"

"Okay. She has a job and lives with a couple of roommates in an apartment in Ballard."

"You've given her life back to her. That's a noble thing, and I'm proud of you."

Sophie waved her hand at Clare and said, "It was nothing, and I was happy to do it."

Clare checked the clock and hopped up. "I want to hear more about this group, but I need to get over to the farm for dinner. I hope you can come. My mom will be thrilled to see you, and there's always plenty of food."

"You're on, but I have to make it an early night. My dad's lonely now that he's retired. I think he'd like me around more. He sees his brothers, and they still fish and crab or catch a ballgame here and there, but since mom died, it's been hard for him. I'll head over to his place after dinner. I picked up some bang-bang-blow 'em-up movies for him."

Clare tamped out the fire, which had burned down as they chatted, then put a screen over the opening. "I'm sure my mom will send a nice plate of food home with you for your dad. Neighbors and friends have dropped off casseroles and salads since the saga of the ladder and leg spread around town. I'm sure by now the gossip mill has him in a full body cast."

***

There was a police car parked in the driveway when Clare and Sophie arrived at the farm. Finn, and a lawyer from her brother Pete's firm, Bill Zorbinski, walked down the porch steps. Grace stood on the porch with her back ramrod straight. Finn shrugged in the direction of Clare and Sophie, then climbed into Bill's car.

"What's going on? Can I come with you, Finn?" Clare walked over to the car.

"Clare, I think you should stay with your parents. I can handle this just fine," Bill said firmly. "This is just routine. We'll be back in a few hours."

Clare stepped back and gave Finn an encouraging smile through the car window as they drove away.

"Mom, how are you and dad taking all of this?" Clare asked as she stepped onto the porch. Sophie was standing next to Grace with her arm wrapped protectively around Grace's thin shoulders.

"I gave your father a pain pill, and he's slept through the whole thing, but soon I'll have to tell him. He's been in good spirits all day. No change since you called this morning." Grace turned and led them into the kitchen as the car carrying Finn and Bill disappeared from sight. "How would you two like some chili and cornbread? Someone brought over some cole slaw. Which should go great with the chili."

"Mom, you seem pretty calm."

"Like you say at times, Clare, what is, is. Not what you want it to be, not what you thought it would be...but what is, is."

Clare and Sophie exchanged a quick glance. Sophie mouthed the words, "in shock," and Clare nodded.

Finn was not home by the time Clare and Sophie left. Grace assured them she would be fine as she hustled them out the door. "I need some time to think and assimilate everything that's been happening." Clare knew her mother would do some yoga stretches. She and her mother used it as a way of relaxing. The simple stretches relieved tension.

Chapter 5

Clare had fallen into a deep sleep as soon as she lay on the sofa after getting home at nine o'clock the night before. Now at five-thirty in the morning she was wide awake and stiff. It was too early to call Finn. She dressed in her running clothes, put on Maggie's harness, and they headed out the door twenty minutes later. Their breath hung in the air with each step. It was getting cold and the smell of snow filled her lungs. This was the time of the morning she loved to run through town. The occasional car would pass, but mostly it was the steady beat of her heart and squeak of her shoes on the pavement. Clare ran up the hill to the house where her son, Mac, was living. The house where she and Stan Parrish had raised their family. The house Stan had designed and built. The garage door opened just as she rounded the corner. Mac backed his car out and paused when he saw his mother.

"Late for the ferry?" She stopped, bent over, and rested her hands on her knees. Her throat raw from the cold air.

"Not today, Mom. It's best I hang around town today. Maybe I can help with Uncle Finn's situation. Right now, I'm heading down the hill for coffee. Join me? I'd like to talk about what's been happening."

"Sure." Clare opened the back door and spread the stadium blanket Mac kept in the car across the seat. Maggie waited patiently for her to finish, then jumped in. Mac had meticulously restored the old '56 Chevy Bel Air when he was in high school. Like his mother, he loved old cars.

They drove down the hill through a forest of evergreen trees and discussed Mac's upcoming December wedding, but avoided any talk about Finn for the moment. She studied her handsome son's profile as he stared intently on the road. With his dark brown hair and eyes the color of melted chocolate, he was the image of his father when Clare met him in college. Mac's nose had a slight bump from a break when he fell out of tree and landed face first onto a pile of logs. She always felt a sadness mixed with regret slip over her that she and Stan would not grow old together attending the weddings of their children and the births of grandchildren. Memories shared and memories lost.

"I'm excited, but a little nervous, Mom. If it was solely up to me, I would have opted for a small ceremony. Just family and close friends." Clare knew her son never liked being the center of attention.

"Mac, the family and close friends in our world add up to a big wedding. But it'll be Caroline's day, sweetie. All eyes will be on her."

"I can't wait to see her walk down the aisle. She's gentle and pretty."

The love Mac and Caroline had for each other was special. Anyone around them basked in the glow of it. Clare blinked back tears of happiness.

Cozy coffee shop smells greeted Clare and Mac as they walked through the door of Bibi's Beans.

"*Bonjour*, Clare and Mac." Bibi filled a bowl of water and set it on the floor. "A refreshment for *Mademoiselle* Maggie." The tiny woman had eyes the color of violets and thick black hair. She chatted with them while filling their order of coffee and scones. Clare loved to listen to her lilting accent.

With Maggie settled under the table in the back-corner booth, Mac lowered his voice and asked, "Have you heard anything from Uncle Finn?"

"No, after I go home and shower, I plan to see him. Why, do you know anything?"

"A little. But let's talk softly and not mention any significant names." Mac eyes traveled around the shop. It was empty except for a lone man with his nose buried in a newspaper across the room. "I got a call last night and another one this morning from the attorney who went with him." Clare nodded for him to go on. "They were there until one in the morning, and…it looks like there will be search warrants issued this morning." He dropped his voice even lower and said, "For the places he's been staying."

Clare's heart sank, Finn had been staying, not only at Pete and Dana's house, but parents' home. He had spent a few nights with her as well. Clare looked up and saw Bibi's husband Brady pick up a coffee pot and head to their table. She held up her hand. "Thank you, Brady, but we're fine." His head and shoulders drooped as he walked back behind the counter. He would have loved to have a new tidbit of gossip to chew over with his customers all day long. Bibi was charming. Clare could never understand why she married this gossipy man with carrot red hair and a doughy face.

"So, I guess the handwriting is on the wall?"

"I think so, Mom, but if they don't find anything—who knows."

The coffee shop had begun to fill up, and Clare noticed people stealing glances at her and Mac. Most of the townspeople loved their family, but they loved a good story and some wouldn't mind seeing a little smudge on the Harrigan-Larsen clan. Grace's aunt and uncle, Lars and Hedda Larsen had helped establish the town in the early 1900s. The Larsen family, and now the Harrigan family, had lived on the farm for almost a hundred years. Lars and Hedda raised Grace from the age of five after her parents, Hedda's sister and brother-in-law, were killed in a train accident. Grace had escaped unharmed.

"Let's leave, Mac. I'm beginning to feel like we're specimens in a petri dish." People's smiles and cherry good mornings paved their way as they walked to the door. Clare and Mac returned the greetings with nods and smiles.

"That was awkward," Mac said once they reached his car.

"Sweetie, they'll find Bets and Uncle Finn will be cleared of any wrongdoing. Please try not to worry." Clare looked up at the concerned face of her son.

"I want to be with you and Grammy and Gramps. Bill Zorbinski thinks the cops might search your house too, and someone from the family should be at Uncle Pete's house.

"I don't like you trying to spread yourself too thin, but I think it's a good idea. Not for me, but for Grammy and Gramps. Why don't you go up to their place now, and I'll jog home with Maggie?" She reached up to hug her son. "Thanks for the coffee. I love you, my sweet son, and I am so very proud of you." She was rewarded with a tender smile as he returned her hug, then placed a light kiss on her cheek.

Mac paused with his hand on the car door handle. "One more thing, Mom. Why is Uncle Finn staying so long on this visit?"

"I've asked that question of him a couple of times. He stonewalled me. I wish I knew, but he acts very strange whenever the subject comes up." Clare shrugged and gave her son another quick hug before she and Maggie turned to jog down the street. The door to the coffee shop opened, and she stopped in her tracks. The man with his nose buried in the newspaper walked out the door. He looked at Clare, smiled, and walked to his car. He was none other than the man with the gun. Had he been there when they arrived or did he follow them? She couldn't recall.

***

Two police cruisers were parked in Clare's driveway when she arrived home. Three officers huddled around the car where Jake Fleming sat with his legs hanging out the driver side door. The police dog in the back of one of the cruisers ignored Maggie's pleas for attention. Clare put her in the cottage and walked over to them.

"Load up, men." Fleming stood and turned to Clare. "We'll be back later to search your house, Clare. Sorry for any inconvenience."

"Somehow I don't think your apology is sincere."

Jake Fleming leaned on the roof of his car and looked her squarely in the eyes. "I'm *really, really* sorry. I'm just doing my job. I have to go where the facts lead me." He got in his car and drove away.

Clare watched them drive up the road, then she noticed the blond bombshell, Bev, who had been parked in her neighbor's driveway, pull out behind them. Uh oh, what the heck is she doing? she asked herself. Please, she begged the heavens, don't let her have a gun in the car. The phone was ringing as she entered the cottage.

"Hello."

"Clare…"

"What are you doing? Bev, please tell me you don't have a gun in the car."

"You know perfectly well I have a license to carry a weapon."

Clare imagined the petulant look on Bev's face at that moment. She inwardly groaned.

"I just want to see where they're going. I came over to offer you some moral support. My dad told me they were searching all the houses this morning."

"But why follow them?"

"I was behind them coming down the road, so I drove right by and parked next door. Then I heard the radio squawking and bam, they're out of there. That means either the police found something at one of the other houses, or it's an entirely different matter. Either way, I'm going to find out."

Clare sighed. "Bev, don't try to play Tonto."

"I'm not, *I'm* the Lone Ranger today. I'll be back in jiff…*Tonto*."

Clare and Bev had placed themselves in some very precarious situations a couple of months ago, and she didn't want a replay of it. But if Finn was arrested…

Clare looked at Maggie, who had a hurt look in her eyes. "I told you, you can't play with the nice police dog. He works for a living." Smiling at her dog, she reached for an apple from the bowl on the kitchen island and tossed it to Maggie. She snatched the apple midair and trotted off to the living room to roll it around, then devourer it.

"A dog's life? Ha! This dog has a great life." She grabbed an apple for herself and went upstairs to shower and change clothes while she pondered what her next step, if any, should be.

Bev walked in an hour later to a worried Clare. "What took so long? I thought I'd have to bail you out of jail. I left messages on your cell phone."

"I followed the police to Pete and Dana's house. It's all covered with crime scene tape but all the activity was behind the house. So, I drove up the hill to the Fulbright place behind Pete's. I ran into Betty Fulbright the other day, and she told me they were going on vacation— back East to visit her sister. You remember how close they were before she moved and…"

Clare, who had been resting her head in her hands, looked up at Bev. "Could you see anything?"

"What? Oh, right. I had to climb up the lattice on the side of the Fulbright's deck. They don't have any stairs leading to the deck from the yard. The trees block the view along the side facing Pete's place. Why wouldn't a person have stairs? I snagged my new sweater. Anyway, I turned off my cell phone—didn't want to draw attention to myself if it rang—and took my binoculars with me, then…"

"Didn't you think they might notice your cotton top hair?"

"No Clare." Bev was indignant. "I had my watch cap with me."

Clare buried her face in her hands. "Watch cap, binoculars, and a gun. *Great.* Please, go on."

"Okay, the police dogs were going crazy, and they had those fore people there, and…"

"Forensic, I think you mean forensic team."

"Will you let me finish, *please*? If you know what I mean, and I know what I mean, stop interrupting. I laid on the deck and scooted with my elbows over to the edge. That's when I snagged my sweater, and I think I have a sliver in my left boob."

Clare sighed. "Were you able to see anything through the trees?"

"Yes…uh…not looking too good. They were taking women's clothing out of the trash cans, Clare," Bev said, "it looked like there was blood on them. And it looked like waitress clothes. A white blouse and a dark skirt. I could see blood on the blouse for sure."

***

Three patrol cars were lined up along the back of Clare's parents' home when Bev and Clare arrived. The officers milled around the vehicles and had not started the search. Bill Zorbinski paced back and forth on the porch. They waited for Chief Fleming to get out of his vehicle. As Clare walked toward him, he ended his call and stepped out of his car.

"Clare, I'm really sorry about all this. I know it's disturbing to you and your family, but…"

"Are you here to arrest Finn?"

"Yes. The judge issued the warrant."

Damn, damn, damn, she thought. "Have you found Bets yet?"

"No, but we did find some pretty incriminating evidence, Clare."

So, it must have been blood on the clothing they found in the trash cans, she thought. "Could I bring him to the station, and he could more or less…turn himself in. Please." Her eyes implored him. She didn't want her mother to witness her youngest son being taken into custody.

Fleming looked away, then stroked his chin for a moment. "Sorry, no. I wish I could, but I have to follow procedure." He looked back at Clare and shook his head.

"Fine. I'll go get him." She took the steps on the old Victorian farmhouse porch two at a time and found her mother and Bev in the kitchen. Grace stood in front of the sink peeling potatoes. "Mom," Clare said gently, as she walked up behind Grace and put her hand on her shoulder, "they've come to—"

"Arrest Finn," Grace interrupted and turned to face Clare. "He's not here, and I have no idea where he is."

"Oh, damn it all to hell! You don't think he ran away? That's the worst thing he could do."

"Watch your language, Clare. He came in after being questioned and went right upstairs. He wouldn't talk to me about what happened. Said he was exhausted and would tell me in the morning what happened."

Bev poured three mugs of coffee and took them over to the table while Clare guided her mother over and sat her down.

"Where's Mac? He said he was coming over here."

"He did, but then he got a call and left for Pete and Dana's."

"The attorney, Bill Zorbinski, called very early this morning and asked to talk to Finn." Grace sighed. "His bed hasn't been slept in. When I looked out, I saw the little sports car was still parked next to the barn. Then I checked for your father's truck—it's gone. I couldn't sleep much last night. During my roaming through the house, I noticed a patrol car driving by every fifteen minutes or so."

"Where was the truck parked?" Bev asked.

"Out behind the pumpkin patch and the corn maze. Mike planned to pull out the last couple of rows of corn and clean up the left-over pumpkins. He throws them in the back of the truck and drives them out to his compost pile at the back of our land." Grace put milk and sugar in her coffee. "How could he get out of the house without my seeing or hearing him?"

"Easy Mom. The same we did when we were kids. Out his window onto the back-porch roof. He shimmied down one of the porch columns, then all he had to do was run along the tree line and veer off into the corn maze."

Grace gave Clare the look. The look that conveyed unspoken words of disapproval and disappointment. Clare looked properly admonished. Damn, she hated to disappoint her mother. Even if it was over something she'd done wrong years ago.

Bill Zorbinski tapped on the door and walked into the kitchen. "Have you heard from him yet?" He jiggled coins in his pocket.

"Not yet, Mr. Zorbinski."

"Call me Bill. Did he take anything? Pack anything? Are his clothes still here?" Bill's Adam's apple bobbed up and down. The collar of his shirt was a couple of inches too large for him, and his tie was askew. He was a slight man who looked like a young boy wearing his father's suit. Thick horned rimmed glasses made his grey eyes bulge even more than they naturally did. Clare thought he might have a hyperthyroid condition. "This is terrible, terrible! Those cops are getting restless out there." He ran his fingers between his collar and neck as he stretched his head around.

Grace kept her voice calm. "All of Finn's things are still in his room. He left his watch and cell phone on the dresser. I did notice the clothes he was wearing yesterday had been tossed in the hamper. He took—" Clare put her hand on Grace's arm and she stopped speaking.

"His wallet, right Mom?"

Grace looked at Clare. "Yes, his wallet is gone."

"I gotta go tell them he isn't here. Okay, that's what I'll do. I'll tell them I'll bring him in as soon as he gets back. This is why I gave up practicing criminal law—criminals are too damned unpredictable. Just too damned unpredictable. Wills, trusts, that's all I want to do. Criminals damn. They lie and then never show up." He turned, pulled his shoulders back and took a couple of deep breaths, then went out the door.

Grace's face hardened at his remarks. "Why didn't you want me to tell him about the truck, Clare."

"If they ask, we can tell them, but it would be better if Finn turned himself in. We'll answer every question truthfully. We just won't volunteer anything unless it helps, of course."

"I suppose you're right, but they will ask." A bell tinkled. "Lord love a duck. That's your father. I don't want him to worry. I promised I would tell him everything. He's getting dressed and up on crutches today." Grace stood and started to walk away, then stopped without turning around and said, "Your brother is *not* a criminal. Find him another attorney, please. It will not do to have a man who does not believe in his innocence representing him."

Bill came back through the door, but he didn't hear Grace's remarks. "They're going to start searching the property." He tossed the warrant on the table. "Call me if you hear anything, *anything* from Finn."

Bev and Clare sat…waiting. Waiting for what? she asked herself. Then Jake Fleming knocked on the door and Clare waved him inside. "We'll need to search the house too."

"Fine. We'll be in the sunroom." Clare said, turning away. She poured another cup coffee for herself. Bev gave him a weak smile, then took a basket of muffins off the counter as she walked out of the room.

A few minutes later the nurse, hired to help out with Mike, came in. Owen Brattleboro had gone to school with the Harrigan clan, played football with Pete and spent many summers swimming in their pool. He had a strong, sweet face with lanky blond hair and bright blue eyes. Clare had had a crush on him for a week one summer, and there had been soft, stolen kisses. Kind and gentle, he could not have chosen a more perfect profession for himself.

"Time to get the old boy up," Owen said, as if it were an everyday occurrence to have police officers and their dogs searching the farm. "No worries, Clare." He bent over and brushed her cheek with his lips.

"Thanks, Owen. Could you bring Dad in here when you're finished?"

"Whatever you want."

The women sat in silence for a while watching the police move about the grounds. After a several minutes, Bev said, "Clare, I think I'll call my dad and see about a new attorney for Finn."

"No need, darlin', I know just the man," Mike said, as he entered the room on his crutches. "I called Dana and Pete last night. They're on their way home." Clare couldn't help but see the emotional and physical pain he was in. "We'll just have to put up with that Zorbinski fella until Pete gets here. I hated to bring them home from their vacation, but Finn's situation comes first. Family first."

"You did the right thing, Dad." Clare and Owen helped him to the sofa and propped up his leg.

The phone rang as Grace tucked an afghan around Mike. Bev picked it up. "Hi Dad," Bev said as she walked out of the room into the kitchen. When she returned, she said to Clare, "Dad needs a little help, one of the waitresses didn't show and the pub is busy. He'd like us to come down."

Clare was eager to have something to do to occupy her mind. She hated to sit and wait. She knew her parents would be fine with Owen there.

Chapter 6

Clare and Bev walked through the gleaming kitchen of the pub. Chef Ollie Moran ran a tight ship. Bev grabbed a clean apron from the storeroom. “I’ll work out front. I make better tips than you anyway.”

“Sure you do. You’ve got bigger boobs.”

Bev smiled at her. “You’re right, although your rack’s not too bad. My Dad didn’t need both of us to work.” She nodded her head toward the office door. “Finn’s in there.”

Clare sighed. She didn’t want to face this alone and stood for a moment with her hand poised on the doorknob. She shrugged, turned the knob and walked into the office. Finn was sitting at a small table their father kept in the office with a full plate of untouched food in front of him. He looked awful. Dark circles hung under his eyes. His shirt and slacks were wrinkled.

“You were right, Clare. I’m the number one suspect, and they asked me the same questions over and over. Zorbinski wouldn’t let me answer many of them. By the way, he’s an ass. I know he thinks I’m guilty. Guilty of what I don’t know. What the hell… I should of have stayed in LA."

"Pete and Dana are on their way home. We'll only have to put up with Zorbinski for a little while. Why didn't you stay in LA?" Clare sat down across from him. Maybe now he would open up to her.

"In a minute." He got up and walked over to the couch and sat with his head leaning back. "I've been trying to figure this out all night. I drove around for several hours, and ended up in Bremerton. Then I came back here and let myself in. I dozed off and on until about hour ago. Up until yesterday I thought Bets' family lived...oh, I don't know…in the Midwest or someplace far away. I can't nail down any specific thing she said, but for some reason that was the impression I had."

Clare looked at him. She didn't want to tell him about the woman Sophie found and took to the shelter in Seattle. No use adding to the load he carried right now.

"Okay. It's true."

"What's true, Finn?" Feared gripped her. He wasn't confessing to doing something to Bets. Please no.

"The part about no new projects until after the first of the year, but normally I would have hung out and played—traveled a bit. I got scared, I needed to feel the real world around me. That's here. That's home."

Clare let out a sigh of relief. "What happened?"

"There was this gal. We dated for about two weeks and suddenly she's talking marriage and how cute our kids will be. What the hell... I freaked out. So, I tried to let her down easy, you know, the usual stuff. Moving too fast—need space—time to think—we barely know each other. I told her I'd call her in a couple of weeks. You know?"

"No, I don't know. I haven't dated in over twenty-five years, and Stan didn't exactly let me down easy."

He ignored her sarcasm and fiddled with his empty coffee cup for a few moments. "I helped her pack the few things she had around my house. She left. I kissed her goodbye and told her again we'd talk soon. Then I took off for a weekend in Tahoe, but when I came home, I found all her things in the house. All her clothes, makeup all over the bathroom. There was a big stuffed bear on the bed with a note about how much she missed me pinned to it."

"I have a feeling you didn't handle this right."

"What the hell..." He ran his fingers through his hair. Finn got up and crossed to the table. He reached for the coffee carafe and refilled his cup while rubbing the back of his neck before he continued. "Anyway, I packed up all her stuff and put it out front, then called her cell and made it clear it was over. She went ballistic. Said her parents were planning the wedding, how could I lead her on this way. Pretty soon I heard her car pull up, then a big bang on the door. After she drove away, I looked."

"And with bang was?"

"A knife stuck in the front door with another note about how I would pay. I called the cops, had to change the locks, and had my cell and home phone numbers changed. She kept calling…leaving crazy messages. I got a restraining order, but they're pretty useless where nut cases are concerned."

Clare heard a soft tapping on the door. Bev poked her head in. "Stan's out front. He wants to talk to you, Clare. He saw your Jeep out back."

"Bev, could you please stay in here with run-around-Finn?"

"I don't need Bev to be my babysitter!" Finn was frustrated, but Clare was afraid he would bolt.

"You have to turn yourself in, but not looking and smelling like a bum. Go in Dad's bathroom. You can at least shave and shower. I'll see what I can do about some clean clothes."

Clare pushed open the door leading to the dining room and scanned the area, looking for Stan. She caught his eye and motioned him to come in the kitchen. They silently walked through the kitchen and out the back door.

"What's going on with Finn? I heard there's a warrant out for his arrest."

"It's true." Tears flowed down Clare's cheeks and Stan pulled her to him. She stood there for a few minutes leaning against him. Why the hell did men tell you they love you right before they jumped into bed with another woman? she asked herself. Stan was a stinker as a husband, but a rock in times of crisis.

Stan reached in his pocket and pulled out a pressed handkerchief. He handed it to her and said, "Tell me."

"I will, but right now I need you to go home and get some of your clothes for Finn. He's in Dad's office showering and getting ready to turn himself in to the police. I can't get him clothes at my parents' house. The police are searching there right now." Stan and Finn were both built the same—tall and slender. They each had the look and build of a Jimmy Stewart, but with a taste in clothing that leant itself to GQ.

"I'll be back in fifteen minutes. You going to be all right?" His brown eyes held a look of concern.

"Please tell me I have another choice."

He smiled at her, shook his head, then turned to leave. Clare opened the tailgate of her trusty old Jeep and pulled out one of the bottles of water she kept in the back. She splashed some onto Stan's hanky and pressed it against her eyes. It would not look good to walk back into the pub with puffy red eyes. She sat for a few minutes on the tailgate, then pulled out her cell phone and called her mother.

"Finn's here, at the pub." She heard Grace breathe a sigh of relief through the phone. "He's fine. I need Zorbinski's cell phone number."

Chapter 7

The fading light of the day barely lit the sunroom of the old farmhouse on the hill. Clare sat, tucked amongst the soft cushions and pillows on her parents' cushy loveseat, going over the events of last few days. Taking Finn to the station had proved more difficult than she had imagined. He looked like a lost little boy. Stan had gone with her to give moral support to both her and Finn. The little *fireplug* had placed a smug look on her face as the booking process began, and she kept it there until Clare and Stan left. As she snuggled deeper into the pillows, she wondered, why does this woman feel threatened by me? She pulled a worn quilt, her great Aunt Hedda had made, tightly around herself. The police never got around to searching her home, but they had hauled bags of evidence out of her parents' and brother's houses. Finn's room and the barn were sealed.

Clare's older sister Hedda walked into the sunroom. She ferried over from Seattle earlier in the day. "Clare," Hedda said as she handed her a glass of wine, "are you spending the night here?"

"No, I'll head home in a few minutes. I have to feed Maggie. With you here, I don't have to worry about Mom and Dad. How long do you plan to stay?"

"Uncle Pug will be here from Ireland tomorrow. His plane gets in right before Dana and Pete land. They'll bring him here, and I'll head out late morning. I cancelled my classes for today, and don't have any scheduled until late afternoon tomorrow. I hate to let my students down."

Hedda stretched her arms over her head then reached back to twist her long hair up and clip it with a barrette. Soft curling blond wisps shot with grey floated around face. Hedda was a professor of women's studies at the University of Washington in Seattle. She had never married, but relished having Clare's only daughter, Emma, live with her. Emma attended Udub, as the university was affectionately referred to. Hedda and Clare both had their mother's peaches and cream complexion and emerald green eyes, but the similarities stopped there. Hedda was tall, slender and elegant like Grace. Clare's auburn hair flew around her head in thick loopy curls. Mike and Clare had soft features and a pug nose.

"Clare, Bev told me you're a little smitten with the new Chief of Police." Hedda sat down next to Clare and folded her legs underneath herself.

"I'll admit I found him attractive at first, but since he's arrested Finn—not so much. Bev should keep her thoughts to herself." Clare waited for Hedda to blast her about not dating since her divorce, instead Hedda laughed and patted Clare's leg. "I've been thinking about our little brother's dating habits. Maybe Bets isn't the only woman he's been seeing since he came home."

"Good point, but I don't think so. That would certainly be in character for Finn, but he told me he really cared for her. That she was different from the women he dated. If something bad has happened to her… *And* I do believe something bad has." Clare stood up. Hedda was not a very demonstrative person, but she stood as well and wrapped her arms around Clare. "Take good care of Emma," she told her sister.

"I will. Clare, before you leave, how is Sean?"

Sean was Clare's youngest son who was studying marine biology in Hawaii.

"What about him?"

"I was curious about when he was coming home."

"Oh. He's not coming home for Thanksgiving. He'll be here

for Christmas, and he's best man at Caroline and Mac's wedding."

"Emma really misses him." Hedda chuckled and said, "I wonder how he will feel dressed in a tux after his days of flip flops, aloha shirts, and frolicking on warm, sandy beaches?"

"It'll be an adjustment. I'd like the whole family to go over for his graduation. We'll rent a house on the beach." Clare relaxed a little. It was nice to talk and think of normal, fun things.

"It's been a lousy year, Clare. We could do with something fun to look forward to. Everyone would love it! That is once we get Finn out of the slammer."

***

Grace had given Clare a casserole and some fresh baked rolls from the bounty the neighbors brought by throughout the day. She slipped both into the oven to warm while she tossed a salad to add to her meal. After feeding Maggie, she took the casserole and rolls out of the oven and loaded her plate. Balancing her plate in one hand, she grabbed a beer and went into the den.

Clare flicked on the television that sat inside an antique pine armoire. Amelia Bay popped up on the screen. "Missing woman...young and beautiful Elizabeth Woodman...daughter of religious cult leader...famous and handsome Hollywood producer, Finn Harrigan...arrested in connection...old family...pillars of the community...charming small town on the banks of Puget Sound...scene of two grisly murders just two months ago." Clare muted the television. She thought, this case has all the makings of the sordid type of story the national media thrived on. Finn's name needed to be cleared and fast.

Clare continued to eat as she watched images of Finn flash across the screen, a different starlet hung on his arm at various locations around the world, at the Academy Awards, and A-List parties. Her town had barely recovered from the murders of two months ago. Clare and her friends would never fully recover from one of them. This mess would turn the town upside-down but mainly hurt the people Clare loved. She turned off the television and picked up the phone to call her parents' house. Hedda answered, and she told her to screen all calls and not to answer the door.

"Jack's here. He's closing and locking all the gates." Two acres of the twenty-five-acre farm were fenced, but the gates were rarely closed anymore. Grace had the fences installed, because she wanted her children to play freely when they were young without the worry of passing cars or one of them wondering off. "He told us one television crew had already been in the pub."

Clare sighed and reached in a kitchen cabinet for a bottle of aspirin. "Hedda, there's a reason Finn needed to leave LA, and it could have something to do with what's happening here. I should have told you earlier."

"Clare, let's not talk about it over the phone."

"Okay. I'll come up there right now."

"Please, stay where you are until morning. Try to get some rest. I believe we'll be fine tonight. Uncle Pug will be here tomorrow. He and Pete will handle the questions from the media."

"If you need me, don't hesitate to call." The line beeped for an incoming call. Clare looked at her caller ID—Bev. "I've got a call coming in. Check with me later."

After fielding calls from her daughter and friends, Clare had just put on the tea kettle when Sophie tapped on the kitchen door.

"I wondered when I'd hear from you. Everyone else checked in."

Sophie dropped an overnight bag on the kitchen floor. "Tomorrow our town will be overrun with the media vultures, of which, I admit I'm one." She shrugged. "I thought you could use a little company."

"You're not like them, Soph."

"I've done my share of shoving microphones in people's faces when they're in times of crisis. Asking stupid questions like 'How did you feel when you found out your husband, the states attorney general, shot your boyfriend in the gonads?' I'm telling you, we're like sharks attacking a plate full of guppies."

Clare laughed. "You're a political analyst, a columnist, and a foreign correspondent."

"I fought my way through the trenches. I still have the scars to prove it—literally."

Clare knew her dear friend had come close to being kidnapped in Iraq and was shot in the leg during Desert Storm.

"I've been thinking about your parents, Clare. This is going to turn into a media circus. We can move them up to my house in Sequim. They'd be out of the fray and safe from reporters."

"That's a great idea, if they'll agree, but how do we get them out of town without the hounds following us?" Clare asked. She glanced over her shoulder, as she took two mugs from the cupboard. "A little Irish tea? I'm making it Gran's style— lots of milk and sugar."

"Sounds great. Your gran made some fun times for us, kiddo. The tea was always the best. To answer your question, if I go out to talk to reporters, maybe I'll take Uncle Pug along, he's such a character the cameras will gravitate to him. We can figure out a way to slip your parents out the back."

"Let's hope it works."

Clare poured steaming water over the loose tea in her grandmother's teapot—a teapot Clare had made for her—then covered it with a tea cozy. There was a soothing ritual that went along with making a pot of tea. Most of the time she threw a bag in a cup with a splash of milk and some sugar, but this she enjoyed much more. Sophie took her duffle bag up to one of the guest rooms while Clare set up a tray with the mugs, milk and sugar. She placed a tea strainer over one of the cups and poured. Before she went into the living room she called Hedda.

By the time Sophie came back downstairs, Clare had moved into the living room, turned on some mellow music, and had a fire blazing in the fieldstone fireplace. Clare's anxiety level dropped. She handed Sophie a mug, and they sat in silence for several minutes watching the fire. Clare told Sophie about Finn's stalker in Los Angeles.

"Wow! So, you think this gal followed Finn up here, got jealous and did something to Bets?"

"I'm thinking it may be a possibility. It certainly bears looking into. Do you have sources or whatever to check out people like her? Also, Hedda pointed out he may have been dating more women than Bets since he's been here, but I don't think so. Jake Fleming is sure he has his man. And he isn't going to look too hard for any other suspects. We might have to start poking around a little."

"Count me in, kiddo, the sooner, the better. Once people start digging into his lifestyle, he'll be tried and convicted by the end of the week."

Clare sipped her tea. "They already have. I think I'll see if I can stop by the jail tomorrow and visit Finn. I'm hoping they'll set bail. So far no body, just the presumed bloody clothes."

Sophie jumped, nearly spilling her tea. "What bloody clothes?"

"Sorry. I forgot to tell you that part. According to our intrepid little Bev, she saw the police taking women's clothing out of the trash cans behind Dana and Pete's house. She *thought* they might be covered in blood. There was blood found at Bets' apartment too." Clare held up her hand. "I know what you're thinking, there's a chance Finn may be guilty. He's *not*. He does not have the heart. I feel that in the very depth of my soul."

"That's good enough for me." Sophie leaned back in her chair. "But it's really stacking up against him."

"I called Hedda when you were upstairs, and she loved the idea of my dad being able to heal in peace. It'll be good for my mom too."

"We can all take turns going up there to check on them, and my neighbor's a retired orthopedic nurse. What could be more perfect! I know your dad has Owen, but he could use a break from time to time."

Maggie nuzzled her nose against Clare's leg and whimpered. "Maggie wants to go outside for her evening constitutional," Clare said, as she hopped up and headed to the kitchen door, only to find Bev coming up the steps to the deck.

"I didn't want to stay home alone tonight." Bev stood on the deck in red flannel pajamas and a bright pink ski jacket. Fuzzy slippers with horse heads on the toes warmed her feet.

"Those slippers are quite a fashion statement." Clare chuckled as she looked down at them.

"Lola bought them for me. That daughter of mine sees anything with a horse on it and she buys it. Actually, they do keep my feet toasty."

"Come on in, girlfriend. I've got two guest rooms. Sophie's claimed one. We'll have a pajama party. Just the three of us."

Bev flopped her horsey feet across the deck and into the kitchen. Clare picked up the duffle bag she brought. "I'll put this upstairs, then get Maggie back inside and join you guys. I don't know what she's barking at out there. Go cuddle up by the fire. There's a casserole keeping warm in the oven and plenty of salad and rolls whenever anyone is hungry."

Clare had just finished decorating both of her guest rooms and was thrilled to have someone here to enjoy them. She sometimes missed her days as an interior decorator. Most of her clients came from Stan's building projects. Since the divorce, she had not tried to develop any new clients. She was happy to make and sell her pottery. A messy *hobby,* as Stan called it. She had been relegated to a dark room off their garage while they were married.

Clare set Bev's bag on the floor with a thud. She peeked inside—sure enough—a gun rested at the bottom of the bag. "What's with this woman and guns?" she muttered. "She's making me crazy." Glancing around the room, her eyes settled on the huge black cannonball bed, with its feather mattress and comforter. This room was done with black and white checked sheets, a red plaid duvet cover and warm, soft golden walls and pillows. Rag rugs her grandmother had made were scattered across the gleaming wood floors. She walked over and turned on the bedside lamps. A warm glow spilled over the room. The room Sophie was staying in had terra cotta walls that set off the pine furnishings and crisp white bedding. She smiled and sighed, she felt so comfortable and at home in this little cottage.

Clare crossed the hallway to her bedroom and looked out the window at Maggie, who was tenaciously barking at something. The moonlight spread its radiance across the backyard, and she could see Maggie digging at something behind the garage. Maybe a raccoon or opossum—heaven forbid not a skunk. She sprinted down the stairs and out the door. She called to Maggie, but the barking and whining continued as the dirt flew out from under Maggie's paws.

Bev and Sophie came out and stood on the deck. "What's she after?"

"I don't know, something's under the pile of firebricks for my outdoor kiln," she called back to them. Grab the flashlight from under the sink." Clare reached Maggie and tried to pull her away.

Bev and Sophie raced up behind Clare. Maggie sat back on her hunches and began to whine. Sophie shined the light onto the pile of bricks, which were now in a haphazard disarray. Clare had stacked them in neat piles along the back of the garage, but someone had moved them recently. She knew it could not have been Maggie, they were too heavy. Sophie flashed the light across the bricks and settled it on folds of fabric. It appeared to be an Indian-style print tablecloth wrapped around something. She knelt down and pulled on the fabric. It was a woman's skirt. Sophie gasped, as she lifted the fabric and revealed a woman's foot. The red polish on her toenails looked garish against the ashen pallor of her skin.

***

Jake Fleming stood in the middle of Clare's entryway. "Clare, I'm…"

"*Don't,* tell me again that you're sorry. I get it, you're sorry."

Jake turned to leave when Clare said, "Look, now it's my turn to be sorry for being so hard on you. Finn has…" Clare stopped, she needed to think things through.

"*Really*? Whatever it is, you can tell me, Clare. I don't want your brother to be guilty, but it doesn't look good for him right now."

"First, let me ask you if the body is Bets?"

"We won't know for a while yet." Jake took a few steps closer to Clare, and put his hand on her shoulder. He smelled fresh and clean, like he just stepped out of the shower. He was smooth and charming. A warmth spread through her body. She looked into his brown eyes and felt she could trust him with her life. Snap out of it, Clare, she thought. You *can't* trust him with Finn's life. Damn, damn. This wasn't good—best to stay angry at him—blame him. That way her head would stay clear. She roughly shrugged off his hand and said, "Will you be searching inside the house too?"

"Yes, the house and the garage," he said crisply, as he stepped back—his official mask slid over his face. "I'll need you and your friends to each make a statement. They'll be available at the station in the morning. All of you will have to come down to the station in the morning to sign them."

"Fine. Please ask your men to be considerate when searching." The thought of people pawing her parents' personal things had made her cringe. Now her things were being pawed through as well. Bright floodlights lit up the backyard and a canopy had been set up behind the garage. “One more thing, we plan to move my parents out of town until things are…uh… settled here. Not far. You can ask Sophie for the address. They’ll be staying at her place in Sequim.”

“I have no problem with that. I’ve already questioned them.”

“Thank you.” Clare felt relieved.

“I’d like to start questioning each of you, to understand exactly how the body was discovered.”

“Who would you like to question first?” Clare asked.

“We’ll start with you. If that’s *all right*?” His voice held a note of sarcasm.

“Of course, and when I come down in the morning to sign my statement, I’d like to visit Finn.”

“I can arrange that. We’re keeping him in a small holding cell, and I’ll try to keep him here as long as possible, but he will have to have an arraignment hearing. He’ll then be transferred to the Kitsap County Correctional Center. Maybe all this will be sorted out one way or the other before that happens. I’ll send an officer in to take your statements.”

“One more thing, my friends and I will be spending the rest of the night at Bev’s house.”

Clare stood for a few moments in the silent vacuum his leaving caused. Sophie startled her when she walked up and touched her arm.

Chapter 8

The blush of dawn peeked over the mountain tops and skimmed across the water. A penetrating cold hung in the air under the thin wisps of clouds. Clare joined Sophie, who was having a cigarette on Bev's deck. Each hugged steaming cups of coffee, and were lost in their own thoughts. They had left Clare's cottage the night before, after they had been questioned. The search of the house was cursorily. None of them wanted to watch the action going on in Clare's backyard.

"Libby will be here as soon as she drops the boys off at school." Bev came out and stood next to Clare. They both stared at the spot where Bev had recently removed a set of steps that had led to the beach. "I couldn't stand looking at them and picturing what happened there. I'm having a new set installed on the other side of the deck. I'll plant a tree where she died—Addie's tree."

Tears spilled down Clare's cheeks and sobs racked her body. "I'm sorry, guys. It's Addie, and it keeps piling on. Now Finn's accused of murder, and they find a body in my backyard. You know damn well it'll turn out to be sweet Bets Woodman who was under that pile of bricks. My dad has a fractured leg, and my son is getting married next month. This should be a joyous time." Bev led her inside and sat her on a chair. Sophie handed her some tissues. She wiped her tears and blew her nose. "Then I finally meet a guy who floats my boat. I like him, and he seems to like me. I have a golden opportunity to maybe spend some time with a really nice guy, but he happens to be the guy who arrested my brother." She blew her nose again. "I get the priority thing. I know that poor girl is dead, but I just need a few more moments on my pity pot."

"Don't worry, kiddo. Everyone has their worries. Sure, you can look around the world, and find millions of people with much deeper problems. But this is your reality right now." Sophie knelt down in front of Clare and held her hands. "We'll find out who killed Bets, your dad's leg will heal, the wedding will come off without a hitch, and…you will have a relationship with a nice fella eventually."

"It's been over a year…uh…since…."

Bev looked at her with disbelief. "You're telling us that you and Stan didn't, you know, *nudge the nugget* a few times before the ink was dry on the divorce papers?"

"I could barely look at him for a year, much less *nudge the nugget*, as you put it." Clare crossed the fine line that lies between laughter and tears. Laughter bubbled up and the tears changed from ones of sorrow. As usual, Bev was the one who pushed them over the line. "Did you do any nudging with your exes?"

"Well, yeah. I was still in my twenties then, but I've had sex with guys I dated, after we've broken up." Bev nodded, and her white blond curls bounced up and down. She sucked in her lower lip, then let it pop out. "You know, for old time's sake, and because I was maybe a little tipsy, and they were available."

"What about you, Soph?"

"Nope. Like Addie always said, 'Men are like buses, there's one along every fifteen minutes.' And once I finish riding that bus, I don't hop on again. I like a change of scenery. A different route." Sophie paused. "Except… Never mind. Anybody want more coffee?" Sophie picked up the mugs and went in the kitchen.

Clare and Bev looked at each other. Their interest piqued as they followed her into the kitchen.

"Who's the *except* guy?" Bev scooted her fanny up on the counter and leveled a steady gaze at Sophie.

"Come on. We tell each other everything," Clare said.

"You two can't stare me down. I've gone up against terrorists. Hell, worse than terrorists, journalists trying to steal my stories. You two are a couple of soft, squishy puppies." Sophie looked at them and laughed. "Maybe when this is all over, we can sit down and discuss our love lives, or lack thereof."

Clare and Bev shrugged. They knew when to pack it in where Sophie was concerned.

"Okay. Let's get dressed. We have a big day ahead of us. By the way, Bev, how did you get your bag out of my house last night? I noticed when I carried it upstairs it was a little…heavy."

"I picked up my bag and walked out. Besides, I *have* a license to carry a concealed weapon! I've told you that before." Bev was indignant as always. "I also have an open-carry license."

"I know, I know, but it scares me sometimes. I'm afraid you'll get hurt."

"These are dangerous times we live in. As has been proven by the events that have occurred in Amelia Bay a few months ago," Bev said. "I seem to remember saving someone's fanny not that long ago. Bet you're glad I had my gun then."

Clare looked over at Sophie, who was leaning against the doorway, and rolled her eyes. "God knows I hate it when she's right. I'm sorry, Bev. I guess I'm taking my frustrations with the situation at hand out on you. *And* I'm really dreading my visit to see Finn this morning. I don't want to see my baby brother in jail."

***

Clare went upstairs, stood under a steamy shower, then wrapped herself in a soft terry cloth robe Bev had hanging in the closet. She wanted to curl up in a chair and stay there all day pretending none of this ever happened. Resigned she dug around in her bag and pulled on a pair of jeans and a navy turtleneck sweater, took a deep breath and thought, Suck it up, Buttercup!

"I'll let my hair go all wild woman today," Clare said, as she looked in the mirror. "As Finn would say, what the hell." A wreath of curls floated around her face. A pair of dangly earrings, and she was ready for her day…well, after a hearty breakfast. The scent of cinnamon wafted up the stairs.

The earlier fleeting promise of sunshine disappeared and

clouds stretched across the sky. Libby arrived just as they were hatching their plan for the day ahead over breakfast. They would all go to the farm first. Libby would pick up several dozen donuts on her way, then help Hedda pack Grace and Mike for their stay at Sophie's house in Sequim. Sophie, Clare, and Bev would go to the station to sign their statements and for Clare's visit with Finn. They all agreed they would wait for Pete and Uncle Pug to arrive at the farm before slipping Grace and Mike out of the house.

"What time will Uncle Pug and Pete's brood arrive?" Libby asked, as she loaded their breakfast dishes in dishwasher.

Clare checked her watch and said, "They should have landed already, and I would guess they'll be at the farm soon. They were all on red eyes. Pete and his family flew out of New Jersey and Uncle Pug left from New York."

Libby was drying her hands when the phone rang. The call was from Hedda. Bev talked for a few moments. "Let's spring into action. The troops have arrived from the airport, and the media is camped out at your house, Clare."

"The media? At my house? Great…just flipping great," Clare said. "Do you think they'll clear out after the police leave?"

"Yes, and hopefully, with a little luck, we can get your parents on their way without the hounds nipping at their heels," Sophie said, giving Clare a quick hug. "It's time to move your fanny off that pity pot, kiddo."

"I know, I know. I gave myself a pep talk earlier. I'll be fine."

Some of the media might have been at Clare's house, but an army of them seemed to be camped around the front gate of the farm. Sophie rolled down her window as Bev slowed down to let the automatic gates swing open. She wanted the press to get a good look at her. Libby had turned off to pick up donuts in her own car.

"Hey Quinn! Sophie! Soph!" shouts rang out from those who recognized her. "What's your in? What's going on?" Bev stopped the car and Sophie leaned out the window. "FOF guys. Friend of the family. This is my hometown you deviants are running roughshod over." They all laughed at her chiding words. "In about thirty minutes Finn's attorney will come out and make a statement, along with some members of the family. Maybe, just maybe, I can rustle up some hot coffee and donuts, even though you guys don't deserve it. I know what it's like to stand in the freezing cold."

"Hey Sophie, this is a big story." A man, Clare thought she recognized from the occasional television news shows she watched, stepped forward and squatted down next to the door. "If you could get me an exclusive with a family member, I'd sure appreciate it. You know...for old times' sake."

"I'll see what I can do, Buck," she said to him quietly. To the rest she said, "Out of the way. Let's give the family a break." Sophie rolled up her window and Bev drove through the gates. "That'll hold the them for a little while. That, and the anticipation of fresh hot coffee and donuts," she muttered.

"Who was that guy...Buck?" Clare asked, looking back at him. He was still a handsome man. His raincoat didn't hide the fact, that too much junk food and, Clare guessed, too much boozing had dealt his body a cruel blow. She had seen men like him all too often in pub during the days before her father turned it into a restaurant. After the changeover, they left and joined the ranks of the others who haunted the gin mills on the outskirts of town.

"Buck Carlson. He was a mentor to me when I first started in the business. He hit a few potholes along the way, but he's pulled himself back up," Sophie said, as Clare turned around. "He's going to be okay."

"What happened to him?"

"Later. Let's deal with the situation at hand."

The atmosphere inside the house was solemn. "Come on, everyone, perk up. Finn is innocent, Pete will spring him, and everything will get back to normal." Clare reached out to hug her sister-in-law, Dana. "Where are the kids?"

"In the den watching *American* television with their grandfather and thrilled to be back home," Dana said with a chuckle. "They'll be much older before we take them on another trip to Europe. I thought the trip would add to our homeschooling experience. When we were in Paris, all they could talk about was going to Disneyland."

Clare hugged her and looked over at her brother, Pete, with his typical tight-ass attitude pinching all the way up to his face. She had a feeling if she hugged him, he would snap in two. "Uncle Pug?"

On cue, Pug lumbered into the kitchen and wrapped her in a

bear-like hug, lifting her off the ground. He had a full head of curly grey hair and bright blue eyes. Unlike his brother, Mike, he towered over Clare. "Ah, my beautiful little Irish lass. You've been kissed by the angels."

"Good to see you too, Uncle Pug." Clare laughed and stood back from him. "You look great. I think the same angels dropped a few kisses on you, along with the gift of blarney."

"Well, if you think I look good, then you've been blessed with the blarney yourself." He gave her a sound pat on the back, but Clare was ready for his classic *good-natured* pat, and leaned forward to soften it. The old boy did not know his own strength.

"Maybe I have, but it has served me as well as it's served you, Uncle Pug. Now let's get busy. I hear the van outside. I hope this works."

"First, look who I brought with me."

Clare turned as Uncle Pug's long-time girlfriend, Fiona, entered the kitchen—her red hair scooped up in a lopsided bun, her apple cheeks glowed, and her blue eyes twinkled. She was pure love. She opened her arms and Clare walked right into them. This woman reminded her of her gran like no other.

Fio, as they called her, held up her left-hand sporting a gold band and said, "The old boy finally made an honest woman outta me. Now let's get down to the business of getting your mother and father into that van and on their way to peace and quiet." Grace smiled, knowing Fio would handle everything in her absence.

Libby's husband, Tom, had borrowed a van from a plumber—who was a friend—to spirit Grace and Mike out of house and through the back gate. At the same time Sophie, Clare, and Bev would leave for the police station to sign their statements by way of the front gate. Pete, Pug, and Libby would go to the gate first and face the press—Libby and Pug to pass out the refreshments and Pete to make the statement. Tom was busy pretending to be a plumber, as Libby came bustling in and started loading donuts and lidded paper cups filled with hot coffee onto the back of an old golf cart Mike had converted for use around the farm. In typical Libby fashion, napkins, sugar, cream, and plastic spoons were placed on a tray.

Clare, Sophie, and Bev followed slowly behind the golf cart down the driveway and stopped at the gate. Uncle Pug and Libby began passing out donuts and coffee while Tom helped Mike and Grace into the plumber's van, which was blocked by the house. Clare heard Pug say, "Top of the mornin' to ya, sports fans. Step up and grab some good ole Irish brew—coffee that is! But sure 'n begorra we can accommodate ya with a different kind of brew if you stop by the pub." Clare laughed.

Buck stepped up to Sophie's window. She reached up and patted his shoulder. As he leaned in, she whispered something to him. He stepped back and winked.

"She turned to the group of reporters and began volleying good-natured jabs with them. Then she rolled up the window, and they headed to the station to sign statements and talk to Finn.

***

Clare, Sophie and Bev dodged puddles as they made their way across the parking lot to the station. Once inside, Clare smelled coffee mingled with a cloying odor. She spotted her future daughter-in-law's partner and dear friend, Chris Reed. His eyes the color of melting chocolate set in a smooth handsome face that reminded Clare of a creamy cup of café au lait. She adored Chris. The wedding was only a month away. Chris would to be one of the groomsmen. But having Finn in jail captured the joy of making wedding plans and held them at bay.

"Hello, Chris. We need to sign the statements we gave last night."

Chris gave her a weak smile. "Sorry, Ms. Harrigan. I don't have the statements. Ms. Rockman, Chief Fleming's assistant, has them. I'm afraid you'll have to see her." The look on Chris' sweet face told Clare all she needed to know about how the department felt about Ms. Rockman. A quick glance around the office showed each face staring at her with open sympathy, including Caroline's. Clare was puzzled and inwardly groaned when she looked at the smug little fireplug sitting outside the office of the chief. She turned instead and walked over to Caroline's desk where she was packing a box with her personal things. Sophie and Bev followed.

"What's going on?" Sophie asked.

Caroline spoke softly. "I had planned to take a couple of weeks off for the wedding and honeymoon, but Chief Fleming thought it would be best if I took more time—starting now—because of a *conflict of interest.*" She tossed a paperback book into the box. "I'm a professional, and I would never compromise a case by revealing information regardless of who is involved."

"I am getting the feeling this guy's a real hard-nose," Bev said, as she perched on the edge of the desk.

"I am pretty sure it was Ms. Rockman's idea. She has a lot of sway with the chief."

"You mean the fireplug?" Clare asked with a wicked smile on her face. She peeked over Caroline's shoulder and saw Ms. Rockman glaring at them. Today she was wearing a bright red dress and with her cap of straw-like hair cut in a dutch-boy bob, she really did look like a fireplug.

"Fireplug? You mean Ms. Rockman? Oh, Clare, I am going to so enjoy having you as my mother-in-law! You made my day."

"Thanks. I shouldn't make fun. Poor thing. People are the sum total of the days they have lived, and her days could have been harder than most," Clare said. Bev and Sophie rolled their eyes. "I guess we have to go over and sign our statements now. Are you ready, ladies? Before we go, Caroline, what is that sickening sweet smell?"

"That would be Ms. Rockman's scented candles. She even keeps one in the chief's office. It's soothing according the her."

As the women approached Ms. Rockman's desk, the chief came out of his office. "Ah, here you are. Ms. Harrigan, Ms. Quinn, and Ms. Hawkins. Good afternoon. I was hoping you would show up before I had to leave. I'll take care of this, Rocky."

He scooped the statements up that were sitting on the corner of Rocky's desk and held open the door to his office. Rocky shot each of them a withering look as they filed into the office. Bev and Sophie took the two chairs in front of the desk. Clare stood next to Bev's chair.

"I'm sorry, Clare. Let me get you a chair." He went to the door and said. "Rocky, could you bring another chair in for Ms. Harrigan?"

Ms. Rockman brought in an old wooden chair with a wobbly leg.

"Thank you, but I'll stand."

"Suit yourself." She picked up the chair and left.

Again, Clare thought, where is a Rottweiler when you need one?

"May we have our statements, please? I would like to move this along so I can have some time with Finn." Clare paused for a moment and looked at the chief. "As you promised."

"Right…sure…not a problem. Look these over and let me know if you can add any information to them." He passed the forms to each of them.

They quickly read through them, signed them, and stacked them on the corner of his desk.

"If that's all, I like to see my brother now, Chief Fleming."

***

Finn walked into an interview room. The circles under his eyes had darkened. and his hair was slicked back and wet. He smiled at Clare. "I just got out of the shower. The food here's not bad. They bring it in from some local restaurant."

An orange jumpsuit hung on his thin frame. It broke Clare's heart to see him. Thank goodness their mother would not see him like this. Hopefully, we can get him out of here before she and Dad get back, she thought.

"They raked me over the coals for a few hours last night about the body they found behind your garage. Then someone came in and called Fleming out of the room. Couple minutes later I was back in my cell, and I haven't heard another word about it."

"I don't know what to make of that. But we only have a few minutes, so let's get to it. What was Bets wearing when she left you? Tell me everything you remember about that night. Leaving out the R-rated parts, please."

This made Finn smile. "Are you sure you don't want to hear the R-rated parts? You could live vicariously through me." Clare pursed her lips and rolled her eyes. At least he still had some of his sense of humor intact. It lifted the serious tenor of the moment. "Okay. I picked her up from the pub a little after ten. So, let's see. She had to be wearing a black skirt and a white shirt. We stopped for a pizza on the way home. Neither one of us wanted pub-grub. Bets made a salad while I set the table."

"Did she bring a change of clothes?'

Finn closed his eyes and rested his forehead on the palms of his hands, then looked up. "She usually does. Why, is that important?"

"I'm not sure, but they found some evidence or at least I think they did. Someone," Clare said, as she mouthed the name Bev in case anyone had a listening device in the room, "saw them taking clothing out of the trash can behind Pete's house."

"How did she manage that? Never mind, don't tell me now. Why's that important? People toss out clothing all the time."

Clare looked through the interior window into the office area. The chief was perched on the corner of Rockman's desk. Both had been staring at her and Finn but looked away and pretended to be engrossed in some paperwork.

"Clothing, with what appeared to have blood stains on them. Pete will know soon enough. I'm sure they have to give him a list of evidence against you. Tell me, how did she seem to you that night? Frightened, happy, what?"

"Serious. She seemed serious and kind of sad." Finn ran his fingers through his hair, and it flopped across his forehead. "One thing was strange. I asked her about her name. She said her name was Elizabeth. That her mother and younger brother always called her Betsy, but that was before…"

"They're referring to her as Elizabeth on the news, but what did she mean by, before?"

"I asked her that very thing, and her response struck me as odd and she didn't really answer. Just said she shortened it to Bets. She started getting cozy with me, and I had the feeling she was trying to distract me. Since cozy is exactly where I like to be—I went with it."

"I have to go now. Bev and Sophie are waiting for me, but I'll be back. Hopefully, they'll find Bets and this'll all be over soon. Can I bring you anything?"

"I'd like something to read—books, magazines."

Clare nodded and leaned over to give Finn a hug, then started to tap on the steel door for the officer to let her out of the room when Finn said, "I remember one more thing. I rolled over when she got out of bed, and she leaned over, touched my cheek, and said, 'Goodbye, Finn.' I fell back asleep immediately. I was out like a light. I woke up around nine. When I think about it now, her words felt kind of final."

The chief stood and went into his office when Clare came out of the interview room. Sophie and Bev waited with Caroline by Chris' desk. Clare walked over to them and said, "My mouth is dry. Let me get a drink of water first, then let's get out of here." She walked over to the water cooler. There stood the fireplug.

"Just so you know," Rockman said, "he is *still* married."

Clare covered her surprise by bending over and filling a paper cup before speaking. "Who's still married? Are you referring to the chief?"

She crossed her arms over her ample chest. "Yes, the chief."

"Good. I think he and his family will be very happy in Amelia Bay." Clare smiled. "That is if he becomes the *permanent* chief. I wouldn't be too hasty signing a lease, if I were him. One never knows what could happen." She drank her water and tossed the cup in the trash, then turned and walked out the door. Inside she seethed. How could that snake of a man even think to make moves, albeit not overt, but moves none-the-less, on me?

***

Clare picked Maggie up from her parents' house before driving home. The lights she had left on glowed through the windows of her cozy little cottage and beckoned her as she pulled into the driveway. Maggie shot out of the Jeep when she opened the door.

"Please, girl, don't find another body," Clare said, as she used her last bit of energy to climb the stairs. She waited on the deck for a few minutes before a whistle to Maggie brought her flying up the steps.

"Let's get some dinner, Mags." Dinner was a word her girl understood and loved. Clare opened a can of dog food and added a few pieces of leftover steak and raw carrots on top.

With Maggie settled, an exhausted Clare went up to her bedroom and pulled on her softest pajamas and a warm chenille hoodie. Back downstairs, she poured a glass of wine, and curled up in a comfy chair. Sleep came over her before she finished her wine. Maggie's barking jarred her awake. Someone opened the kitchen door. Clare was groggy, but froze for a moment, then looked around for a something to use as a weapon. Fireplace poker? Why didn't I lock that door and set the alarm? Wait a minute, I did lock the door, she thought. Maggie's barking stopped, and Bev poked her head around the door.

"You scared me! I was getting ready to clobber you. Why are you here so late?"

A beautiful Wheaten Terrier stood timidly behind Bev. Maggie walked over and licked the pup on the nose. They sniffed and circled each other for a few moments.

Clare dropped to her knees, held out her arms and called to them. Maggie trotted over along with her new friend. "Who is this darling?"

"Her name is Ginger, and she lives with me now. She belonged to a navy couple, and they're both deploying overseas. Something they hadn't planned on. They asked my dad if he wanted her, but I took one look and knew we were meant to be together."

Clare buried her hands in Ginger's silky coat and kissed her on the nose. "Love at first sight. She's beautiful, Bev, and Maggie has a new friend." Maggie's tail thumped on the floor.

"It's not that late. Let's take the dogs and let them run on the beach. We need to do something to clear our heads."

"That's a great idea. Might help us figure out what's what."

Bev held up a bottle of wine. "I have a bag of clams. I brought cheese, and bread. I'll pop the bread in the oven when we get back to make it all warm and crispy. I also brought cream puffs for dessert!"

"You're on. I am starving anyway. I had a little snooze and could do with a little booze. Funny, huh?"

Bev rolled her eyes and groaned. "Okay, a little funny, but definitely corny. You bundle up, and I'll lay the wood so we can have a fire when we get back."

Clare stood up and stretched her arms over her head to work out the kinks from being curled up like a cat in the chair. She grabbed an anorak from the closet and pulled on her Wellies, tucking in the legs of her pajamas. She handed Bev a pair, who put them on, then poured a couple glasses of wine. They followed the dogs toward the beach.

Bev stopped—transfixed— by the area where the body was found. The firebricks had been moved and were stacked along the side of the garage. The ground had been raked and sifted for evidence. Even Maggie stopped for a moment and sniffed the area. She looked up at Clare, gave a short bark and ran to the waves that gently lapped the beach. Ginger trailed behind her.

"I'm going to get rid of it. There are plenty of potters who would love to have an outdoor kiln. Come on, Bev." Clare took her arm, and led her to the Adirondack chairs near the water. "Let's shake off the bad vibes. At least for tonight."

The wet sand on the beach shimmered in the moonlight as the tide washed in. They watched the dogs chase the waves and gazed at the stars trying, but failing, to name the constellations.

"At least we got the Big and Little Dippers right," Clare said. "A feat I'm sure any grade schooler could accomplish."

Clare slid open the french doors to the walkout basement where her studio was located as the phone rang. She checked the caller ID to make sure it wasn't a reporter. "Hi Pete, what's up?" She listened for a couple of minutes and said goodbye. "The body behind my cottage is *not* Bets. She was killed with blow to the head."

"Oh my gosh! Who is it?" Bev sat on a bench next to the door to remove her boots.

"No one we know. Pete said her name is Everest Johansson." Clare plopped down next to Bev and pulled off her boots.

"Everest is an odd name. What on earth could she have been doing behind your garage, Clare?"

"I can see why someone would dump the body here with all the cover from the trees, but…none of it makes sense. Some stranger in town, I guess. Maybe she went for, what she thought was a romantic walk along the water with a guy, and he killed her."

"It's possible. It isn't too far to the hotel from here. She might have been a reporter snooping around." Bev frowned and sucked in her lower lip, then asked, "Did Pete say she was raped?"

"No, and I think he would have mentioned something as serious as that." Clare rinsed off their boots with a hose she kept for washing clay splatters into a drain in the floor. The dogs did not escape a rinse with the hose and a brisk toweling off, before they all went upstairs. "This doesn't get us any closer to solving the mystery of what happened to Bets."

"She could have taken off to get away from her family. Maybe her mother gave her a heads-up before The Evening Star showed up at the pub."

Clare took a moment to think about what Bev said as they went upstairs to the kitchen. "I don't think Mrs. Woodman could get too far away from that evil man she's married to. Finn also told me Bets has a brother."

"Younger, older?" Bev turned on the oven and took the loaf of french bread over to the sink. She wet her hand and ran it over the top crust of the bread, then sprinkled coarse sea salt onto the loaf before she popped it in the oven. She turned her attention to fixing a tray of cheeses, grapes, and apple slices.

"He told me younger." Clare pulled a large sauté pan with a dome lid out of the cupboard and dropped in a stick of butter to melt. She chopped onion, garlic, and parsley, then added them to the creamy butter. The heady aroma filled the kitchen. She filled two wine goblets with her favorite Louis Jadot Chardonnay and poured the rest in the pan. You should always use the wine you drink for cooking, was Clare's motto. After adding few crushed red pepper flakes, in went the clams and on went the lid. "Ten minutes, and we'll indulge ourselves with the gifts of the sea."

While Bev lit the fire, Clare carried the tray into the den, then went back to rustle up some treats for Maggie and Ginger. By then, the clams and bread were ready.

Clare and Bev sat cross-legged on floor pillows by the coffee table. Their feast spread before them.

"I love this room, Clare. I love that you have used Gran's furniture. It brings back wonderful memories for me. She took the place of the grandmothers I never knew."

They each pulled off a chunk of bread to soak up the buttery wine sauce while lost in their memories of days gone by. Days when the cottage was filled with the smell of Gran's cooking and baking, her singing of Irish folk songs as she taught them to dance the jig. Every morning when Clare woke up, she thanked her gran for leaving her this little piece of heaven.

Chapter 9

Clare stopped by the local convenience store to pick up some magazines and a bag of the bite-size Snicker bars that she knew Finn loved. She had perused her bookcase and found some spy thrillers, belonging to her sons. She hoped they would help take his mind off everything. The officer on duty at the front desk was Harley Stevens. He checked her bags before letting her in to see Finn. He approved everything. She knew he trusted her since he spent many days and nights at her house with Sean during their school years. She would always be Mrs. Parrish to him—the woman that made the world's best blueberry pancakes and homemade blueberry syrup. Harley led her back to the interview room. A haunted expression masked Finn's face as he entered the room. Harley looked at her, blew out a breath, and shook his head as he closed the door.

She stepped forward and wrapped Finn in a hug. "Did Pete tell you they found a body behind my garage?"

He nodded. "Bets?"

"No. The police told Pete the body behind my house isn't

Bets." Finn raised his bloodshot eyes. "It isn't Bets," she repeated. "A woman we don't know with an odd name." She hoped it would make him feel better.

"I'm relieved it isn't her, but why would someone hide a body behind there? What the hell..."

"Her name is Everest Jo—"

Finn threw up his hands. "Stop right there." His face crumbled, as he closed his eyes and formed a fist with his left hand and pressed it to his mouth. He sucked in deep breaths of air, then said, "Clare, get your cell phone out and turn on some music. Please."

"Why? What is…?"

"How did she die?"

"Pete said it was a blow to the head. Murdered."

Finn's head dropped, and he remained silent for several moments. Then he looked up and moved his eyes around the room. He silenced her with a shake of his head. Clare reached for her purse and turned on her Blackberry. She slid it onto the table, pressed the music icon, then adjusted the volume.

Finn let out a heavy sigh. His voice was a whisper. "There cannot be too many women in world named Everest Johansson. How did they identify her? Never mind that. It doesn't matter."

"How do you know her? Is she the stalker you told me about? Where did she ever get a name like that?"

"Oh dear God. You have to find her son. What else do you know? Clare, you have to look for him. *Now.* And no, she is not the woman who stalked me. That woman's name is Elena."

"I'm not budging until you give me an explanation." Clare crossed her arms across her chest and leaned back in the chair.

"Okay, fine. The little guy's name is Cole. He's three years old. The nanny's family lives on Bainbridge Island. Eve, or Everest, and I had lunch together a few days ago. She came up to work on a script with a fellow writer. Maybe Cole's with him and his partner. They live in Seabeck. He's probably with his nanny though. Finally—and this is the most important thing—he's my son. Now move. Find my son. *Please*."

Clare was stunned into silence for a few moments. Her mouth opened, then shut. "You have a son…and…you never thought to tell the family? This is a big deal, Finn!"

"Clare, please keep your voice down."

Harley opened the door and stuck his head in. "Is everything okay in here, Mrs. Parrish?"

"Everything's fine. Finn is upset about his…circumstances. This is a very frustrating time for him and our entire family. I'm sure you understand."

He nodded. "You just let me know if you need anything…anything at all." He cast a meaningful look at Finn and closed the door.

"Are you sure he's your son?"

"Yes, DNA tested. *And* one look at him you will know he's a member of our family. I found out in January. I planned to tell the family over Thanksgiving and introduce him and Eve. That kid owns my heart, Clare." Tears spilled out of his eyes. Clare reached in her purse for tissues and handed them to him. "Never thought I would have a kid. When Eve told me, I was blown away. It was a one weekend fling. She was on the rebound, and I was available. I care for her as a friend and the mother of my son. I can't believe she's dead. Cole will be devastated. His mother is dead, and his father's in jail. What the hell…" Finn shook his head. "What the hell…"

Clare blinked back tears. "Okay. I can wait for more information. Tell me how to find Everest's writing partner and the name of the person he lives with. Also, the nanny."

"The nanny's name is Mia. The number's on my phone." He shook his head. "Damn, the cops have my phone. I'll put Pete on it when I see him today. Gage, the guy she was working with on a script, and Rene, his partner, have been in the pub a few times. I had a drink with them not too long ago."

"Does she have any family I should contact?"

"No. Her parents were killed in a climbing accident. They were adrenaline junkies. They'd climbed Everest. It was their second or third climb, and they didn't come back. She was in college at the time." Finn stood to leave and leaned over the table with tears glistening in his eyes.

Clare sat in the visitor's room for a few minutes after Finn had gone back to his cell, studying the names and directions to Gage and Rene's house. She needed to gather her thoughts and plan her next move. Should she involve anyone else in this? Her mother? Yes, Grace had a right to know.

As Clare was leaving the station, Jack was coming in the door.

"Hey Clare, I'm here to drop off the flyers for the Children's Christmas Party the pub's sponsoring this year at the Community Center." He looked her for a moment. "Did you get to see Finn? You okay?"

"I'm fine. It's just everything, Jack. I've got to hustle." He leaned over and gave her a hug. She smiled at him and hugged him back—hard. Jack's hugs were rare.

***

Clare called her mother and asked her to meet at the Park and Ride in Port Gamble on the Kitsap side of the Hood Canal Bridge. She hoped no submarines on the way to Bangor Base to offload weapons, before returning to the Naval Shipyard for repairs, would cause the floating bridge to open. Delays of up to sixty minutes could back up traffic at times. Luck was on their side, and Grace pulled into the parking lot five minutes after Clare arrived.

"All right, Clare, now what was so all-fired important I had to race down here?"

"First, how's Dad?" Clare stalled for a moment. She didn't quite know how to tell her mother this story. She put her Jeep in gear. "We'll drive and talk."

"He's fine. He waved me out the door. I told him I was meeting you to plan Thanksgiving, and I had some shopping to do. He and his two nurses, Owen and Brian, the next-door neighbor, were teaching penny ante poker to one of Brian's nephews when I left. Cute young man—rather shy, though. He is staying with Brian and his wife to recover from an accident. I can only hope they don't turn the darling boy into a juvenile delinquent. Brian's an orthopedic nurse—a retired gentleman. Your father's in good hands. Now, Clare, enlighten me, please."

"The long and the short of it is a body was found behind my house, and it's not Bets." Grace's hand flew up to her mouth, but she remained silent. Clare went on to explain what had transpired. "I talked to Finn, and he knows the woman whose body was found. She was murdered." She took a deep breath and said, "There is no easy way to say this. The woman is the mother of Finn's three-year-old son."

"Finn...is...uh...I don't understand. A father? If Finn wasn't in jail, and I didn't feel so frightened right now, I would wring his neck for not telling us. At the very least he could have told his own mother about this! Lord love a duck. Poor little baby. His mother is dead, and his father's in jail."

"That's exactly what Finn said. He just found out about Cole—that's the little guy's name—in January. They had DNA testing done. Finn said, he and Cole's mother were friends. It was a one-time thing."

"That poor woman. What's her name? Where is he? We have to go to him immediately. He belongs with family. I don't understand. How? What? In your backyard?"

"We don't know much. Pete told me Eve died of a severe head wound. How she ended up in my backyard is a mystery. The problem is we don't know where Cole is. According to Finn, the little fella's mother, Everest Johansson, has no family. Her parents are dead."

Grace's hand began to tremble. She took some deep breaths. "Cole. Okay. What do we know?"

"Very little." Clare explained as they drove out to Seabeck. She didn't have the exact address for Gage Brinker, but Finn had been out there for a party and gave her good directions.

They pulled into the driveway of an enormous house with fieldstone and cedar shakes covering the exterior walls. Clare parked. She and Grace walked up to the massive double-front doors and rang the doorbell. A voice came over an intercom.

"Yes, how may I help you?"

"I'm Clare Harrigan, Finn's sister. My mother is with me. We would like to speak to Mr. Brinker about Everest Johansson."

An exasperated sigh came over the intercom, followed by another voice. "Rene, who is it? A delivery?"

Clare looked at her mother and raised her eyebrows. Grace shrugged, then leaned forward and spoke into the intercom. "Mr. Brinker? I need to speak to you concerning Ms. Johansson and her son—my grandson. If you could give us a few moments of your time, I would appreciate it."

"Certainly." The door opened and a darling man in a red

plaid flannel shirt and jeans, who could easily play the perfect Santa Claus, stood next to an incredibly handsome, and much younger, man wearing a sweatshirt that read, *Sorry Girls, I'm Gay*. He was tall with glossy black hair and brooding eyes. He would make a terrific model for the covers of romance books.

"Welcome, welcome. We've been to Harrigan's Irish Pub many times," he said, glancing his partner. "Am I correct in assuming you're the owner of the establishment?"

"Yes...yes, my husband and I own the pub. Let me apologize for not calling before my daughter and I came, but it was rather spur of the moment, and…well…a bit of an emergency."

"An emergency, you say? Please come in." He ushered them into the house and introduced himself and his partner, Rene Bertrand. "Here, allow me take your coats."

Clare noticed a low shelf unit with a couple of pairs of shoes on it, along with a basket containing neatly folded pairs of white slipper socks. She looked at Rene, and he nodded. Both women got the message and slipped off their shoes, then sat on a nearby bench to put on the socks.

"Thank you. My Rene is such a fussbudget when it comes to keeping things tidy. Come this way," he said, indicating toward the back of the house. "Rene, would you be a dear and bring us some refreshments. Coffee, for you ladies?"

They nodded and Grace said, "Thank you, that would be lovely, but we are in rather a bit of a hurry, Mr. Brinker."

Rene frowned and headed off to the kitchen. "Excuse him, please. He and Eve are sometimes at odds. I assume she's the reason you're here. And please, call me Gage."

Clare glanced at her mother with a bemused look as he showed them into a room with a wall of windows that looked out to a breathtaking view of the Hood Canal and the snow-capped Olympic Mountains. "Mr.…uh, Gage, we want to find out what you might know about Everest Johansson's movements since she arrived in Washington. Also, I am very concerned about my grandson, Cole. We don't know where he is."

"Hmm…let me think. Eve was due to be here this upcoming Saturday to go over some of the changes we were making to a script we've been working on. She planned to stay here for…"

"You mean a script *you* were doing all the writing on, and *she* was taking half the credit for?" Rene interrupted Gage as he entered the room carrying a tray and placed it on the coffee table.

"Eve is an award-winning writer, and I'm lucky to be working with her, Rene. I will not have this conversation with you…*again.*" He leaned forward and poured the coffee, then gave the cups to Grace and Clare before picking up his own. "She has written for some of the most popular sitcoms on television today. You see, ladies I have done full-length comedy movies, but writing for sit…"

"*Please,* Gage. Eve has been murdered. Now, is there any information you can give us?"

"*Murdered*, you say?" Gage turned to face Rene. His hand shook as he set his cup down and coffee sloshed onto the saucer. Rene's face was defiant. He jumped up, grabbed a napkin to sop up the mess, then picked up the tray and left the room.

Gage watched him leave, then he shook his head and shifted his attention back to Clare. "Perhaps…yes…that must be it." He muttered to himself as he stood, "I guess I'll have to complete the script on my own. I don't know how I'll do it without her. Much of the new work is on her laptop. She hadn't sent it to me yet…"

"I don't understand what you mean when you say, that must be it?" Clare felt puzzled by the odd remark.

"Uh…uh…why I haven't heard from her, of course. I guess I wouldn't if she's dead, now would I?" He walked toward the kitchen with a dazed look on his face. "Excuse me for a moment."

Clare got up and headed for the kitchen door as Grace whispered, "What are you doing?" Clare rolled her eyes and stood next to the opening.

"Rene, did Eve phone here? This could be serious. Now be honest with me, my pet."

Clare heard Rene sigh, and she imagined a sulky look on his face.

"Yes, she phoned twice. First, to say she was in town and staying at the Silverdale Beach Hotel. I spoke to her then. The second time I let the machine pick it up. I certainly wasn't going to let her disturb you, love. Something about needing help and couldn't get hold of Finn. Yadda, yadda, yadda. You know what a drama queen she was."

"You didn't think to relay the message to me?"

"I'm not discussing this with you anymore. You can get rid of those women and clean the coffee mess. I'm going out."

"You get back here, Rene. Please, pet...*please*." A door slammed.

Clare hurried back to the sofa and sat next to Grace before Gage entered the room. "Sorry, I don't know what has gotten into that naughty young man. He's very high strung. I wish I could help you ladies find young Cole, but I must say, I'm devastated about Eve. How horrible. We weren't particularly close, but I wouldn't wish… Murder, you say. Dreadful, simply dreadful."

"Thank you for your time. We really must be going…*Mr. Brinker*." Grace stood. She and Clare made their way to the door. Gage helped them into their coats and waited while they put their shoes on before he opened the door.

"If you think of anything that would be of help, here's my card." Clare paused and placed her hand on the door to hold it open. "Why didn't Eve and Rene get along?"

"Oh that!" He waved his hands. You know…actors," he said with a hollow chuckle, then cleared his throat. "Rene wanted a part in a sitcom that Eve wrote, and she didn't think he was right for it. She thought he was too good looking. You think the silly fool would have seen it as a compliment, but no. Actors, what can I say?" He shrugged and closed the door, causing Clare to jump back. But before it was completely shut, they heard him bellow. "Rene!"

Once they were back in the car, Grace turned to Clare and said, "Did you notice he never even asked how it happened? Really? He seemed to be worried about the script. Certainly, not my grandson! *Or his mother*."

"I noticed. I ran into so many people like the couple we just met when I lived in Los Angeles the first year of my marriage. Self-serving. There are lots of wonderful people there, but oh, so many them are just like those two." As Clare backed out of the driveway, she noticed the garage door going up, then it stopped and went down, then started to go up again. Hmm…a battle of wills? I have a feeling Rene will win, Clare thought, as she rolled down the passenger-side window. "Can you hear what they're saying, Mom?"

"No. I can tell they are having a heated conversation, but not what's being said."

Chapter 10

Clare dropped Grace off at the carpark and promised to call her the moment she knew anything. Rain pounded her windshield and fog began to roll in. Clare switched her wipers to high and turned on her lights. She glanced in her rearview mirror and saw blurred headlights bearing down on her. She checked and yes, her lights were on. Maybe he wants to pass, she thought and edged over to the side of the road. The Jeep's wheels caught on the berm and slid onto the rain-soaked shoulder just as the vehicle behind her hit her bumper.

"What...?" The Jeep flew off the road and jerked to a stop as it sank into mud. "What the hell just happened?"

Dazed, she flexed her arms and legs. Nothing seemed to be broken or injured. She reached up to rub the back of her neck. Her Jeep didn't have an airbag, but her seatbelt had held her tight against the seat. She turned the key to restart the stalled engine—nothing. The rain continued to beat down and darkness was all she could see. Someone pounded on the window of her tailgate. Rivulets of water ran down the window, distorting the face that appeared in the window. The pounding continued. She screamed, and her voice reverberated around the Jeep. I will never make light of Bev and her guns again, she thought. Was this guy trying to kill me when he ran me off the road and now he wants to finish the job? she asked herself. Clare unhooked her seatbelt and scrambled around looking for her purse. If she could just find it and call the police to send help. It had dumped its contents onto the floor in front of the passenger seat. She grabbed the phone and looked up to see the contorted face appear in the window of the passenger side door. Clare screamed again. Her fingers fumbled on the key pad. Damn, 911. How hard can it be to hit the right keys, she thought.

"Clare, it's me, Glen Wynter. Unlock the door so I can get you out of there!"

"Glen Wynter? Why did you run me off the road?" She leaned back in her seat and lowered the window three inches.

"I didn't run you off the road, hon, but I saw it happen. It was a dark pickup truck. I recognized your Jeep. Not too many people have one of these old beauties. I figured it was you. Are you hurt?"

She shook her head. Glen would never run her off the road. He was a friend of her brother, Pete. Clare pushed the button to unlock the door.

"I'm up to my knees in mucky water and mud. If you can roll the back window down, I'll open the tailgate and get you out that way, but only if you're sure you aren't hurt. I don't want to see you further injured. Sometimes a person is in shock and can't feel anything."

"I'm pretty sure I am okay, Glen." Clare pushed the switch to lower the back window. It slid down, and she crawled over the seats. Glen lifted her out and guided her up to the road to his car. Once she was in the car, the tears flowed.

Glen pulled a blanket from behind the seat and wrapped it around her. He reached into the glovebox for a wad of napkins. "Is your key still in the ignition so I can put the tailgate and window back up? Then I'll call Pete, and we'll get the sheriff out here. First, I want to get you to the clinic and have you checked out."

Clare nodded and wiped her tears. "No clinic. I'm fine. Please take me home. Let's keep this quiet and see what Pete thinks first. I'm afraid…this has something to do with what's been happening with Finn. I do want the police to check this out, though." She sniffed and smiled. "Glen, thank you."

"Always at the service of a damsel in distress." Rain dripped off of his slicker and he grinned.

"Oh, I think I could have rescued myself, mister. I am not a shrinking violet who suffers vapors."

Glen smiled. "I have heard of some the exploits you and Bev went through a few months ago. No, you're definitely not a shrinking violet."

***

After Glen brought Clare home, she popped a couple of aspirin, fed Maggie, and poured a glass of wine. She searched through the fridge and found the leftover casserole. It passed the smell test. Dinner was served. A half an hour later, she slipped into the soaking tub she had installed before she moved into the cottage. She used her toe to coax the faucet into trickling more hot water into the tub. She had already talked to Pete and told him what had happened. He had been a little testy that she had not called him before going out to Seabeck. She let him lecture her, then finally tossed some little sister guilt at him, *'After all I've been through today...'* He calmed down and said he would talk to Finn in the morning and make a plan, but felt since Eve had a nanny, Cole would most likely be with her. He had already put in a request to examine Finn's phone. Clare relaxed while sipping her second glass of wine.

Chapter 11

Clare crawled out of bed the next morning. Every muscle in her body cried out with each step. Glen was right about her body being in shock last night. She pulled on sweatpants, socks, and a warm cashmere sweater of Stan's that had seen better days. Somehow it had escaped being thrown out the door with him, his cheatin' heart, and all of his other possessions. She winced as she put her hair up in a clip. Maggie danced around, letting her know the call of nature was pressing and not to be ignored.

Clare let Maggie out and was brewing a pot of coffee when Pete tapped on the back door before he walked into the kitchen. "You should keep your door locked. After all that has happened…I'm worried about you"

"You're right, big brother. Coffee?"

Pete nodded and sat at the table in the kitchen alcove. He tossed a key on the table. "Dana is going to pick me up here in a little while. I'm leaving a vehicle for you to use while yours is being checked out and repaired. It's my Land Cruiser. I want you in a solid, heavy car." He leveled a steady gaze at her. "Are you sure it was intentional?"

"Yes, very sure. Glen Wynter saw it happen. And thank you, Pete. Sorry I've added to your burden. You have enough to deal with right now with everything else that's going on," she said, setting his cup on the table. "You look beat. How about a breakfast burrito?"

"Sounds great. I could eat two. I've been up all night. I went to the scene with the sheriff's deputy. They searched, but couldn't find a thing. There are no skid marks, and the rain washed away any hint of tire treads. Your car's in the station impound lot, and they're checking for paint scrapings. I'm not holding out hope. Looks like it was bumper to bumper, and you went flying, little one. You were really lucky the Jeep didn't roll." He shook his head and sighed. "We got a statement from Glen. It looked intentional to him too. How are you feeling this morning?"

Clare pulled out the eggs, "In the words of Gloria Gaynor, I will survive. I'm worried about Finn, his son, and Bets. What, if anything, have you found out?"

"I did find Cole. He's with his nanny. Finn remembered the lady's last name and knew she had family on Bainbridge Island. He's safe. I told her what happened to his mother and asked her to keep him with her for a few days until we can sort things out here. I called Mom and told her. We'll handle all the expenses for the nanny's time."

"Now for Bets, and here's where it gets interesting. It seems no Elizabeth Woodman has ever graduated from Oregon State. Which is where she told Jack her degrees were from."

"Whoa! She lied to all of us then." Clare cracked eggs into a bowl and added a little cream, salt, and pepper before she whisked them. Then she sliced open an avocado, grated some cheese, and pulled salsa and sour cream out of the refrigerator.

"It would seem so. I have an investigator checking around Portland. So far, he found she did one semester at a community college, but that's it. He's going to keep digging—try to find some friends down there or where she worked. She could be staying with someone in Portland trying to avoid her father."

"I'm gobsmacked. We're so gullible. We take people at face value."

"There is one more thing—evidence. They found some blood residue in my kitchen. Someone had wiped it up, but there is still plenty of trace evidence there. It's the same blood type that was on the clothes found in my trash cans and at Bets' apartment. The clothes by the way…belonged to Bets. Her waitress skirt and blouse. They took some samples of DNA from her apartment. The labs are busy, but the cops did put a rush on it. So, we'll see. They also found a wad of bloody towels in my trash can along with the clothes."

"To state the obvious, this looks bad for Finn." Clare diced some tomatoes and onions, then started to build the burritos. She laid a large flour tortilla on a plate and layered the ingredients down the center, then folded the bottom and sides up, creating a pocket to hold all the goodies.

"Also, they found Dana's car at Bets' place. Finn told me he loaned it to her. She claimed her car was in the shop. I've checked all the repair places in town—no car belonging to her. I'm going to head back to Mom and Dad's. Dana isn't looking forward to moving back to our place. It should be released soon. The entire house has been searched—there's fingerprint dust everywhere. She feels our home and our lives, have been violated."

"You need to get professional cleaners in." Clare called Maggie and filled a plate with scrambled eggs for her.

"She wants everything stripped, washed, and I think she'll call the painters for a complete redo. I hope new furniture and a completely new kitchen aren't on her agenda!"

"Can't say I blame her." She placed his breakfast on the table.

***

After Pete left, Clare popped a couple of aspirins, took a quick shower, and dressed in a cozy, yellow turtleneck paired with black leggings. She slipped on knee-high boots and zipped them.

"Come on, Maggie. Let's check out our fancy wheels." She spun doggie circles around Clare, then headed to the door. She pulled on her denim jacket and opened the door, then set her alarm system before they left.

Wow, she thought, as she slid across the leather seats and ran her hand over the woodgrain trim. "We're riding in style, girl." Maggie seemed to understand and took on a regal stance with her golden head held high, as she sat on the passenger seat—where Clare had placed a towel. "We could afford one of these babies with the money I inherited from Addie, but it's little too extravagant for the likes of us. You and your muddy feet, and me hauling pottery around. We'll stick with our old Jeep for now." She ruffled Maggie's fur. "It'll be fun to cruise around in it for a while, though. It even has a dropdown television for Dana and Pete's little guys to occupy themselves with cartoons! Maybe I could rustle up some old Lassie flicks for you to watch. I'm glad you weren't with me last night, girl. I will definitely get you a doggie seatbelt."

There wasn't an available spot on the street with all the media in town. She cruised by Bibi's Beans, but could see the place was packed too. She would get some breakfast at the pub. Sunday was the one day of the week the pub served brunch. She parked behind the pub.

Ollie waved at her and pointed to the office when she entered the kitchen. "Bev and Sophie are in there. They came begging breakfast. I guess Bibi has more than she can handle today. I've got bacon and pancakes going. Crab eggs benedict are the special today. Coffee pot's already in the office. I'll let you know when everything's ready. You gals can serve yourselves. We're jumpin' around like drops of water on a hot griddle trying to keep up with all the orders."

Clare smiled and blew him a kiss. "You're the best!" She grabbed a cup and pushed open the office door. She loved her father's office with its soft, worn leather furniture and dark woods. Pictures of his Irish homeland covered the walls along with photos of family and friends. A small round table was placed in the corner where Bev and Sophie sat drinking coffee.

"Well, well, well. Where have you been, kiddo?" Sophie asked as she filled Clare's coffee cup.

"Yesterday was a long day—a lot happened. Let's wait for our breakfast, and I'll tell all. Where's Libby? Are she, Tom, and kids coming for breakfast?"

"She's putting on the Christmas pageant at Saint Amelia's this year. It'll be with real animals this year. She's thinking of tracking down a few camels. It's not for another month, but she's busy getting all her ducks, or perhaps I should say camels, lined up in neat rows. We won't see much of her."

"Let's go get some sustenance to see us through the day ahead. I'm starved."

Clare and Bev carried in a platter of oatmeal-wheat pancakes, bacon, and a bowl of mixed fruit. They each filled their plates and topped the pancakes with pure maple syrup, as Clare filled them in, starting with her trip to Seabeck and ending with the revelations Pete shared with her.

"I'm stunned about Bets, Finn, and his son! Now we find out his little boy's mother is dead. How does all this tie together, if it ties together? Is Bets missing, kidnapped or worse?" Bev asked, biting into a piece of crisp bacon.

"Why would Everest Johannsson's body turn up behind your house, Clare? It doesn't make sense. You didn't even know her."

"I need to have another talk with Finn."

Sophie pulled out a notebook. "Let's make a quick list of people we need to interview and those who play a significant role in this mystery. Then we'll get crackin' on it to help Pete any way we can."

1. Body behind the garage. Why there?
2. Everest's writing partner and his significant other. Rene run Clare off road? Jealous?
3. Bets - kidnapped, run away or dead?
4. True Bergman - claims to be Bets' fiancé. And his father, Josiah.
5. Burl Woodman - Bets' father
6. Mrs. Woodman - Plays in how?
7. What about Finn's stalker? Here or in Cali?

Bev looked at Clare and raised her eyebrows, then turned to Sophie. "You're more organized than we were when we were searching for information about Addie. We sort of stumbled along."

"That's true, but somehow we managed. Even if we almost got killed in the process," Clare said. "There is one more thing, and it may have nothing to do with any of this. There's been this fella hanging around the pub who, according to Jack, is not what he claims to be." Clare told them of her conversation with Jack about the African American fella with the gun.

Sophie added this to the list.

8. Who is the guy with the gun and what is he up to?

Ollie tapped on the door and stuck his head in. "Sophie, there's a guy out front asking for you. Jack wants to know if you want to talk to him. Guy's name is Buck."

"Thanks, Ollie." Sophie turned to Clare. "Would you mind telling him to go around to the delivery door? I don't want to go out there. Too many reporters will gather around me. Also, check to see if gunman is out there too and casually point him out to Buck. If anyone can figure out who this guy is, he can. He's a Pitbull if he thinks there's an exclusive in it for him. I'll give him the behind-the-scenes story when this is all said and done."

"Sure. Do you want to bring him in here?"

"No, I'll talk to him in the alley."

Clare handed her the keys to the Land Cruiser. "You can sit in the luxury of my loaner from Pete."

"Wow. Sweet ride," Sophie said, as she looked at the key fob. "Maybe I should have become a lawyer instead of a journalist."

"There's still time."

Clare walked into the bar area and recognized Buck from the other day at the farm. She walked over to him and sat down. "I'm Clare. Finn's my brother. Do you see the muscular fella sitting at the end of the bar?"

Buck picked up his coffee cup and smiled at Clare, then nonchalantly leaned back. He let his eyes drift over to the bar area. "Yep, I've seen him here a few times. He's not any reporter I know."

"No, we don't think he's a reporter. Sophie wants to talk to you about him and other things. She'll be waiting in the red Land Cruiser parked behind the pub." Clare stood and patted Buck on the shoulder. “It was good to see you again. Take care.”

Clare found Sophie waiting in the kitchen. “He’s coming, but man, all this cloak and dagger stuff… I feel like I’m in a Vince Flynn spy novel. Code words…Does the blue dog howl at midnight? Only when the purple moon shines.”

Sophie rolled her eyes and headed out the back door.

“Mission accomplished, Bev,” Clare said, once she was back in the office.

“What are we going to do today?” Bev poured coffee for herself and Clare, then pointed to a casserole of warm rice pudding with a bowl of whipped cream sitting next to it. “Ollie brought it in a few minutes ago.”

Clare groaned. “I guess I can make room for one more nosh.” She filled bowls for herself and Bev. Every syrup laden breakfast should be topped off with desert, she thought. “I’ll have to run a few extra miles as soon as my body is feeling better.”

There was a tap on the door. One of the new waitresses peeked around it. “Mrs. Harri…”

Clare laughed. “It’s Clare and you are…?”

“Yes, ma’am. I’m Maria. I keep forgetting. My upbringing…well…anyway, Mr. Hawkins said you might be back here. There’s a gentleman asking about you, a Mr. Glen Wynter. Do you want to see him?”

“Please send him back, and thank you.” Clare smiled. Nice to see some of the younger generation still had some old-fashioned manners. “That reminds me. Since Glen helped me out yesterday. I was thinking I would give him a set of my pottery wine goblets. He told me he recently moved from Port Angeles back to his parents’ house here.” She paused. “Um…he didn’t mention a wife.”

“No. The wife got the house in Port Angeles. They’ve been divorced for about two years. His dad was MIA in Vietnam and his mom died a few years ago.” She gave Clare a curious look. “He’s a writer. His books are pretty popular. My dad and boys read them. I think they’re FBI or CIA thrillers.”

“Interesting.”

The door opened and Maria showed Glen into the office. Maggie jumped up and ran to him for love and pats. He knelt down and ruffled her fur. She rewarded him with a lick on his nose.

“Hello there, my knight in shining armor.” Clare had softened, knowing she would have been a mess without him coming to her rescue.

"You bristled at my reference to a damsel-in-distress comment last night?"

"I've since reconsidered." Clare grinned. "Thank you, Glen. Coffee?"

"No thanks. I just wanted to see for myself that you're doing okay. I stopped by your house, then took a chance you might be here, and…uh…here you are looking fine and…lovely."

Clare stood and walked over to him. "Thank you, again."

"Well, I've got to run. See you around…I hope."

"Uh…hi, Glen. Remember me—Bev?"

"Of course. Sorry, I didn't notice you sitting there. Hello, it's been a long time. Gotta run." Clare closed the door behind him and leaned against it.

"My, my. What was that all about? Knight in shining armor, damsel in distress, looking fine *and* lovely. Oh, thank you, Glen. Chuckle, chuckle. Men are falling at your feet. First Fleming and now Glen Wynter."

"Stop. It wasn't about anything except grateful, that's all. He's seems to be a very nice man."

"Sure. If you say so. Now back to what we should do today."

"I need to talk to Finn. I know Pete is keeping him and the family updated. Also, I wouldn't mind tossing a few nasty looks at that worm Fleming—coming on to me and still married. If he fell at my feet, I'd be tempted to step on him."

"Maybe he and his wife are separated. It was Ms. Rockman who told you that he was married. How far can you trust that woman?"

Clare stared at Bev. "He's probably on the rebound, but I'm not going to catch him. I'll stay angry. It's safer that way. He has a target on Finn, and he's not looking for anyone else."

"You're right."

"We could talk to Mrs. Woodman if we can find her without her husband around. I guess we'll have to drive up to their compound. I think it's along the Olympic side of the Hood Canal," Clare said.

"The compound is there, but she's not. She showed up in town yesterday and is staying at Bets' apartment. Caroline stopped by the pub while I was helping serve. I guess Chris told her. He said, it looked like she had taken another beating from Woodman."

Sophie came back into the office and poured herself a cup of coffee. "I put Buck onto ferreting out some info on our gun fella. I want to give Jack the okay to tell him everything he knows about the guy. Plus, I need to mingle with my colleagues. They may have come up with something we aren't privy to yet."

"Sounds great. We're heading over to talk to Mrs. Woodman. We'll meet back at my place for lunch in a few hours."

Chapter 12

The apartment Bets lived in was on the first floor. As Clare and Bev approached the door, traces of blood were still evident on the sidewalk. They looked at each other and winced. The door opened before they could knock. Mrs. Woodman stepped back—surprised. Clare was shocked at the way she was dressed. She looked completely different from the meek veil-covered lady she had been at the pub. Wearing jeans topped with a bright pink sweatshirt, she held a pail of soapy water in one hand and a scrub brush in the other. Bruises were evident on her face, and her arms showed signs of bruising where the sleeves of her sweatshirt were pushed up. It looked as though someone, Mr. Woodman, Clare thought, had gripped them hard enough to leave marks.

"Hello, Mrs. Woodman? I'm Clare Harrigan and this is Bev Hawkins."

"I know who you are. Call me Brenda. I am no Mrs. Anyone now." She followed their gaze to the blood on the sidewalk. "The police told me I could clean this up." She didn't invite them in but stepped outside and closed the door.

"We were hoping you could help us by answering some questions about Bets. Do you have any thoughts on where she might be?"

Brenda hesitated for a moment and looked away before answering. "I don't know anything. Now if you women will excuse me, I have work to do."

"Of course. If we can be of any help to you, or if you think of anything that would help us find Bets. Mrs…uh…Brenda, I know some very good people who deal with...uh…injuries such as yours. Also, my brother is a great attorney. We only want to help."

"I. Don't. Need. Anything." She stared down at the sidewalk and spoke through clenched teeth. "And I don't want your help." Her tense body radiated her desire for them to leave.

Clare and Bev stepped back. "Thank you for your time. Goodbye." They turned to go. There was no response in kind. Clare looked back over her shoulder, and Brenda was already on her knees scrubbing the sidewalk. Was she scrubbing her daughter's blood away? Clare's stomach clenched.

***

"She was lying to us about not knowing anything," Bev said, as they drove away. "Did you notice the look on her face when you asked about Bets? And…*and* where is the ex-Mr. Woodman? Hmm? Yeah, where's he at? That's what I'd like to know. She was dressed in Bets' clothes. I've seen Bets wearing that Victoria Secret's Pink sweatshirt."

"You're right on all points. I can't see her sporting that kind of outfit around Woodman. Obviously, she's mustered up the courage to leave him. I wonder how she escaped? Still, I think she seemed frightened and anxious to get rid of us."

They stopped by Skate's Market on the way to the cottage to picked up deli meats and Skate's sweet potato salad. Once home, Clare stored everything in the refrigerator until Sophie arrived.

"How many are coming to Thanksgiving dinner, Clare?"

"Let see, your family, Libby and her crew, my family, and Sophie—her dad. My Emma plans to go to Tahoe to spend the time with Stan and his family. She doesn't see her dad's family that often." Clare would miss seeing her daughter, but understood that divorce means trade-offs. She counted off people on her fingers. We should invite Buck too. Should be around twenty-four.

God-willing, Finn and his son will be with us. With all the bad that's happened—Eve's death, Finn in jail, and Bets missing—we need to focus on what we do have to be thankful for. Thinking about my dad's fractured leg seems minor now. Pete and Dana and their gang are going to her parents' house."

"Will your table seat that many? Oh, before I forget, have you talked to your mother today?"

"Yes. I called her this morning. Pete talked her off the cliff. Her spirits are good, and she seems convinced Finn will be vindicated. The important thing is we'll all be together to support each other. And yes, the table will seat twenty-two with all the leaves in—twenty-four if everyone squeezes together. But we'll have to bring it through the archway into the living room."

"Why don't you invite Glen Wynter?" Bev asked. "He's alone. His parents are dead and I think his daughter lives out of state. It's a nice way to say thanks for pulling you out of the muck. My dad and boys would be over the moon to have their favorite author here."

Clare cast her a sidelong look. "You wouldn't be trying to play matchmaker? Because…"

"Oh, Clare, stick a sock in it. Of course, I am. He's great-looking and an all-round nice guy. I can tell you're attracted to him. Oh…by the way…he's not married like come-to-me-hot-mama, Chief Fleming."

"*Fine*. Twenty-five and it will be tight. We'll invite him." Clare sighed and moved on to cover her slight feeling of embarrassment. "I've ordered creamy linens from the supply company and I'll pick up the lovely yellowy-gold dinnerware the pub uses for special events. We'll use my mother's silver combined with the silver Gran left to me, which should give us more than enough place settings. I have plenty of crystal glassware. I left my silver and china at the old house when I moved. Caroline loves the patterns of both. They were too modern for me. I need to get busy and make some pottery dinnerware."

"I'll handle the floral arrangements and candles. We can work on the grocery list later."

"I have some pretty low bowls and candleholders I made that will be perfect for the arrangements. We'll dig them out of the store room later. You can decide if you want to use them. Thanks, for all you help with the meal, Bev. With all that is going on, I'd be overwhelmed without help."

Sophie breezed in and announced, "To steal a phrase from Clare, I'm starved."

Clare smiled, pulled the deli meats out of the refrigerator, and warmed the potato salad. She piled everything on serving plates and bowls. Within ten minutes, they were sitting down to eat.

"How did your meetup go with Mrs. Woodman?" Sophie asked, while biting into a sandwich.

"She's holding something back."

"Holding something back? Clare means she flat-out lied to us. Like daughter, like mother. But I suppose if you lived the life they have lived with that evil man, Burl Woodman, you would become pretty adept at lying."

"I guess," Sophie said, "but what could have been Bets' motive for lying to everyone about her college degrees? By the way, this potato salad is delicious."

"I bought it at the market. As far as Bets goes, maybe she thought it gave her some gravitas," Clare said, before she went on to relate to Sophie exactly what happened at the apartment. "She seemed nervous, but not overly worried about her daughter. As I think about it now, maybe she knows where Bets is, or she has had so many bad things happen in her life she accepts what's thrown her way."

The three women finished their meal in silence. Each pondered their next move when the phone rang. "It's your dad," Clare said, handing the phone to Bev.

"He wants me to work. With all the media, he needs experienced help. The new gals he hired are still being trained. I'll be behind the bar. He'd like you to help with serving. Lynn still isn't back from the burns she suffered. Poor kid."

"Okay." She turned to Sophie. "I've been thinking about your friend, Buck. Why don't you send him out to Seabeck to interview Gage and Rene? It's the exclusive story you promised him."

"Perfect," Sophie said. "The victim's writing partner. I'll fill him in on the background of what happened when you and your mom were there."

Clare looked over to Bev. "The blond bombshell should be able to wheedle some information out of our mysterious man-with-the-gun if he's there. What do you say, Bev? You game to give it a try?"

***

Jack was behind the bar when they arrived. Sophie hung back and came in a few moments after Clare and Bev so the media didn't put two and two together and start hounding them. They went right into the kitchen and grabbed aprons.

Clare turned to Jack and asked, "Where do you need me?"

"In the bar area. We have the dining room covered. Thanks for coming in."

The mystery man, John, was sitting at the end of bar when Clare walked in. Bev was working her way down toward him, chatting and flirting as she refilled drinks and wiped the bar. Clare sidled over to the empty table behind John and began to clear it. She kept an ear turned to Bev, who had made her way to the man.

"Hi. I haven't see you around. Are you one of the reporters looking for a story?" Bev smiled.

"You got a story to tell, hon?"

"Not really. My name's Bev. I'm Jack's daughter. Filling in for him for a little while. Used to work here. How about you, you got a story to tell, mister?" Bev leaned her elbows on the bar and put her chin on her hands. Her liquid brown eyes gazed at him.

Clare chuckled to herself and kept wiping the table. Yep, these chairs could use a wipe down too, she thought.

"Name's John. Maybe you could help me. I'm looking for a gal. She recently moved up here. Daughter of a friend of mine. Since I'm new to the area, I thought it'd be nice to see a familiar face." He reached in his jacket pocket and pulled out a picture. "She's in her twenties—about your age. Slight build."

Bev laughed and raised her eyebrows at him. "You *are* a charmer. My daughter's in her twenties. But I'll take the compliment. Thanks." Bev picked up the picture and studied it. "Can't say I've seen her." A fella at the other end of the bar asked for a beer. Bev winked at him and said, "Duty calls. I'll keep my eye out."

Clare picked up her tray and headed to the end of the bar to drop off the bar glasses. Then she took the plates and silverware into the kitchen. Ollie handed her a couple of plates. "Take these to the back booth." When she came out, she saw their man heading out the door. She looked at Bev and shrugged.

Jack introduced the new waitresses, both cute, young gals with long blond hair piled on their head and big brown eyes, Maria and Lily. Jack put them right to work bussing tables and serving orders.

"Nothing like being dropped into the deep end of the pool." She smiled at the new waitresses. "You'll do fine. If you have any questions, just ask me or Bev." She nodded in Bev's direction behind the bar.

Clare thought the day would never end. She was getting too darn old for waitressing. Her feet were tender by the time she finished. She and Bev went into the office, took off their shoes, and collapsed on the sofa.

"Who was that man Sophie was talking to all afternoon?" Bev asked. "I saw her leave with him. He didn't look like the other reporters. Very distinguished-looking."

"No idea. Tell me about the picture you looked at."

"It was of a pretty girl—young. Short dark hair with astonishing dark blue eyes. I was hoping to get back and talk to him some more, but he left." Bev rubbed her feet. "Did you hear our entire conversation?"

"I did. Now, it's home and bed for me."

They gathered their purses and put the torturous shoes back on their aching feet, when they heard a tap on the door.

Clare opened the door and one of the new waitresses, Maria, came in. "I'm sorry to bother you, but…well…this turned up when we were cleaning the booths, Mrs. Harrigan." Maria said.

Clare smiled and shook her head. "Clare, please call me Clare. You can put it in the lost and found basket behind the bar."

"It might be something important."

"What is it?" Bev stepped forward.

Maria reached in her apron pocket and pulled out a passport. "I think…we think it belongs to the lady whose body was found behind your house. The name's been mentioned so many times tonight, and mixed up with snatches of the story, from all the reporters…" she said.

She opened the passport, and Clare and Bev peered over

her shoulder. "Where was it?"

"It was between the bench and the wall in one of the bar booths. The corner was sticking
out."

"We can't find Mr. Hawkins. So, I brought it to you." Maria nibbled on her fingernail.

"You did the right thing, but now we have to turn it over to the police." Clare picked up the phone and called. After she explained the situation, she hung up, turned to them and said, "An officer is on his way. He'll want to know exactly where it was found and take statements. We'll wait out front. Bev, you go home."

"You're my ride."

Clare unlocked the front door to the pub and Jake Fleming walked in a several minutes later. Did the man never sleep, she asked herself? Maria had placed the passport on the bar. Clare introduced him to her.

"Who touched this?" He pulled an evidence bag out and slid the passport into it.

"Well…I did, and…" Maria said.

"We've tracked Ms. Johansson's movements as best we could. I don't believe she had ever been in the pub, but it's possible." With a gentle tone in his voice, a tone Clare now found phony, he turned to Maria said, "Walk me through where and how this was found, please."

Clare and Bev watched. Bev leaned over to Clare and whispered, "To state the obvious, this does not bode well for Finn."

Fleming came back over to Clare when they had finished. "Isn't this is an interesting turn of events? That's the booth you and Finn were sitting in the day I first meet you both. In fact, I believe it's the side where Finn sat. I do thank you, though, for handing over this evidence."

Clare stared at him with a blank look. "It was the right thing to do. That's the way my parents raised me, my sister, and brothers. *Always* do the right thing and…*always* tell the truth."He rolled his eyes and sighed, then left.

Clare dropped Bev off and drove home. Maggie did her doggie pirouettes when she walked in the door. She dropped down and hugged her fiercely before letting her out into the yard, then filled a food bowls. With Maggie back inside, she knew she had to call Pete. He wasn't too happy with what she had to report about the passport. Earlier in the evening, Ollie had handed her a bag—bread pudding and a container of rum sauce. Clare slipped it in the fridge. Exhaustion washed over her as she climbed the stairs. A soak in the tub would be nice, she thought, but I'm too tired. I'd probably fall asleep and wake up in cold water. She washed her face, brushed her teeth and burrowed under her covers.

Chapter 13

Maggie's bark dragged Clare out of a deep sleep. Confused and groggy, she looked at the clock—two o'clock. The smell of cigarette smoke drifted through the window. She usually left it cracked at night to let in fresh air. She put her hand on Maggie to quiet her and reached for the phone as she slid off the bed, and crossed the room. She leaned against the wall and pushed the curtain aside. There was a figure on the deck, but it was too dark make out who it was. The kitchen doorknob rattled. Did I set the security alarm? Damn. Why didn't the motion light come on? she asked herself.

Clare tiptoed away from the window and dialed 911. "Someone is trying to break in my house. I saw them on the deck by my backdoor. Harrigan. Clare Harrigan. Yes, that's correct. Hurry. Please."

Within less than a minute, the sound of a siren came closer and closer. Clare crept back to the window in time to see the figure sprint across the yard and vanish behind her garage. Car lights appeared, and she threw open the window as Chris Reed and another officer got out of their cruiser.

"He took off and disappeared behind the garage," she called

from the window.

Chris directed the other officer to give chase, then looked up at Clare. "Where was the guy trying to get in? The kitchen door?" Clare nodded. "Then let me in the front door."

Clare pulled on a sweatshirt over her pajamas and went down the stairs to open the door. Chris stepped inside and Clare said, "I know this probably isn't appropriate, but I need a reassuring hug from a friend." Chris opened his arms, and she walked into them. "Someone ran me off the road and now this. The motion lights didn't come on. They worked when I came home tonight."

Jake Fleming pulled into the driveway. He was dressed in civilian clothes. "I heard the call on my radio. Chris, do you have a kit to check for prints in your cruiser?"

"Yes, sir."

The officer who had given chase ran up to the group. His name tag read, William Wells. Clare had never met the young man before. "Whoever it was is long gone, Chief. He ran along the bank and up a path to the road. By the time I got to the top of the path, the vehicle had already taken off. Fast. All I saw were tail lights in the distance."

"Damn." Jake kicked his boot against the step. "Thanks, Bill. Go with Chris to see what, if any, evidence you can find." He turned to Clare with a concerned look on his face. "I doubt whoever it was will be back tonight." He hesitated for a moment. "Are you sure you saw someone? You know, maybe you were dreaming."

"Yes, I am completely sure, and so is Maggie. She alerted me that someone was there, then I smelled cigarette smoke."

"Okay, if you're sure. I read the report on the incident the other night. You claimed someone tried to run you off the road. There weren't any skid marks or paint chips."

Clare felt her hackles go up. What was this guy implying? "What exactly do you mean? Officer Wells heard a car drive off."

"Clare, sometimes people, especially women, feel a need for attention. Now I like you, but…"

"First, you hit on me, and I find out you're still married, I will add. And now, *now* you imply I'm some needy, neurotic bimbo?"

Before Fleming could answer, Chris and Officer Wells walked up. "We found few prints on the door, but I am guessing they will be yours, Clare, or some of your friends. I think whoever did this was wearing gloves since nothing was found on the lightbulbs. They'd been unscrewed just enough. Bill tightened them. They're working fine now. We did find a discarded, cigarette though."

"Thank you, Chris." She turned to Jake Fleming. "You think I loosened the lightbulbs? What about the cigarette?"

"I believe I've seen your friend Sophie smoking." His smile was laced with pity, then he turned and said, "Thank you, Chris, Bill, you both can leave now."

Chris shrugged and looked at her with understanding before he turned to leave.

Clare turned her attention back to Fleming when he started to speak. "These incidents could also be a way to throw suspicion off your brother. I have to consider all options."

"Well, option this!" Clare went inside and slammed the door behind her. "Option this? Great comeback, Clare. You really put him in his place. Come on, Maggie, let's make sure everything is locked and the alarm is set."

Clare opened the refrigerator when everything was secure. She pulled out the bread pudding and warmed it and the butter rum sauce in the microwave. She needed comfort food.

Chapter 14

The next morning Clare was looking at the ground around the garage when Sophie and Buck pulled into the driveway.

"What are you up to?" Sophie asked after she got out of the car. Buck pulled in behind her and walked over to Clare. "You remember Buck? I brought him along so you could fill him in on the guys in Seabeck. He'll head out to interview them today. He also has an interesting story to tell about Chief Fleming."

"Good to see you again, Buck. I had a little bit of a scare here last night. Right now, I'm trying to see if there are any footprints." Clare told them what happened and Fleming's remarks to her.

Buck reached up and touched the light easily. "Pretty low, anybody could have reached it without a ladder."

"Good point. Come on in the house. I've got a delicious tomato basil quiche in the oven that I picked up from Skate's Market. They make them fresh every day. I baked some blueberry muffins and put together a nice fruit salad this morning. I never know who might drop by, so I have plenty. I haven't eaten yet, and I'm starved."

Once inside, Clare placed strips of bacon in Gran's old cast iron skillet and tossed the fruit in a bowl with a little honey. The sizzling bacon and scent of coffee filled the kitchen. Sophie grabbed plates and utensils and poured cups of coffee for herself, Clare, and Buck.

"First, what happened to you is frightening, Clare. The remarks made by Fleming… They don't surprise me," Buck said as he settled onto a chair at the kitchen table. "A few years ago I was sent out to cover a story in Portland. Had all the ingredients for sensational headlines. Sex, attempted murder, adultery, and throw the head robbery/homicide into the mix... They're all the makings for quite a whale of a story."

"Was Fleming involved in it?" Sophie asked.

"Up to his neck! He was the head of robbery/homicide. It seems he was having it off with the mayor's secretary. A gorgeous gal. Susan Mason. She was married to another cop." Buck pulled a notebook out of his pocket and flipped it open. "When I got here, and found out Fleming was the guy in charge, I checked back on my laptop to refresh myself. I keep all my stories on it. This all happened several years back."

"Oh, my gosh." The timer went off and Clare pulled the quiche out of the oven, then filled a basket with blueberry muffins. "Let me get everything on the table, so we can talk and eat. I don't want to miss a word of this story. I'm not much of a newshound, so I don't remember anything about this. Portland isn't that far away. I should pay more attention."

Buck piled his plate with quiche, a couple of muffins, bacon, and fruit before he told them the story. "To start off, Fleming's wife is not a stable woman." He looked at his notebook and flipped through a couple of pages. "Here it is. Name's Amy, Amy Fleming. She went ballistic when the rumors of the affair reached her. I got a gal who works in the mayor's office to open up to me." Buck looked up at Sophie with a grin and said, "I haven't lost all my charm with the ladies."

"You always did have a way with women, Buck. I can remember a few who were quite taken with you and your cuddly teddy bear look."

A sly grin spread across Buck's face and he raised one eyebrow. "Okay. According to my gal, Amy Fleming started calling Mason at work and harassing her. Came by the office a couple of times and even confronted her at her house. Finally,

Mason's old man started believing the rumors."

"That must not have gone over well in the department." Sophie scooped up a bite of quiche. "Go on, Buck."

"Basically, Amy Fleming waited in the parking garage for Mason to leave work one afternoon and tried to kill her. Lucky for Mason, Amy drove one of those little Mini Cooper cars, and her aim wasn't so good. Our little Amy did manage hit her hard enough to throw her onto the hood of a parked car, though, but not enough to kill her. Mason ended up in the hospital. Said she wasn't watching where she was going, and Fleming's old lady said it was an accident. The cops got her for leaving the scene—hit and run. She told the them she didn't realize she'd hit someone. Something about…she remembered hitting a bump and losing control for a minute, but had been on medication and really didn't recall."

"Didn't the garage have security cameras?" Sophie asked as she leaned back and picked up her coffee cup. She held up her hand and shook her head when Clare offered another muffin. "No thanks. I'm stuffed."

"Oh, yeah! There was some camera footage. Fleming was parked nose out and hit the gas the minute Mason walked off the elevator. Our man Fleming went on television and actually squeezed out a few crocodile tears. Denied everything. Claimed his wife needed a *rest.* She had been under a lot of stress since the *accident*, and they were all so sorry for the hurt that was caused to the Mason family. In fact, he claimed he was taking early retirement to devote all his time to his wife's healing and the care of their son. A *real* stand-up guy."

"What about the Mason family?" Clare asked. She cut another piece of quiche for herself and one for Buck.

"Thanks, Clare." He reached for another muffin and more bacon as she placed the quiche on his plate. "She left town as far as I know. Got divorced—her old man got the house and the dogs.

"I'll bet the cop shop took sides in this," Sophie said.

"Most, if not all, took the side of Detective Mason. Probably the reason Fleming decided to retire. The handwriting was on the wall, literally, I heard. Lots of name calling and veiled threats posted here and there. He'd lost the trust of his men. Even though the papers were on Fleming's side, it didn't help him with the other officers. The media painted the Mason woman in a bad light—even alluded that maybe Mason started the rumor herself because she was infatuated with him. Mrs. Fleming looks like the milk of human kindness pours out of her rosebud lips by the gallons." Buck shrugged. "He's got those all-American boy good looks."

"Where's Amy Fleming now?" Clare asked. "There's been no talk around town that Chief Fleming brought his wife or son with him."

"That I don't know. I'm checking on that angle. I put a call in to my lady friend. We parted on good terms. Even thought when I finished here, I'd head down to see her. Also, I'm thinking I might be able to hang some of Fleming's dirty laundry out and tie it into this story. We'll see how it plays out."

Sophie poured herself another cup of coffee and topped off Clare and Buck's. "I can tell you one thing for sure. You hang this laundry out in Amelia Bay, and he won't be acting chief anymore. He'll be history. Chief Bradshaw isn't going to like this. How the hell did he not trip to this situation before he and city council hired him?"

"Like I said, he's smooth operator." He looked at Clare as he blew on his coffee, "You're awful quiet."

"Buck, I don't know what to say. After the way, he treated me when the prowler lurked around my house and now this..."

Sophie loaded the dishwasher after Buck left for Seabeck. "I think those two fellas, Gage and Rene, will love giving a human-interest story to Buck. He took his camera with him, and thinks he can sell the story to one of the show biz tabloids. Those types thrive on publicity."

"I hope he can get them to open up. Do you have any plans for today, Sophie?"

"I do, but I can change things around if need be, kiddo. Otherwise I'm going to get going."

"I'm going to call Pete to get the address for Cole's nanny and see about going over there. I want to meet my nephew. I'd like him to get to know us. Maybe I can convince the nanny to bring Cole, and they could spend a few days with my parents at your place in Sequim."

"I have no problem with that. There's plenty of room. Most of the media have moved on from your parents' place. I think they could come home in a couple days."

Bev breezed through the kitchen door as Sophie headed out. "Did I miss breakfast?" She plopped down on one of the new parson's chairs upholstered in gold toile that Clare had purchased for the kitchen. "Wow, these are comfy."

"I think so too. They look great with the gold and cream check curtains. The color plays nicely off of the dark wood cabinets." Clare sliced a piece of quiche and popped it into the microwave along with a muffin. "Have you heard any word about Bets?"

"Sorry, nothing to report. It's like she vanished into thin air. Dad said the police checked all the hospitals for miles around and no one of her description showed up with cuts."

"I have to call my mom and see if she wants to go with me to visit her newest grandson—after I call Pete for the address."

***

Clare and her mother had agreed to meet in a coffee shop on Bainbridge Island. She parked and spotted her mother through the window. Grace twisted her napkin between her fingers. She had been at the birth of each one of her grandchildren. Now she had to forge a relationship with a grandson she had never met. They all did for that matter. Clare pulled open the door, and the sounds of *Redneck Woman* floated over the airwaves. Her mother loved Willie, Dolly, Daniels, and Strait. Hank Williams and Patsy Cline were right up there with all the rest. She sang her favorites to her children and her grandchildren when she rocked them to sleep and hummed the songs while she puttered around the house cleaning and cooking. *Crazy* was one of Clare's favorites, and Grace with her beautiful voice could do that song justice.

"Hi Mom." Clare leaned in for a kiss and hug. Grace clung to her, and when her mother finally released her, she could see tears in her eyes. "I'm nervous too, Mom."

"Oh, Clare, what if he doesn't like us? I know he'll be frightened."

"What's not to like?" Clare extended her hand and pulled Grace to her feet. "Let's go. The nanny sounded nice on the phone. She hasn't told Cole about his mother yet." She put some money on the table and nodded to the waitress.

Clare drove along the bay to Beach Drive. The house sat down by the water while the garage was at street level. They got out of the car, and Clare took Grace's hand as they made their way down the wooden steps to the house. "According to Pete, Doctor Jackson is a dentist, his wife is a teacher, and their daughter, Mia, is Cole's nanny."

"It's a lovely home." Grace's voice was taut, but she took a deep breath, cleared her throat, and pulled herself up ramrod straight before she rang the doorbell.

The sound of tiny feet raced toward the door, and a reedy voice hollered, "I get it, I get it!"

"No, Cole. You never open a door unless we see who it is first."

The curtain on the sidelight pulled aside and the image of Finn as a young boy peered up at them. Grace's hand flew up to her mouth, and she gasped. The door opened and a, now shy, little boy ducked behind a young woman's skirt. He peeked at them and said, "You're my grammy. Daddy and Mommy showed me your picture. Will you read me a story?" He grabbed Grace's hand and pulled her to a rocking chair tucked in a corner with a table covered in books. She looked back at Clare and grinned.

"Mia Jackson. You must be Clare." The nanny laughed and held out her hand. She was a lovely, with an infectious laugh. "Precocious little guy. He's been waiting—*impatiently*. I hope you're hungry, if not, fake it. My mother's a feeder. If you're not eating, she's not happy."

"Actually, I'm hungry. I love feeders, because I'm always hungry." Clare followed her to the dining table set with a lavish spread of sandwiches, a tureen filled with soup, and a casserole of mac and cheese. A plate of cookies sat on a sideboard—homemade by the looks of them. She sighed, "I think your mother is my new best friend."

A woman breezed into the room carrying a cake. "Hello, I'm Mia's mother, Anna." She held up the cake. "I hope you like chocolate. It has a delightful layer of whipped cream in the center. She placed the cake next to the cookies. She was petite woman with salon styled blond hair that had a pinkish cast to it. Anna reminded Clare of the actress, Helen Mirren. Mia was a younger version.

"You have a lovely home." Clare walked over to the windows that looked out on Puget Sound. Gentle waves lapped the shoreline. "And the food… Thank you, we never expected this."

"You're welcome."

Cole—cuddled in his grandmother's lap—was losing the battle to stay awake.

"Mia, I see Cole is dozing off. It's past his naptime. Why don't you put him down, and we can have a nice visit with these ladies?"

Mia rolled her eyes and walked over to pick up Cole. Clare could see Grace was reluctant to let the little guy go as Mia picked him up. "He's been so excited waiting for you. He's worn himself out."

"Clare, if you'll sit there and Grace there, I'll ladle the soup—vegetable. Made with mostly winter veggies from my garden." She placed a bowl in front of each of them after she sprinkled some cheese in the center of each bowl. She filled one for herself and sat down. "Grilled ham and cheese, also plain cheese. One never knows if someone is a veggie person. If you're a vegan…I guess I can rustle up some water crackers."

"No, everything is perfect. It looks delicious. Clare is right, we certainly did not expect this. Thank you."

"You're welcome, Grace. My pleasure. Mia will be with us in a few minutes. So, I will get right down to it. She and Eve were very close, and this has devastated her. She loves that little fella like he was her own. She can't have children, you know. You see, she was married to cad of a man. Once he found out she couldn't bear his offspring, he left her. Just like that. Found out one day and was gone the next."

"Mother! You don't need to tell them all my personal trials." Mia walked in and took a seat. She reached for a bowl to fill, but her mother outreached her and filled the bowl.

Clare thought Anna might jump up and tie a napkin around Mia's neck.

"I'm sorry to hear that." Clare selected a sandwich and bit into its gooey cheese and crisp, bread, then slid the plate over to Mia. "Finn has every intention of keeping you on as Cole's nanny."

"Humph, and if he goes to jail, then what? I'm sure you will take him away from her and absorb Cole into your family. I understand you have quite a large family?"

"Of course, he isn't guilty of murder. He's a loving man and good father." Mia reached for a sandwich. Eager to change the subject, she said, "Look, here comes Dad and Tomas. My father and brother have been fishing. Hope they caught dinner."

Clare glanced out the window at the returning fishermen.

"My son is guilty of no crime, Anna." Grace directed a gimlet-eyed look toward her, then took a composing breath. "We were hoping Mia and Cole would spend a few days with us at our home. My older son, his wife, and children are staying with us while their house is being…uh…renovated."

Anna looked out the window and tapped her index finger on her lip for a few moments. Clare raised her eyebrows at Grace.

"I think that will be acceptable. For a few days, only. I'll come along and drop them off. I'd like to see where they will be accommodated."

"Shouldn't we ask Mia?" Clare looked over at her. Her mother acted as if she wasn't seated at the table or a capable woman.

Anna smiled at her daughter and said, "Mia is a good girl. She does what is expected of her. Then it's settled. Shall we say tomorrow afternoon?"

Anger flashed in Mia's eyes. "Mother, I'm capable of making my own decisions. Yes, Mrs. Harrigan I would *love* to spend time with you and get to know Cole's family. They finished their lunch and settled on a time for them to bring Cole over before they left.

"I think Mia will be thrilled to be someplace that woman can't control her every move," Clare said, as she and Grace climbed the stairs back up to the street level.

"Your father and I are anxious to be home. Since most of the media hoopla is focused on other areas now—we should be safe. The swelling in his leg has gone down, and he needs a cast put on the lower part of his leg." Grace stopped abruptly at the top and stared at the SUV. One of the rear tires was slashed and the word *murderer* was scratched across the fender. "This simply will not do."

"What the…?" Seething, Clare took a couple of deep

breaths, then opened the tailgate. She found the jack and the spare. She looked around and a shiver ran up her back. She had the sensation of eyes watching her even though she couldn't see anyone. Irish sixth sense. "Let's get this done and get out of here."

Grace's hands trembled as she tried to help. Clare pulled Pete's leather jacket out of the backseat and wrapped it around Grace's shoulders. "Sit on that rock, Mom. I can handle this."

Chapter 15

"I don't know what to think, Bev. Someone must have followed us out there, and I had the feeling whomever it was lurked nearby watching us. After getting run off the road, I should have been more alert." Clare placed a plate of buttered toast and a jar of jelly on table. Maggie and Ginger scooted over to Bev and looked at her with sad eyes.

"Could it have been someone at the Jackson house?" Bev broke off a couple of pieces of toast to feed the oh-so-neglected-dogs.

Clare stood at the stove stirring a pot of oatmeal. "I don't see how. Mia was gone for a few minutes while she carried Cole in for his nap. I watched her father and brother pull their boat onto the beach. They took the fish out and started filleting them on a worktable. I didn't watch them every second, but why?"

Bev sipped a cup of coffee and bit a slice of toast slathered in jelly. Clare filled four bowls with oatmeal—one for each of them and the dogs. She placed brown sugar and a pitcher of milk on the table.

"I have had enough of all the nasty stuff that's been going on. I'm going to start acting—not reacting, Bev."

"Count me in, Kemosabe. Where to first? The Lone Ranger

and Tonto ride again." Bev hesitated, then said, "Only this time…let's be more careful."

"Agreed. We are going back to see Bets' mother. She knows more than she let on to us, and I'm sure she lied. Then we are going out to that commune or cult or whatever those Evening Star people are."

They ate in silence until the phone rang. "Hey Pete, what's up?" Clare listened for a few moments and blew out a breath. "Thanks, Pete."

"The blood type found at Pete's house and Bets' apartment is a match," Clare said after she hung up the phone. "But wouldn't that mean she was injured at Pete's house, but still alive when she reached her apartment? Fleming should have realized that all along."

"How did she get from Pete's? She didn't walk. It's too far, especially if you are losing blood." Bev sipped her coffee. "Didn't Finn tell you he picked her up from the pub, and they brought a pizza back to the house?"

"Yes, now that I think about it. Did you see an extra car at Pete's place the day you were playing secret agent?"

"An extra car there is like asking if I noticed an extra beer mug in the pub." Bev stood up and took Clare's bowl away. "Let's go, now." She rinsed her cup, and the bowls.

Clare frowned. "I wasn't finished."

On the drive, over to Bets' apartment, Clare noticed a truck seemed to be following them. "Bev, don't turn around, but I think we are being followed."

Bev reached up and pulled down the visor and slid the mirror cover over. "How long have they been back there?"

"Since we pulled onto Salmon Run. I'm going to drive past the Marina Apartments and head toward the police department. Can you make out a license number?"

"The whole front is covered in mud. I can't even see the make or model. If I hazard a guess, I would say a Ford, because it looks kind of like the shape of my dad's truck. It does look like the driver has a ballcap on and sunglasses."

Clare put her signal on to turn into the parking lot of the police station. The truck dropped back, turned, and zoomed up a side street. Clare drove around the parking lot and headed back to the apartments.

They parked and walked up to the apartment. Clare noticed the curtains were drawn. A footed urn sat next to the door, bursting with purple and white ornamental kale. She rang the bell and the curtain flicked slightly. She waited, then knocked. "Please, open the door, Mrs. Woodman. We know you're in there. We only want to help."

"How...how can you help? Leave...me...alone." Tears choked her voice. "I don't know...I don't know what to do. I'm not going to listen to you. Go away! Your brother killed her. That's what happened to her."

"No, he didn't. She got a phone call in the middle of the night, and she left. If he killed her, why was her blood found here? We want to find Bets. If you don't know where she is, maybe we can help. Please, open the door." A few moments slipped by before the sound of a lock clicked. The door edged open. Clare hadn't noticed the other day that she had the same strawberry blond hair as Bets. But the scattering of freckles was partially obscured by the red blotches on her tear-soaked face. She was dressed again in what must have been her daughter's clothing—jeans and a sweater. She opened the door all the way, stepped back and turned away. The bruises on her arms and face had turned to a sickly yellowish green.

"Mrs. Woodman, we only..."

"Don't, don't call me that! I told you, I'm nobody's Mrs. Anyone. Brenda, *please*. I never married that man. Oh, some trumped up ceremony performed by some pretend minister. I was forced."

"Oh." Clare and Bev said in unison.

"My husband took off and left me with nothing. Betsy, Jonathon, and I were living in a small trailer. We were getting by. Just barely though. I was waiting tables. Every week I'd go to the farmer's market in Sequim. I met The Evening Star people there selling their wares. The women brought handmade items and quilts. They grew all their food—made cheese from cow and goat's milk. Everyone pitched in and helped each other. It seemed the idyllic life to me. Boy, was I wrong."

Clare and Bev let her ramble. Occasionally murmuring sympathetic responses.

"That's when the monster decided he wanted me. By then they had taken my wreck of car and all my belongings, which weren't much." She looked up at them. "I was pretty back then."

"You're still pretty now," Bev said as she reached out and touched her arm. "It's good to get all this out. A friend of ours helped a woman, who left the group and got her settled in Seattle."

Brenda looked away for a moment. "Must have been Arlene. I wondered what happened to her. She told them she had to use the restroom, and the booth at the farmer's market was so busy, they let her go alone. Usually a man accompanied you and stood outside and waited. Betsy ran away when she turned eighteen. She managed to have a friend sneak me her cell phone number a few months later when I was working the booth. Then my son left. I don't know where either of my kids are right now. I'm so afraid Betsy and Jonathon are dead, and I'll never see them again." She broke down and started sobbing.

"Brenda, when was the last time you saw Betsy or spoke to her? Have you called her cell phone?" Clare reached in her purse for some tissues and handed them to her. "And who was this friend? Whoever it is might know where she is."

Brenda waited a split second too long to answer. "I don't remember."

"Was it a man or a woman?" Clare watched her closely.

"I…I don't know. We were busy that day. And of course, I've called her cell phone. It goes right to voicemail, and the last time I saw her was at dinner the night she ran away. I want to find my kids and leave this place."

"Where is Woodman now?"

Again, she hesitated before answering. "I don't know…uh…I guess at the compound."

"Your son?"

"Look, I understand you want to help, but you can't. I'm worn out, and I need you to leave…now. Leave me alone and don't come back here." Brenda stood and walked to the door. Clare and Bev got up and followed her.

"Here's my card. Call me if you need anything. Anything at all."

"Yeah. Sure. Thanks." She took the card and slipped it in the pocket of her jeans, then opened the door, and Clare and Bev stepped outside. The door closed behind them. The locks snapped back into place.

Once they were in the car, Bev said, "She still isn't being honest with us. I can understand how frightened she is after the life she's lived. I had my dad to turn to when things went south for me. If she last saw Bets the night she left, how did she know she had shortened her name to Bets?"

"Yeah, I agree. She's holding something back and lying. We're going to find out just what that something is." Clare turned the key and the SUV roared to life. "Let's grab some lunch. I didn't get to finish my breakfast." She gave Bev a pointed look. "I have to drop this baby off at the garage later to get the tire repaired and hopefully, get the scratches rubbed out."

The crowd in the pub had diminished since the last time they had been there, but it was still pretty busy. Lynn was sitting on a stool at the hostess station. Clare looked down at her legs. She was wearing slacks.

"I'm healing nicely, but need to take it easy for a while." She smiled and started to get up.

"You sit right there. We can manage. It's good to see you back at work. Anyway, no special treatment for non-paying customers." Clare picked up a couple of menus. "Is the table by the fireplace okay?"

Lynn nodded. "This such a nice place to work. I was paid for the time off and all my medical expenses. Jack wanted me to stay home, but I was getting bored."

"If you need anything, let one of us know," Bev said.

Crisp white table squares over hunter green tablecloths and orange napkins heralded the arrival of autumn and Thanksgiving. Little pumpkins nestled among pots of mums that decorated every table.

Once they were seated, Bev said, "Look who just walked in. Stan and Clay. Let's ask them to join us and...*behave* yourself, Clare. I don't want a repeat of the last time we had lunch with them." Bev lifted her arm and waved them over to the table.

Clare rolled her eyes, then smiled as her ex-husband and his business partner approached the table. She was always happy to see the charming Clay, and Stan had, literally, been a lifesaver to her a few months ago.

The waitresses were hopping. Lily, one of the new gals, came up to their table and reeled off the specials. She was a quick learner. "Do you need a few more minutes?"

"Easy choice. I'll have the bangers and mash with the red-wine gravy." Clare's mouth was watering at the thought of this treat. "I'll have the steamed cabbage with it, please."

"Make that two," Bev added.

Clay glanced at Stan who nodded. "Make it easy. We'll all have the same thing." He looked around the table. "Coffee for everyone?"

"You all do make it easy. I never even heard of this dish until today!" Lily told them. "It's so good." With those parting words, she spun around and headed to the kitchen.

"Clare, I'm sorry to hear about Finn. Also, sorry to hear of the scary things that have happened to you. Stan and I were talking to Pete earlier." Clay paused for a minute as Lily brought their coffees to the table. She placed a thermal carafe in the center of the table. "Thank you, Lily."

"How's your dad?" Stan asked. "It feels like a black cloud is hanging over the family. Finn, Bets' disappearance, Mike's broken leg, and someone ran you off the road? The keying of Pete's Land Cruiser… And what's this I hear about Finn having a…son?"

"You left out slashed tire, someone trying to break into my house, and the body of Cole's mother found behind my garage. Wow, when you put it all together, it really is a medley of misery plaguing us."

"Cole, I assume, is the son of Finn and the poor woman who died?" Clay asked.

Bev nodded. "There is good news. Mister H. will be getting his cast on today, and the best part…" Bev turned to Clare and smiled. "Cole's nanny has agreed to spend a few days at the farm so the little fella can get to know his family. I am sure he'll soon be asking questions about his mother and father, though."

The servers arrived with their lunches of steaming mashed potatoes and pork sausages smothered in red-wine gravy. A perfectly steamed mound of buttery cabbage was piled on the side.

"I can't afford to eat like this every day," Stan said. "I need to watch my waistline."

"I've been watching my waistline grow for quite a while lately." Clay glanced down at his paunch. In days gone by, it would have been said, he looked successful, which he was. But successful today means a person can afford a personal trainer and an exclusive gym membership.

Bev reached over and placed her hand on Clay's. "You look just right." He put his other hand on top of hers and let it linger there for a few moments.

Clare looked at Stan. Even though they were divorced, they could still communicate with the special looks couples, who have been married for many years, share. A smile twitched the corners of Stan's lips. The moment was over and everyone resumed eating and oohing and ahhing over the pub grub.

Stan laid his napkin next to his plate. He reached for his wallet and Clay held up his hand and shook his head. "Thanks, Clay. I have to get moving. I'm heading to the airport. My family is gathering at their cabin in Tahoe for Thanksgiving. Looking forward to doing a little skiing with Emma and relaxing. He bent over and kissed Bev's cheek, then looked at Clare, who smiled at him. He kissed her cheek and whispered, "Watch your back, Clarabelle. Happy Thanksgiving to all of you." With that, he turned and left.

Clare watched him go. The cabin in Tahoe boasted seven bedrooms, *en suite,* along with a gentleman and his wife who were the caretakers and lived in an apartment over the garage year-round. She thought about it…nope, she did not miss that lifestyle. "How about you, Clay? What are your plans?" Clare asked.

"Stan invited me to go with him, but I find his family a little…"

"Shallow and self-absorbed?" Clare laughed. "No arguments. You're going to have dinner at my place. There's so much that has gone wrong lately. I hope all of us being together, we'll find things to be thankful for and offer love and support to each other. Of course, there'll be no staff cooking, serving, or cleaning up after us."

Clay laughed. "I'd be delighted. I'm not much of a cook, but I will say my cleaning skills are topnotch. Maybe, just maybe, it will be a celebration of Finn's release, and this whole ugly mess will be over. What are you ladies up to this afternoon?"

"We decided to head out to The Evening Star compound to try to find some nugget of information that might shine a light on what happened to Bets."

"You both thought the two of you would go out there all alone…after all that's happened?" He looked back and forth between the two of them. Are you nuts? I know you both did some crazy things and nearly got yourselves killed a few months ago, but think about it. Your luck is bound to run out sooner or later."

"Clay, we can't just sit around cooling our heels while Finn sits in a jail cell, and Fleming isn't looking for another candidate to pin a murder on."

"I'm going with you. We aren't opening the office until next Wednesday and the holidays are always a slow time." Clay reached for his wallet and dropped some bills on the table. "Let's go."

"I have to drop off Pete's Land Cruiser for repairs first. If you'd follow me to the garage, we can leave from there."

Chapter 16

Clay stopped his truck at the entrance of The Evening Star compound. Surprise lit up each of their faces. Instead of an unwelcoming and foreboding place, what greeted them seemed to bid them to enter. It was a welcoming place. Wrought iron gates, that hung on stone columns, stood open. The driveway curved to the left, and evergreen trees, ferns, and azaleas, which must be breathtaking when in bloom, covered the banks. Clay shifted into drive and pulled through the gates. A break in the trees opened up to a pasture on the left, with cows and sheep leisurely grazing. A few curious heifers looked up as they passed, then turned their heads back to the business-at-hand. To the right, they saw pristine white buildings clustered around an open lawn area with a large pavilion that held rows of seats. Two bright reds barns stood beyond the field of animals.

"No wonder Brenda thought she found paradise for herself and her children," Bev said. "I thought they were some rag-tag bunch of religious nuts living in huts and tents."

"This type of operation cost someone a great deal of money. I wonder where it came from?" Clay pulled off to the side of the driveway and parked.

"I've heard when people join these cults, they have to give up all their money, property, and possessions. Whoever built this has vision," Clare said, as she stepped out of the truck.

Standing near one of the buildings were two men and three women. One of men indicated the women should go inside. Two went inside but the third woman followed the men, who made the walk across the expanse of lawn in record time. Clare recognized both of them as two of the men in the pub the day Bets went missing. The woman clutched the younger man's arm. She looked at him with hunger in her eyes.

The older of the two spoke. "What are you doing here? Leave immediately. You are trespassing on private property." He glared at them.

Clay stepped forward. "We have a few questions to ask first. But we would like to ask them of Mr. Woodman. Would you please let him know we're here? And may I ask, what is your name, sir?"

Clay was not large in stature, but he possessed a commanding presence when the situation called for it. Clare had often thought of him as a cuddly teddy bear with his graying hair he wore banded in a short pony tail at the nape of his neck. He spoke with an endearing, barely discernable, lisp.

"I am Brother Bergman, and this is my son, True. Brother Woodman is not here. He is on retreat, and I have no idea when he will return. He often goes for a week or two at a time."

"Perhaps we could speak with Mrs. Woodman." Bev asked, trying to spark a reaction from the men. "We are also concerned about Bets...Elizabeth."

"Not that it is any of your business, Sister Woodman is with her husband. He, of course, requires someone to tend to his wishes and needs as he prays to lift his soul to a higher plane of understanding. Something people like you would not be able to comprehend." His face began to turn the color of a beet, and his eyes started to blink rapidly. "Sister Elizabeth..."

"Father, please. Calm yourself." True Bergman placed a soothing hand on his father's shoulder in attempt to relieve his father's distress. "My betrothed, Sister Elizabeth, is not here, and we do not know where to find her." He turned to Clare and said, "I truly hope your brother has not *soiled* her or done her harm." He turned to the young woman. "Sister Leah, go to the women's lodge with the others."

Anger flashed in her eyes. "Elizabeth is not worthy of you, True. She deserves whatever harm has come to her! Don't you see? If she loved you, she would not have left. She has soiled herself and has not held pure for you."

"You are just a child and cannot understand. Do not say such hateful things." He disengaged her hand from his arm. "Go to the lodge. Father, attend to Sister Leah, please."

With reluctance, Brother Bergman took Leah's arm.

Once the pair left, True turned to Clare and her friends. "Now go! Never come to our compound again. You might regret it if you do." His voice held an ominous tone.

They climbed into Clay's truck, and he reversed down the drive. True followed the truck. Once they were out, he closed the gates, wrapped a chain around them, and put a padlock in place.

On the way, back to Amelia Bay, Clay asked, "Where to now, ladies?"

"I want to go to the farm and see my parents. Dad should be home from getting his cast on his leg. I also need to make sure everyone is ready for the arrival of Cole and his nanny, Mia. It'll be a full house with Pete, Dana, and their crew there. I'm hoping for good news for Finn too." She paused. "Clever of you to ask about Brenda, Bev."

"Clearly they don't know what's going on. Why is Brenda living in Bets' apartment, and where is Woodman really? Is he praying for enlightenment or shootin' craps in Vegas?"

"Interesting. The whole commune thing could be some kind of scam," Clay said. He reached over and patted Bev's hand.

***

The farm was a beehive of activity and excitement when Clare, Bev, and Clay arrived with the dogs to add to the cheerful pandemonium. Pete's youngest, Delia—Dilly as she was called by all who loved her—grabbed Clare's hand. "We have a new cousin. Not some old ones like Sean, Mac, Ben, and Emma. I mean I love them and all…but they *are* old." She sucked in her lower lip and looked at Clare to make sure she hadn't hurt her feelings.

"I understand, Dilly." Clare smiled and scooped her up in

her arms, as she walked into the kitchen. "What's cookin' Mom? It sure smells good."

"It's Southwest pumpkin soup. Terrific for a chilly day. How about if you pull the corn muffins out of the oven and toss a salad?"

"You bet," Clare said, plopping Dilly on the counter before she pulled two one-dozen tins filled with golden muffins from of the oven. She piled them into the baskets her mother had lined with napkins.

Dilly looked at her aunt with emerald green eyes exactly the color of her own. Her auburn hair sprung out in corkscrew curls all over her head. She was the image of Clare.

"They're still hot, Miss Dilly. I'll put one a plate for you, but let it cool." Satisfied, she jumped from the counter and scampered off.

Clay walked over to Grace and kissed her cheek. She turned and placed her hands on his shoulders and looked directly in his eyes. "How are you doing?"

"Better every day. Lonely, though. I'm happy to be out of a stagnant marriage. I bought a little condo down by beach and joined the local theater group. I'm not sure if I'm much of an actor, but I sure can design the sets. The group was pretty happy when they found out I was an architect. So, all in all, I'm making new friends. I left the country club folks to Jane and the new friends…they're whole lot more fun." Grace kissed his cheek and hugged him.

Clare and Bev pulled the salad fixings out of the fridge and pantry. Leafy lettuce, a crisp apple, feta cheese, Grace's homemade poppy seed dressing, and walnuts.

"Shoo, outto here. Go see your dad, Clare. Clay, will you help with the salad while I set the table." Bev picked up and unfurled the persimmon tablecloth she found sitting on the kitchen hutch. "Eating in the kitchen on a chilly day is perfect, Mrs. H."

"I thought it would make Mia and her mother feel more comfortable."

Bev placed gold napkins and cobalt blue dishes at each place setting around the big farmhouse table.

"It looks welcoming and cozy, Mom. Thanks, Bev. I think I will go see Dad." Clare walked into the sunroom to find her father surrounded by four little munchkins armed with magic markers.

"Don't worry, Auntie Clare, we are saving a special place for Cole to draw on." Dilly informed her. "Our new cousin's name is Cole. Isn't that a nice name?"

"Why don't you little ones help Auntie Bev set the table?" They scattered and left blissful quiet in their wake. "Dad, you certainly look a lot better than the last time I saw you." Clare sat in the chair next to him and reached for his hand.

"Your mother and I are glad to be home. But tell me all you know about Finn."

"I don't know much. I'm sure Pete is much more in the loop than I am. I can fill you in on some of the strange people churning around Bets. Pete told you she lied about her education?" Mike nodded. She told him about the visit to The Evening Star compound. "Bets' mother, Brenda, is living in her apartment. I know she's lying to us, but about what, or maybe everything, I have no idea." Clare did not tell him about being run off the road or that someone had tried to break into her cottage. "The two guys in Seabeck are really odd. Mom told you we went to see them? Very shallow guys. Sophie sent a reporter friend of hers out to try to wheedle some information out of them under the guise of doing a human-interest story about how devastated they must feel about Eve's death."

"Your mother told me about your visit to their home. Also, what happened to Pete's fancy SUV and the body behind your house of Cole's mother. Hmm… Aren't you leaving a couple of things out, darlin'?" Mike raised his eyebrows and leveled look at her.

"Oh…you know about those things? They were nothing really, Dad."

"Clare, didn't we go through enough a few months ago? I would have thought you learned your lesson. You, and Bev, and Eddy are lucky to be alive."

"Dad, the new chief is convinced Finn is guilty of Bets' disappearance or worse. It's up to Pete and me."

"Pete has professional investigators working on Finn's case."

Clare sighed and thought, people are more likely to talk to me than a *professional*. Bev and I solved it last time with Libby's help. Maybe it wasn't pretty, but… "I better go help Mom in the kitchen. Your new grandson will be here shortly." She leaned over and kissed him on the top of his head.

Clay motioned Clare into her father's study before she made it to the kitchen. "I know what you're up to. Bev has been spending a lot of time at the pub helping. Your dad's out of commission and…" He paused. "You need a new sidekick. And I'm available to be your Pancho. I want to keep you and Bev out of trouble and…danger."

"I don't need babysitting, but I do understand the concern, and I know my objections will fall on deaf ears. Libby's tied up with her Christmas pageant, Sophie is helping on the peripheral, but there is something going on with her." Clare had a puzzled look on her face. "I'm going to find out exactly what." Clare laughed. "So, you want be Pancho? Bev told you about that, did she?

Clay looked at her with a knowing smile. "Putting that aside, Bev told me she and her equalizers are moving in with you until everything is settled. I'll watch over you and her."

"As long as you promise not to serenade me in your underwear, I'm okay with it." Clay's head snapped back with a deer in the headlights look. Clare smiled and shook her head at the memory of Bev singing Carol King's *Where You Lead* using a shampoo bottle for a microphone a few months ago. "She didn't tell you about that?"

Clay became solemn with a hint of smile playing at the edges of his mouth. "I'll swear to that one on the architectural bible of Frank Lloyd Wright."

The doorbell rang, dogs barked, and a cluster of small feet raced to the rarely used front door. The new cousin had arrived. Clare watched her mother herd the kibbles and bits away from the door. Grace looked into the mirror that hung in the entryway tucked a few strands hair back into her chignon, squared her shoulders, and opened the door. "Welcome to our home."

"And a lovely home it is," Anna Jackson said, as she sailed through the door. She slipped off her coat and handed it to Clay and gave him a tight smile. Looking around, she said, "Mia, you and Cole should be quite comfy here for a few days. As I told you, it is important for the Larson family to get to know you and the young fella if they are to be a part of your lives." She headed for the kitchen with Grace following behind her.

Grace's backward glance of astonishment told Clare she had to take over for her with Mia.

Mia hung back a little, holding Cole's hand. He pulled free and pushed through the door. Dilly approached him, grinning ear to ear. "Come on, you have to meet our grampy." The kids were gone in a flash.

"I…I think I should go with Cole. He might feel a little uncomfortable."

Clay stepped forward and picked up their bags after laying Anna's coat on the hall bench. "I'm sure he'll be fine in Dilly's capable hands. Please, come in."

"I know this must feel strange to you, Mia," Clare said, as she helped her with her coat. "Complete strangers and all… I understand."

"Not really. I've been all over the world in stranger's homes. Working for Eve is the second nanny position I've held. I taught first and second grade for a few years." Mia said, looking around. "Your parents do have a lovely home."

Dana, who had been in the background observing, said, "Hi, I'm Dana. I am married to Clare's older brother, Pete. Those four kids you almost met are mine. We have a room all ready for you. The house is full right now. There's a cot for Cole in the room, but I have a feeling my rowdy bunch will want him to bunk with them. Clay, would you bring the bags while I lead the way?"

"Take your time to getting settled, and when you're ready, come down to the kitchen," Clare said.

The trio started up the stairs, and Clare heard Dana say, "I am having my house redecorated. That's why we're staying here." Poor Pete, this was going to cost him and Dana a bundle. She followed her nose into the kitchen.

***

Clare checked her text messages as Clay drove her and Bev over to the cottage. "Sophie and Buck are at the cottage waiting for us. I'm anxious to hear what Buck has to say about his visit to the fellas in Seabeck."

"What are those fellas' names again, and what do they do?" Bev asked. "Refresh my memory and update Clay."

"Gage Brinker is…was Eve's script writing partner, and Rene Bertrand is Brinker's life partner. Bertrand was *not* a fan of Eve either. He's the whinny sort…kind of resentful of her. I guess she turned him down for a part in one of the sitcoms she wrote for because she thought he was too good-looking."

"Oh, I can see where that would be hurtful. I say with my tongue planted firmly in my cheek," Clay said as he pulled into Clare's driveway behind Sophie and Buck's cars.

Sophie and Buck were standing on the deck, coffee cups in hand, looking out toward Amelia Bay. Steam drifted off of the cups and vanished into the brisk afternoon air.

"Be careful and don't lean on that rickety railing." Clare called out to them, as she bounded up the steps. "I have to ask Eddy to come over here to do some repairs before someone is hurt." She paused on the top step to catch her breath. "Better start running again. I sure miss kayaking in the winter months too. Have you two had lunch?"

"Yep, we ate at the Amelia Bay Hotel Restaurant. Buck's staying there. But I wouldn't say no to dessert."

"You're on. I have a delicious carrot cake with pineapple, walnuts, and coconut topped off with cream cheese frosting. With all the fruit and carrots, how could it be unhealthy? My *new* Aunt Fio baked it, but Mia's mother brought a dessert so, Mom served that and sent this home with me."

"Uncle Pug and Fiona tied the Celtic knot, so to speak? I've always adored her. Clay, this is Buck," Sophie said as she helped Clare get plates and napkins onto the table. "How are your mom and dad doing…and Finn?"

Bev reached into the refrigerator and pulled out the milk. She poured a glass for Clay without him asking. Sophie looked at Clare, who shrugged with an I-know-as-much-as-you-do look.

"All pretty good. Mom—she's holding up, the way she always does. Finn—I'm going to see him later today. I'm afraid they are going to transfer him to county. I know Fleming's been keeping him here, so he's trapped in his web."

Once everyone was settled around the table delving into the delicious cake, Clare looked at Buck. "How did it go in Seabeck?"

"Those two guys tried to avoid telling me much. Some croc tears from that Brinker guy. And that Rene fella…whoa. That guy's a piece of work. I brought my camera with me and they loved that. I told them I was freelancing for *People* magazine. They really loved that! Also, People was going to put out a special edition because this story is so explosive."

"Are they?" Bev asked, her eyes big as saucers.

"Nah. At least not that I know of. Mostly they gushed about Eve, and who could ever 'extinguish the bright light' of such a wonderful person. She was a joy to work with and talented, yadda, yadda, yadda. What was to become of her darling little boy? Both of them phonies." Buck finished off his cake. "This sure is good."

"I agree they are frauds. Can I get you another slice of cake, Buck?"

"Just a small one, thanks. I had a strange feeling when I was there. They were both nervous. At one point, I thought I heard a noise in the back of the house. A door closing…maybe. Could have been my imagination or something outside."

Clare handed him another piece of cake and topped off his coffee.

Buck nodded. "Thanks, Clare. Anyway, they told me they had an appointment. So, I folded up my tent, thanked them, and asked if I could give 'em a call if I had any follow-up questions. Now, here's where it gets interesting."

The others sat listening, giving Buck the floor. Clare gave Maggie and Ginger each a treat, and they trotted into the dining room.

"I decided to follow them. No special reason, but you never know. I parked in a driveway at the end of the road opposite their place. A couple of minutes later, they pull out in a sweet, canary-yellow Mercedes sports coupe. I followed them to an auto body shop in Bremerton. The young guy jumps out and heads inside. A few minutes later out he comes and hops into a shiny black pickup truck."

Clay let out a low whistle and leaned back in his chair. "Clare, wasn't that the color of truck that ran you off the road?"

Clare nodded. "Glen and I both think so, but it was dark."

"That's what I thought. I let the guys head out. Figured they'd go back to Seabeck. An old guy, I thought might be the owner, comes out and gets in a truck, and leaves. A bit of luck there. Then I went in the garage. A young kid was sweeping the floor. I asked him what kind of damage they'd repaired on the black truck that just left." Buck took a bite of his cake and a sip of coffee. "Kid shook his head, and I laid a couple of twenties on the counter. He scooped them up and said they replaced the bumper. There was damage to the right front. Not bad, but they wanted a new one."

"Did you ask if they paid cash or used insurance?" Sophie asked.

"I did. Cash. Not a credit card or a check."

Chapter 17

A gentle mist swirled around Bev's Cadillac Escalade as she drove Clare to the jail to visit Finn. They had picked up magazines, books, and some special treats for him. Clare knew her mother had been visiting him, and he most likely had more than enough goodies. Their heads still reeled with the bombshell Buck had dropped on them earlier.

Still not ready to talk about what she had learned, Clare said, "This is some luxury car, Bev." Clare ran her hands over the leather upholstery.

"I didn't buy it new, and my dad got a pretty good deal on it for me. After what happened to my previous car, I wanted another heavy, solid vehicle. It does have a lot of nice bells and whistles, though." She paused and said, "Okay, let's stop beating around the bush. Do you think those fellas, Rene and Gage, could have killed Eve?"

"It kind of adds up in a way."

Bev parked her car in the lot and the women walked into the station. They were startled to see Pete pacing the reception area.

"What's up, Pete?"

"Plenty. The DNA results came back, and they're a familial match."

Clare put her hand on his shoulder. "Exactly what does that

mean?"

"Let's step outside." Pete directed them to his car and opened the door. Bev and Clare slid in the back seat. "It's private here and out of the cold and wind," he said once they were settled. "Simply put, the blood DNA is not a perfect match to the DNA the lab tested from articles taken from Bets' apartment. It could be a sibling, her mother, father, or even another close relative. But the blood is *not* from Bets."

"That's good news, right?" Bev asked.

"You're not smiling, Pete. I sense there is some bad news coming." Clare leaned back into the plush leather seat and tented her fingers pressing, them against her lips. Pete nodded. Sadness stole over his face.

"Let me go on with the rest of the good news. Finn is being released."

"But that's fantastic news," Bev said.

"Wait a minute. Why am I just hearing about this now? You could have called and let someone know! I..."

Pete held up his hand. "It's been a crazy day. I didn't call anyone because things have been flying at a furious pace. Now all they have on Finn is some circumstantial evidence that doesn't point to a crime, but..."

Here it comes, Clare thought. She braced herself waiting for an axe to drop that would slice their joy and relief for Finn and the family in half.

"Bets' body was found last night. She was found in a wooded area next to her apartment building. There's a lot of underbrush and trees." Clare and Bev recoiled. "She's only been dead for about twenty-four hours. That puts our boy in the clear for her murder *and* for the murder of Cole's mother, Everest Johansson."

Clare felt anger surge through her body. Who could be killing these beautiful young women? She got out of Pete's car with determination to help find this evil killer.

"Let's bring our guy home, then will see what the next steps should be," Pete said, as pushed open the doors to the station and held them for Clare and Bev.

"Hello, Ms. Rockman." She stood by the coffee station stirring clumps of powdered creamer into her cup. Five sugar packets were scattered on the counter. She swept the empty packets into the trash and scowled at Clare before picking up her cup.

A smug smile appeared on her rather squashed-looking face. "The chief is busy. He's talking to his *wife*."

Pete stepped up to her. He towered over the woman. "We've come to pick up Finn Harrigan. Is he ready to leave?"

Rocky didn't answer. She turned and started to walk away.

"Excuse me, Ms. Rockman, I would like an answer. Is Finn Harrigan ready to leave?"

Clare glanced over to the chief's office and saw him in a heated conversation with a woman who was shaking her finger at him. So, that's the hit and run driver, she thought. At that moment, Jake Fleming jerked his head in their direction, and his wife turned to see what had taken his attention away from her. He stood and walked out of his office with his wife close behind. Mrs. Fleming walked over to Rocky's desk and slid onto to it and crossed her legs. Rocky leaned over and whispered something to her. She smiled and nodded. They both stared at Clare and Bev.

"That little woman took an instant dislike to me, and I don't understand it," Clare said.

Fleming crossed the room in quick strides and motioned Pete over to a desk. Finn walked through the door that led to the cell area. His clothes were rumbled, and he appeared traumatized. Certainly, not her glib brother who loped through life.

"Finn." Tears glistened in Clare's eyes partly for the release of the tension she had felt for the last several days, but mostly for Bets. The lovely woman with the cloud of strawberry blond hair who had known so little happiness in her short life. Anger bubbled up inside of her again. I will not let this go, Clare thought. She turned and took Bev's arm. They walked over to the men who were signing some paperwork.

"You're free to go, Harrigan. But I know in my gut you're guilty of something, and when I get the goods on you, I'll haul your ass back here and lock you up. Those bloody clothes mean something."

Sparks flashed in Clare's eyes and she asked, "Hmm… Tell me, Chief Fleming, was their blood on Ms. Mason's clothing after the hit and run?"

"What…how…how the hell…?" Shock radiated on

Fleming's, now beet-red face.

Pete and Finn shot her a questioning looks. Bev smiled. Clare turned and looked at Mrs. Fleming, who slid off the desk in a less than graceful way. The fireplug's mouth popped open. She knew they had been listening. Clare smiled sweetly and locked her arm through Finn's. Bev took his other arm, and they walked out of the station with a confused Pete following behind.

Once they were outside, Pete asked, "What do you know that I don't know, Clare, and I would guess Bev too?"

"A lot, but nothing to do with Finn's case. It seems little Amy Fleming aimed her car at Ms. Mason, the woman the chief was doing the nasty with. Fleming was head of the Robbery-Homicide Division of Portland at the time. She fled the scene."

"She looks so sweet…but I guess she's a lot crazy," Finn said. "I have met beautiful and seemingly sweet that turn into crazy."

"Get in the car, Finnegan. You're coming home with me. Mom and Dad have a full house, including your little guy."

***

Clare looked out her kitchen window at Finn schooling Cole in the art of digging clams. Maggie tried to help by digging holes in the sand. Pete lounged at her kitchen table nursing a beer.

"It's a madhouse up at the farm. It was all I could do to pry Cole out of there. Between his nanny wanting to come with me and my kids wanting him to stay. Hey, what's for dinner?"

Clare stepped away from washing vegetables in sink and plunked them on her chopping block. "Pizza and salad with homemade ranch dressing—Finn gave me the recipe Cole loves. I adore the idea that a kid his age loves salad. Hot fudge sundaes will finish off the meal. According to Finn, these are Cole's favorites. The little fella was so overjoyed to see his daddy."

Clare pulled out an old wooden salad bowl and rubbed two toes of crushed garlic around the inside. She tossed sliced scallions, diced the tomatoes, lettuce, and a medley of bright red, yellow, and orange pepper cubes into the bowl. Toasted walnuts, feta cheese, and grated apples topped off a perfect garden salad.

"Knock, knock." Bev and Clay walked in each carrying a

stack of take-out pizza from Tony's in Bremerton. Old Tony was gone, but the legacy of this fine man who was filled with warmth and a generous spirit lived on in the hearts of all who knew him.

"Wow! That's a lot of pizza." Shrieks of delights caused Clare to turn her attention to the backyard. Libby and Tom's two youngest boys raced down to meet Cole. "Aha. I see why we needed so much pizza. I better double the salad."

Libby and Tom walked in carrying bottles of wine and six packs of beer.

"I've missed you two," Clare said, as she wrapped Libby in a hug. "How's your Christmas Pageant coming along?"

"What's that saying? Busier than a one-armed, wallpaper hanger. That's me these last few weeks. You have no idea how difficult it is to find a camel willing to work over Christmas. Their demands are overwhelming. Actors!" They all stared at Libby—puzzled, then laughed. She rolled her eyes. "Geez, you guys are slow."

"Come on, let's eat." Clare stepped onto the deck and rang the little bell her grandmother had mounted next to the door years ago to call everyone inside. Finn hustled the children and dogs into the walk-out basement that housed Clare's ceramic studio. They could shed their wet jackets and shoes and wash their hands before coming upstairs.

"I'll go down and help Finn," Tom said. "Where do you want them to eat?"

"I'll pop in a movie, and they can eat in the den around the coffee table. Libby, Bev, will you set some extra places at the dining room table?"

Everyone spun into action, and in no time the table was set, the boys were settled in front of the movie *Cars,* and adults munched on their favorite pizza. After Maggie and Ginger polished off their dinner and joined the boys in the den, hoping for a morsel of their dinner, which they were only too happy to share with them. Clare closed the doors so the adults could talk freely.

"Finn, you've been arrested," Tom said, "and released." Tom lifted his glass to him. "I'm relieved about that. But on the flipside, Clare, you, Bev, and Sophie found a body in your back yard, and now we hear the sad news of Bets. This has been one hell of week."

"What the hell…" Finn buried his face in his hands. Libby reached over and patted his back. He picked up his plate and glass. "You all talk about this and fill me in later. I still need time to process Bets and Eve's murders. I…I can't wrap my mind around this. These two women…these women I cared about." His voice was ragged. He took a deep breath and said, "I'll help any way I can, but right now I'm going to watch a silly movie and hang with the boys for a while."

"Go, Finn. If we come up with any questions you might be able to answer…well, tomorrow's another day." Clay said.

Clare waited until she heard the french doors leading to the den close. "There's that fella hanging around the pub who's carrying a concealed weapon. He lied to Jack about where he was from, and…he showed up when all this started."

"I think my dad's guess about him could be right. He might be some kind of a private investigator. He said his name was John, and he showed me a picture of woman he was looking for. Either that, or he's a hitman."

"I doubt that, Bev. You didn't recognize the woman in the photo?"

"No. Cute with short dark hair and big blue eyes.

"We'll keep an eye on him. That's all we can do," Pete said.

"I'd like to throttle Fleming for all he's put us through. I think he'll do everything he can to cause trouble for Finn."

"I think you might be right, Clare, where Fleming is concerned. Okay, let's hear who you have on your suspect list. I've been busy trying to spring our brother out of jail." Pete took a bite of cheesy pizza and washed it down with a swig of beer.

"There are so many people and ways to point fingers. Bev and I were thinking the couple from Seabeck, Gage and Rene. They'd maybe have a reason to kill Eve, but not Bets. One of them might have run me off the road. That Rene fella didn't like Eve at all, though."

"One thing that has not been found is Eve's laptop. The question is, who benefits most from having that?" Pete finished off his pizza. "I'd say the guys from Seabeck."

"Gage told my mom and me he was working on a project with Eve. So, that makes sense."

Clare lifted the wine bottle, but Clay, Tom, and Pete shook

their heads.

"One glass is the limit for designated drivers."

Libby tapped her glass. "Bev and I aren't driving, and this is excellent wine."

Clare topped off their glasses and went into the kitchen. Bev followed her and they pulled out the makings for the sundaes. Bev heated the chocolate fudge sauce, and they loaded two trays with the sundaes that had been topped with whipped cream and nuts. Bev took one tray to the den. Clare served the folks in the dining room and brought a thermal coffee carafe and cups to the table.

"Okay, where were we? Burl Woodman. He's a candidate for sure. Wife beater and all round louse, and let me add, scary guy."

"Clare, Bev, and I spoke to True Bergman, who claims to be Bets' fiancé, and his father this afternoon. The father got pretty hot, and True tried to calm him," Clay said. "I wouldn't put it past either of them. The kid ordered us off the compound property in a threatening way."

"Finn had a stalker in California. From what he told me she was capable of doing someone in."

"I checked her out," Pete said. "She has a little house in Santa Monica. I had an investigator follow her for a few days. Nothing much—shopping, restaurants, and a walk on the pier. I told him to swing by every couple of days to keep tabs on her. She seems to be sitting tight." He licked the last of his ice cream off his spoon. "This is really good, Clare, but it's time for me to head up to the farm."

At that moment, Finn walked out of the den carrying a sleeping Cole. He handed him over to Pete. "I'm beat, guys. I need a hot shower and a comfortable bed. I bid you all good night. And thanks to all of you for all that you've done to help me."

Clare walked over and hugged him. He held her for a moment—his silent tears dampened her cheek, then he turned away. She watched him climb the stairs, gripping the bannister with each deliberate step.

The remaining group sat in silence until Clare faced them with determined look. "Yes, as you said earlier, Clay, tomorrow is another day.

Chapter 18

Clare, Bev, and Clay met at the pub the following morning. They had slipped in the back door and pleaded with Ollie for breakfast. The pub didn't open until eleven, and they knew Bibi's would be packed with reporters chewing over the news of Finn's release. That, along with the discovery of Bets' body, would be the hot topics of the day.

"Libby's back on camel duty, so it's up to us to find out anything we can to help Finn," Bev said, as she poured coffee for them.

One of the new waitresses brought out plates laden with fruit salad, Irish fried potatoes with whipped honey butter melting on top of them, along with bacon, and sausage.

"Oh, my gosh, I'll never be able to eat all this, but I'll give it my best shot. Thank you, Lily." Clare knew she'd be able to eat copious helpings of all.

"Uh…I…uh, well, I wanted to say I'm happy Finn was

released from jail. He's a really nice guy…from what I hear and all."

"Yes, he is. Are you planning to stay on once all the hoopla is over and things settle down?" Bev asked.

"I think so. My family lives in Salt Lake City. It's pretty and all, but I like the lush green trees here. Well, I'll let you get on with your breakfast."

"Thank you, dear. Everything looks great, but what are these…pancakes?" Clay asked.

"Irish fried potatoes—basically, potato pancakes. We were raised on them," Bev said.

Clare scooped up a forkful of pancakes and said, "I think we need to pay a condolence call on Bets' mother, even though she told us not to come back. She has no one to turn to, and she must be beside herself with grief."

Jack came over to the table with a coffee cup in hand. He leaned over and kissed Bev on the cheek before sitting down.

"Dad, did you learn anymore about that gun guy?" Bev asked as she sliced a bite of Irish potatoes. "Hmm, heavenly."

"Yes, and I'm not proud of it. All of you nosing into people lives has had its effect on me." Jack sighed. "I noticed him going into Bibi's this morning and took the opportunity to check out his car. It was unlocked, so I snuck a look at his rental agreement." Jack shook his head and blew out a breath. "His name is John E. Taylor. Address, 282 Bellows Street in Chicago."

"So much for him being from Portland," Clare said.

***

They drove over to Bets' apartment with a floral arrangement and a casserole Ollie had provided for them. No answer.

An elderly lady poked her head out of the next-door apartment. "She isn't there. I saw her pack up and leave with some fella yesterday evening. The police were still searching the area. I had just finished my dinner and was cleaning up. I always like to get the trash out to the dumpster every night. You know, keep everything clean and tidy just like my mama taught me. It's pretty scary for me, you know. A lady alone. Especially after they found that poor young woman's body."

"You possess very admirable qualities, ma'am. I can certainly understand you feeling fearful. I hope the keep the area is well-lit for you at night. My name's Clay. These ladies are Clare and Bev. About what time was it you took out your trash?" Clay asked, in a gentle voice.

She preened at his praise. "I'm Elouise Barker. Folks call me Miss Elly. Hmm…?" She tapped her finger on her cheek. "Now let me think. I finished watching my show and wanted to clean up before my next show started. It's just me, so I eat and watch my shows." She smiled. "I guess I'd say about…oh…around seven. The police were still over behind the garages."

"So, it was pretty dark? Could you tell us anything about the fella she was with?"

"No, he was behind the doors of the van loading boxes and a couple of suitcases. She didn't even look my way, either to say goodbye or kiss my fanny! I had coffee with her once and she acted all nervous. Brought her some of my homemade cookies one day. But I saw those cookies in the trash all wrapped up pretty just like when I gave them to her."

Clare and Bev bit back smiles and let Clay's charm take over.

"I thought they were kind of…sneaky-like. If you know what I mean? Like they didn't want the cops to know she was leaving. She kept looking over her shoulder as she hauled the things out of the apartment. Then they both got in the van real quick-like and hightailed it outta here. But those cookies… If that don't beat all."

"Perhaps she's diabetic and couldn't eat the cookies. But I must say, you have a keen sense of observation. Since she isn't here, and it doesn't look like she'll be back, would it be presumptuous of us to offer you this casserole and these flowers?"

"Oh, my goodness, of course. You are a lovely gentleman. Not many of those around these days. Thank you. I guess you'd be

bringing her flowers and a casserole because of poor Bets?"
"Yes, we heard about her daughter. Let us carry these inside for you." Clay stepped through the door she opened wide for them. Clare and Bev followed him through the door into a cozy apartment. Baskets of yarn sat next to an overstuffed chair, and the tantalizing aroma of fresh-baked cookies filled the air. Clare placed the flower arrangement on the round wooden dining table.
"Would you like me to put the casserole in the fridge?" Bev asked.
"Just put it on the counter. I'll tend to it in a bit. Thank you, dear. Please make yourselves comfortable. Sit. Can I get you all something to drink? Coffee?"
"No, but thank you. We're fine." They settled on the comfy furniture, and Clay asked, "Did you happen to see or hear anything unusual before Bets' body was found?"
"No. The police questioned everyone in the building. She was found clear over behind the garages. That yellow tape is still over there. I don't drive no more. One of my grandchildren takes me wherever I need to go. You know, the doctor, the grocery store, and the like."

"Yes, I do know. Would you be so kind as to tell me which apartment the manager lives in?"
"Why, that would be Mr. Springer in apartment 1-A."
"If we have any more questions, could we call on you again?" Clare could swear Miss Elly batted her eyes at him, as she nodded. The manager's apartment was at the far end of the wood and cedar shake building. Clare pressed the doorbell and a burly man opened the door. He looked to be in his late sixties.
"I'm not talking to any reporters. Just go away." He started to shut the door when Bev stepped forward and flashed him a smile.
"We aren't reporters, Mr. Springer. We worked with Bets at Harrigan's Pub. I'm Bev Hawkins and this—"
"You Jack's girl? Come on in, all of you. Call me Fred."
Miss Elly's place was cozy. This was the polar opposite. One well-worn recliner, a Formica table with two chairs, and a sagging

loveseat with a pressboard end tables next to the chair and loveseat. A television sat on an old trunk.
“Strangest thing about that gal. Pretty little thing she was. If I were forty years younger... I cut quite a swath in my youth. Yes, I did.” He paused and shook his head. “Real sorry to hear someone did her in, though.”
“I’m Clay Fuller, this is Clare Harrigan, and you’ve met Bev. Tell us what was so strange about her?”
He pulled the chairs away from the kitchen table. “Go ahead and sit down. Don’t have nothing to offer you to drink except water.
“Thanks, but no. We’re fine.” Clare said.
“As to your question, I’m sorry, but I don’t carry tales about my tenants, or repeat their personal going-ons.”
Bev sat, crossed her legs, and leaned forward. Clare noticed she had undone an extra button on her blouse. The white lace on her bra peeked through the opening. “Of *course* not.” Bev leaned forward a little more. “Anything you could tell us that might help find out who killed her would be appreciated. You said strange?”
Fred’s eyes traveled to Bev. He cleared his throat and let out a breath. “Well, she is dead and all. So, I guess it can’t hurt. Not so much strange, but the company she kept. That tall, handsome fella—the one they arrested and then let go. Guess that might be your brother, Miss Harrigan?”
Clare nodded. “Finn is my brother.”
Clay leaned against the doorjamb, and Fred perched on the edge of his recliner with his still eyes locked in on Bev.
` “A couple of days ago, some crazy fellas in white robes showed up and banged on the door. Bets’ mama wouldn’t let them in. They were yelling at her. I finally went down and run ‘em off. Told them I’d call the cops.”
“So, just Finn, and the people in robes?” Bev asked.
“Nooo. Before that, before she went missing. A couple of those homos come by and… oops…sorry.” He looked at Clay. “I don’t mean no offense. People can live their lives any way they choose. I

just don't hold with all that PC stuff, though. So again, no offense."

Clay bit back a smile, dipped his head, then said, "Uh…none taken."

"You with that little ponytail, and that kinda funny way you talk…I just thought… Anyway, the one was wearing a T-shirt announcing to the world he was a…well…you know, a pansy boy."

"So, Fred, tell us, were you able to hear any of their conversation?" Bev asked, pulling his attention back to her legs and lace.

"As a matter of fact, I was checking my mail when they were leaving her apartment. The door was open, so I couldn't help but hear. I don't snoop on my tenants. No siree bob!"

"Of course not." Bev swung her leg.

Fred blew out another breath. "The older one, he looked like Santa Claus, handed her an envelope and said, 'There's more where this came from when we have what we need.' She didn't look none too happy. Then the younger one moved forward in a kinda threatening way—sudden like. Bets looked scared. So, I cleared my throat. Just to let them know I was there."

"Anything else?"

"Nope. The young guy gave her and me a hard look, and they walked off. She shut the door. That was the last time I'd seen her."

"What kind of car were they driving?" Clare asked.

"Weren't no car. A black truck. They was parked in a handicap spot too. Didn't look handicapped to me!"

Clare glanced at Clay. "One more thing I'm curious about. When Bets' mother left, did you happen to notice who she left with? Or anything unusual about it?"

"Nope, the Seahawks was on, and I was watching the game. The rent's paid up on that apartment until January. She'll probably be back."

"Thank you, for all your help, Fred." Clay stepped away from the doorjamb to help Bev out of her chair. He put a proprietary arm around her waist when she stood, leveled a look at Fred, leaned over, and kissed Bev's cheek as he guided her out the door. Clare smiled at the display of machismo between the two men.

Once they were outside, and the door was closed, Bev rolled her eyes at Clay and said, "Okay, manly man, you can let go now."

"Well…I…didn't want him to think I was…you know. Not that there's anything wrong with that." Clay blushed. The ladies laughed.

"No, there isn't, Seinfeld. Let's head over to my place and regroup. We have to figure out our next move," Clare said. "I'm ready for lunch, and I know Maggie needs a call of nature. Also, we need to check on Finn."

Chapter 19

Maggie did her doggie twirls around the kitchen when they arrived home. They lavished attention on her, and Clare handed her a couple of treats. When she felt, she had received the love she so richly deserved, she raced out the door. Clare went upstairs to look for Finn. She tiptoed down the hall and opened his door. He was sleeping, but she could see he been up. A coffee cup and a plate with toast crumbs sat on the nightstand. Poor guy, she thought, he must be exhausted from his time in jail, and the ordeal he's been living through.

"Clare, is that you?" Finn rolled over and sat up. "Mom called earlier. I told her I still needed to sleep, but I'm ready to get up now. And I'm hungry."

Clare walked over and brushed his hair off his forehead. He looked much better with a good night's sleep.

"Bev's rummaging through the kitchen. Something wonderful will be ready soon, knowing her. Clay's downstairs too. We had a couple of interesting chats with Bets' neighbor and her apartment manager. Hop in the shower and get dressed."

"What the hell..."

Finn padded across the room wearing his pajama bottoms. Clare waited until she heard the shower to make his bed. She picked up the dishes and headed downstairs.

Onions and garlic sizzled in a pan, filling the kitchen with a heavenly scent.

Bev poked in the refrigerator and said, "It feels like a grilled cheese paninis and tomato soup day kind of day."

"I don't think I have any cans of tomato soup."

Bev sighed. "I'm making tomato bisque soup. You have everything I need. Although I'm using canned not fresh tomatoes. Do you have any sherry? It isn't necessary, but it adds a nice flavor." Bev dumped a large can of crushed tomatoes into the pot, along with chicken stock and spices.

Clare found a bottle of sherry and handed it to Bev. Clay had piles of cheese, ham, and a couple of sliced avocados ready to go. The panini grill was on the counter.

"I'll let this simmer for fifteen or twenty minutes, then I'll add the cream."

"Perfect. Finn will be down in a few minutes." Clare pulled out bowls and plates she had made on her potter's wheel—blue with swirls of cream in the glaze. She had to get back to her wheel, she thought. The tension of the last several days would slip away after a few hours of making beautiful art. "Is it too early for a glass of wine?"

"It's five o'clock somewhere," Bev and Clay said at the same time.

Clare set wine goblets on the table, along with her favorite wine, Louis Jadot Beaujolais.

Finn walked in looking refreshed. He looked at the wine on the table. "What time is it? How long did I sleep?"

"It's almost two o'clock. We are indulging a little early—feeling European with French wine. Coffee? Would you rather have breakfast food?"

"Yes to the coffee, and whatever Bev's busy doing at the stove smells great. Look, I've been thinking about Eve. She doesn't have any family except Cole." Clare placed his coffee on the table and sat down across from him. "Thank you. I want to handle all the funeral expenses and have her buried here, in Amelia Bay. If it were me, I'd go for cremation, but I know Cole will need a place he can go to visit his mother. This will be home and family for him."

"That's lovely, Finn." Clare reached across the table and took his hands in hers. "I think there's space at Cherry Hill in the Larson family plot. She's connected to us through your son. I'll find out all the particulars. I'm so thankful you are home."

Clay pushed the lid down on the panini grill, poured himself a glass of wine, and sat down. "Finn, are you up for answering a few questions?"

"What the hell… Anything I can do to help. I'm ready."

"Eve's laptop is missing. The police don't have it, and it wasn't found in her car, according to Pete."

"I don't know why the cops don't have it. Eve left it in my car, or I should say Pete's car that I was using. I know they impounded it. Bets had asked to borrow it a few days before she disappeared, and I forgot the laptop was in there. Her car's not too reliable. She told me it was in the shop, but Pete couldn't confirm that."

Clare ladled soup into the bowls and topped them off with a dollop of sour cream. "Did Bets drive your car when she left?" Bev sliced the sandwiches and piled them on a serving plate.

"No, my car was at her apartment complex. I picked her up at the pub after she finished work. She walked to work that day because she knew I was picking her up. I was driving Mom's car that night."

"We now know the blood was from a family member. Her mother maybe? But Bev and I didn't notice any cuts on Brenda—just bruises." Clare said, taking a bite of her ham and cheese panini. The avocado blended with cheese. "These are delicious."

"Thanks. Brenda seemed pretty strong to me when she was scrubbing the blood off the sidewalk." Bev picked up her wine glass and sipped. "Maybe it's from the elusive brother, or…or what about her birth father? Brenda said he walked out on them. Maybe he walked back into Bets' life."

"And what? She stabbed him? What the hell…"

"You picked her up, you ate, made love, and she put her waitress clothes back on? That doesn't make sense. She couldn't have left the house bare-assed and buck naked." Clay scraped the bottom of his bowl. "Is there any more of this soup?"

"Yes. Sit, I'll get it for you." Bev grinned, got up, and refilled his bowl. "I'll take this as a compliment."

Clay nodded. "It's delicious!"

"She brought an overnight bag with her. In fact, now that I think about it, she changed her clothes before we ate. I think a pair of leggings and a sweatshirt."

"What did the sweatshirt look like?"

"I don't know—a sweatshirt. Why, does it matter?"

"No reason." Brenda was wearing one of her daughter's sweatshirts when she was scrubbing the walk. But, Clare thought, she herself had a half a dozen sweatshirts.

Everyone remained quiet for a few minutes as they mulled over the unanswered questions.

"How can we find out who her birth father is…or if he is still alive? I wonder why she continued to use Woodman as her last name," Bev said.

"Maybe she didn't know her real last name, or maybe Woodman legally adopted her," Clay said. "Do we know how old Bets was when she entered the cult?"

"I have no idea really, because I don't believe much of what Brenda has told us. *And* I'd like to know where is Sophie?" Bev asked, as she finished off her sandwich. "She might be able to help us figure out some answers."

"I have a delivery of dishes to make today. I promised the lady who ordered them I would drop them off today."

"I'll drive you over there," Clay said. "Where does she live?"

"The other side of the Hood Canal. It's a bit of drive."

"I have to get over to the pub. I told my dad I'd organize some paperwork. They've all been so busy. Things are piling up." Bev said.

"We have to stop by there before we leave for the delivery."

Clay and Clare cleaned the kitchen after Bev left.

Finn yawned. "I think I could sleep for a week." He took a cup of coffee and headed into the den. When Clare checked before she and Clay left, he was sleeping with Maggie curled up next to him on the sofa and Ginger on the floor in front of them. She covered him with quilt and tiptoed out.

Chapter 20

"Hey, Ollie, is Bev here?"

"Yep. She's in the office with Pug. He came down to pick up some food to take up to the family. I'm working on getting it ready right now."

Clare walked in the office. "What's up?"

"Food to stave off the ravenous throngs storming the kitchen gate. You'd think they hadn't eaten in a week! Mind you, darlin', there's plenty of food, but none to suit their tiny taste buds! So, here. Ollie cooks and I deliver!"

Clare laughed and eyed the stacks of order forms and computer spreadsheets.

"Normally one of our dads handles all this stuff. My dad's so busy, and your dad hasn't been in since he broke his leg," Bev said. "I'm trying to help Uncle Pug put some orders in and balance out the monies, which I will add are considerable."

"I would imagine so, considering the crowds we've been serving. I'll take the food up. I want to see Mom, then I'll deliver the pottery I mentioned earlier. The lady lives on Discovery Bay." Clare smiled and glanced at her watch. "Clay's waiting for me."

"There's another thing, Clare, I've been wanting to talk to you about. With all that's been going on, I'd like to take you out to the target range and teach you to shoot straight. Nothing else may go wrong, but you should be able to protect yourself." Bev said.

"Okay, but guns scare me."

Pug, who had been oblivious to their conversation, looked up at them over his cheaters and said, "Shush yourselves, my darlin' girls, I'm going to call in some orders." He reached for a chocolate candy square and used it to scoop up a blob of peanut butter. Pug's favorite treat. "Thanks, Clare, for helping me out. I'm needed here."

Clare headed out the door and found Jack in the kitchen picking up a couple of orders.

"Hey, Jack. Have you learned any more about our mysterious gun-toting stranger?"

"No, he's hasn't been in lately. I did see him going into Bibi's a couple of times. Maybe too much noise and too many people here. I'll keep my eye out, though."

Ollie helped Clay carry the boxes of burgers and fries out to his truck while Clare prepared a Thermos of coffee for herself and Clay.

They were mobbed by the little ones when they entered her mother's lovely Victorian kitchen. Grace had recently remodeled but had been careful to retain the charm of the Victorian farmhouse she had called home since she was five years old. Soft creamy cabinets with glass paned doors lined two walls and set off the Carrara marble countertops. Grace had lived in this house since her parents were killed in a train accident, and she came to live with her Aunt Hedda and Uncle Lars.

Mia got their lunches onto plates and tried to settle the children around the table. They nudged and shoved, wanting to sit next to Cole. Mia stuck her lower lip out and said, "Doesn't anyone want to sit by me?" Dilly immediately sat next to her.

Grace smiled and said, "She's very good with children. I can see why Cole's mother hired her, and trusted her with our little Cole. I haven't had children playing hide and seek in this big, old house in years. Later they're going to do crafts."

"This is a nice break for Dana, as she plans the total redo of her home." Clare chatted with her mother for a few minutes, and felt assured she was doing well.

"Hey, little one." Mike came into the kitchen leaning on a cane. His walking cast was covered in fanciful artwork. "Can I bum a ride with you down to the pub? I'm itchin' to get back into the swing of things." He leaned over and whispered in her ear. "Your mother thrives on having her kibbles and bits around, but this old leprechaun could do with a little peace and quiet."

"I think Pug and Bev could use your help." Clare hugged her father. "Clay's driving me to deliver some pottery to a client on the other side of the canal. We can drop you off on the way."

***

Clare and Clay were drinking sweet, milky cups of coffee. Clare felt satisfied and happy. The woman had loved her dishes and the goblets.

"What's going on up ahead?" Clare asked.

An ambulance and sheriff cars lined the sides of the road. A firetruck blocked their way forward. Clay slowed the truck and parked behind one of the cruisers. A woman and man stood off to the side by the tree line. They looked like hikers. She was crying, and he had his arms wrapped around her trembling body.

"I've got some more to-go cups in the back of my truck. Maybe they could use some coffee." Clay emptied the Thermos into the cups and took them over to the couple. "Hi, I'm Clay Fuller, and this is Clare Harrigan. We're from Amelia Bay."

They readily accepted the coffee.

"Thank you. I'm Bill Darling, and this is my wife, Denise."

"What's going on?" Clare asked, as she reached in her purse and offered the woman some tissues. "They're clean—just wrinkly."

"We were walking along the beach, and we looked up and saw what we thought was a bed sheet billowing in the wind. But Denise noticed it seemed to have some fancy embroidery on it. Turned out to be a sun and a star."

Clare looked at Clay and raised her eyebrows. "And then what?"

"I climbed up the bank and found there was a body wrapped up in some strange kind of robe. He'd been dead for a while." His wife hiccupped and started to cry again. Bill pulled her closer. "I won't get rid of the smell or mental picture any time soon."

A young officer walked over to them. "The firetruck and ambulance will be out of here in a few minutes, then you folks should move along."

Clare glanced at his badge. "Officer Barnes, I'm Clare Harrigan and this Clay Fuller. I might be able to identify him. I'm guessing he's from The Evening Star compound south of here. I'm not crazy about the thought of seeing a dead body, but if it would help, I will."

"That would be helpful. There was no ID on him." The officer motioned for his partner to come over. "This lady thinks she can identify the body." He introduced the new officer as Pendleton.

Clay put a protective arm around Clare. "I'd rather you didn't do this. Someone from the compound will do it in good time." He looked at the officer and asked, "What kind of shape is he in and how did he die? Was it foul play?"

"We didn't observe any outward signs of trauma. He might've been banged up a bit from the fall. Your friend's right ma'am. I think it would be better if you held off. Do you have any idea of who we should ask for at this compound?"

Clare breathed a sigh of relief. "I don't know if their leader is there. His name is Burl Woodman. If not, ask for the man who calls himself Brother Bergman. He has a son, True Bergman, who might be able to help as well."

"How do you know so much about these folks?" Deputy Pendleton asked. He seemed a little suspicious.

"Mr. Woodman's daughter worked at my father's pub in Amelia Bay. Harrigan's Irish Pub, do you know it?"

"My wife likes to go there," Deputy Pendleton said. "Leave me your name and phone number. We'll contact you if any further information is needed."

Clay turned to the Darlings and asked, "Do you two need a lift home?"

"We're staying at a B&B in Sequim. We could use a lift to our car, though," Bill said, as he looked at the deputies. "Can we leave now?"

After Clare and Clay dropped the Darlings off at their car, Clare said, "I give pretty good odds that body is Woodman's. What do you think?"

"I'm not a betting man, but I'd make book on the fact it very well could be the missing Brother Woodman.

***

Clay dropped Clare off at the cottage. Bev and Sophie's cars were parked in the driveway, along with another car she didn't recognize.

"Looks like the gang's all here," Clare said, as she stepped out of the truck.

Bev came out the front door and crossed over to Clay's truck. "Clay's going to drop me off at home. I'll be back later to spend the night. Oh, and guess what?" She stood on the running board of the truck. "I've decided to run for mayor in the special election. Blame Sophie, Finn, and Glen."

"Wow! You've got my vote, sweetie!" Hmm…Glen is here, Clare thought and smiled.

Clare peeked in the living room. Everyone sat around the coffee table where a magnificent feast of *hors d'oeuvres* was on display. "Whoa, this looks heaven-sent."

"I was bored and started poking around in your freezer and pantry," Finn said. "Didn't know your younger brother could cook."

"Finn's been telling us how he takes cooking classes in various countries wherever he's shooting a film. Also, filling us in on the sometimes strange, and rather unique habits of some of our favorite stars." Sophie picked up a crab-stuffed mushroom and popped it in her mouth.

Glen poured Clare a glass of wine. She dropped to the floor, and sat cross-legged on one of the cushions she had stacked near the fireplace hearth. Maggie and Ginger curled up next to her. Everyone seemed gobsmacked when Clare told them the events of the afternoon.

"But how do we find out if it's Woodman, and how he died?" Clare asked.

"Let me handle that," Glen said. "I've got a buddy who works in the coroner's office. It's probably too soon to know, but I'll call him now and give him a heads-up that I'm interested.

I need to pick his brain from time to time when I'm doing research for one of my books." He walked into the kitchen to make the call.

"It's Woodman for sure. The deputies called the compound and someone arrived at the morgue shortly after the ambulance dropped the body off. It was pretty difficult to identify him facially because…"

"Please stop, Glen." Clare held up her hand. "I don't want to hear what you have to say. I'm just glad I didn't have to do it." She shook her head and quivered.

"But what caused his death won't be determined until tomorrow. It was a man named Bergman who identified him. Woodman has a tattoo of the sun and a star on his right back shoulder. They'll do DNA and dental records to confirm absolutely."

"So, we have Bets dead, Eve dead, and now this Woodman character. What the hell…" Finn dropped his head into his hands.

"Bets' mother, Brenda, has disappeared with some guy. Maybe her son. Maybe not."

Chapter 21

"Rise and shine, Clare. We're heading to the shooting range. It's a clear, sunny day." Bev opened the shutters on the windows and let the pesky light into the room.

"No." Clare rolled over and buried her head in the pillows. Even Maggie lifted her paws and covered her eyes. Although she was most likely scratching her nose. "Go torment Finn. I tossed and turned all night. I barely got any sleep. How can I shoot straight with no sleep?" She looked at the clock—nine o'clock. Guess I did get more sleep, she thought. The shower was on, and Clare knew the handwriting was on the wall—further sleep would not be forthcoming. With a groan, she stretched. Maggie refused to budge.

"I've already been out grocery shopping, and I picked up bagels. You'll feel fine after a shower. Dress warm, it's chilly. Make sure you wear comfortable clothes."

"Yes, Mother," Clare said under her breath. Dang these women are taking over my life, she thought. It put Clare in mind of mornings during summer vacation when Grace would sweep into the bedrooms of her children, throw open the curtains to the blinding sunlight, and cheerfully announce, "Wake up my sweet darlings the bookmobile will be here soon!"

Clare forced herself from her cozy nest and headed to the shower. She toweled off and pulled on a pair of leggings, a denim shirt, and grabbed a thick wool cable-knit sweater. Digging through her closet, she found her ancient pair of Frye riding boots. Stan had given them to her years ago. She would never spend that much money, but she loved having them.

"Toasted bagels smell so good," Clare said, as she entered the kitchen and poured a cup of coffee. She dropped onto a chair and eyed the spread of goodies on the table—cream cheese, pancetta, and sliced onions. "Do I get to wear a holster and practice quick draws? Maybe instead of Pancho and Cisco, we could be Wyatt Earp and Doc Holliday."

"There is something I'd like to say right now, but it wouldn't be ladylike. Finish your breakfast and get your cute patootie out the door. We have a bit of a drive to the shooting range."

Clare and Bev had just gotten on the highway when a police cruiser came up fast behind them with lights flashing. They pulled over and Bev watched Chief Fleming in her rearview mirror as he got out of his car.

"I wasn't speeding, Chief."

"No, you were not, but I noticed your license plate is falling off. Looks like the screws have come loose." He looked across Bev, smiled, and said, "Good morning, Clare."

Clare nodded and stared through the windshield. Bev started to open her door when Fleming said, "Stop. You never exit a vehicle during a traffic stop unless instructed to do so by the officer."

"Permission to exit vehicle, *sir.*" Bev blew out an exasperated breath as Fleming opened the door. She pressed the button to open the tailgate, stepped out, and walked around the back of her SUV with Fleming following. "I have a toolbox in the back."

"Are there firearms in those cases?" Fleming asked when he looked in the back.

"Yes, and yes, I have licenses for each one of them. Would you like to see them? Clare and I are going to the shooting range to practice."

"No, I trust you. Grab your toolbox, and I'll help."

"Thanks, but Clare and I can handle it."

"Fine!" Fleming got back into his patrol car and torn off with his tires spitting gravel in their wake.

"What an ass," Bev said, once they had made the minor repair and were cruising down the highway.

***

"Well, deadeye, how'd you do?" Finn asked. "I'm starting to go a little stir crazy. There were some reporters camped outside for a while this morning, so I've been hiding out back here. I'm marinating skirt steak for fajitas for dinner."

"I hit the target, and that's a good thing. Maybe not every time, but enough." Clare took off her jacket and reached for the coffee pot. "We might be able to figure out a way to move you and Cole up to Sophie's place in Sequim. But I do like having wonderful cooks for friends and now, a brother. I'm not sure I want you to leave."

Glen tapped on the kitchen door, and Clare let him in. "I come bearing dinner ingredients for Finn, and I have some news." He handed a bag to Finn that released the heavenly scent of cilantro. He audaciously stepped forward, hugged Clare, and kissed her smack on the lips. "That's just cuz I think you're cute, and I wanted to get that awkward first kiss out of the way."

"My, aren't you a cheeky fella? What makes you think they'll be a second one?"

Glen raised his thick, dark eyebrows reminiscent of Groucho Marx. He lacked the stogie and mustache, though.

Clare smiled and shook her head. "What's your news?"

"I talked to my friend at the morgue. It seems Woodman died of a heart attack." Glen poured himself a cup of coffee and added a little milk. "He was pretty banged up from the fall. There wasn't a car anywhere around, so how did he get there?"

"Hmm… 'Curiouser and curiouser,' to coin Lewis Carroll's famous line. Maybe whomever brought him there followed Alice down the rabbit hole and is having tea with the Mad Hatter and the Cheshire Cat." Clare walked over to the refrigerator and pulled out a platter of cheese left over from the previous night. She put an artichoke-spinach casserole into the microwave to warm.

Everything went on the table, along with baskets of crackers and the crostini.

Glen laughed. "An interesting thought. There was some bruising on his chest, though. Could be from two hands giving him a mighty hard thrust. The rest of the injuries were from the fall."

Bev tapped on the kitchen door and pushed it open with Ginger at her heels.

Clare said, "Madame Mayor, Lady Mayor, or just plain ole Mayor Hawkins? I'm so proud of you for taking this step, Bev. What even made you think of doing it?"

"Sophie suggested it, and it snowballed from there. So, from your lips to God's ear. It'll be fun…I think, and I know a lot of hard work. At least I want to try. I've been taking classes for the last twenty years, and I finally have my degree. It's in history, but I can make sure the bad history from our previous mayor doesn't repeat itself in our little town."

Finn chopped the cilantro and tossed it into his marinade. He poured it over the steak and put the bowl in the refrigerator. "Good for you, Bev. What the hell… There aren't enough honest people in politics these days. I'm heading upstairs. I want to call Pete and see how plans are going for getting out of town with my son for a little while."

Glen waited until Finn was out of earshot before he started to speak. "I also asked about Bets and Eve, but didn't want to bring it up in front of Finn."

"What did he say?" Bev asked. She slipped a couple crackers to Ginger and Maggie.

"He said Eve was hit with what they think might have been a baseball bat. Something with a rounded shape. Whoever did it hit her three times—hard. Any one of the blows would have done her in, but she was hit again and again."

"Oh, dear God! And Bets?" Clare felt tears well up.

"Looks like someone came up behind her, hit her over the head, and strangled her with a wire. She struggled to pull it off. They didn't find any DNA evidence on either one of them or around the bodies. Although there is a bruise in the middle of Bets' back. I feel awful for not knowing the answer to this question, but where was her body found?" Glen asked. "I heard in a wooded area."

"The thicket of trees and bushes to the left of her apartment building and behind the garages. For all we know she could have been staying with her mother and hiding for whatever reason. Or maybe she was trying to get to her mother by the back way so she wouldn't be seen?"

"What do they think caused the bruise on her back?" Clare began clearing the table and loading the dishwasher. Finn might be a good cook, but he was lousy at cleaning up after himself.

Bev refilled Glen's mug and her own. "Maybe a knee to hold her down caused it. I'm not going to go into more details with you ladies. What I've told you is gruesome enough. Besides, I have a plane to catch. I'm heading to New York for a meeting with my agent and publisher, and I'm running a little late, but I'll be back on Wednesday. Wouldn't miss Thanksgiving. Thanks for the coffee and the good eats."

Glen leaned over and kissed Bev's cheek, then turned to Clare. She stuck out her hand and said, "Goodbye, Mr. Wynter." He grabbed her hand, pulled her to him, and kissed her cheek. He laughed, and Clare rolled her eyes and chuckled. She was beginning to like this Mr. Glen Wynter.

Bev answered her cell phone, listened, and hung up. "Dad needs me to work. Hmm… Mayor by day, barmaid by night. I like it. Can I leave Ginger here?"

"Of course. She's a sweetie and Maggie likes the company. Bev, I hope you win this election. You'll make a great mayor." Clare said, "You know the girlfriends will work night and day to make it happen." She hugged her. Bev petted the dogs and was out the door.

***

Clare puttered around the kitchen and chopped vegetables for Maggie's stew. Today she made extra for Ginger. Once that was finished, she headed down to her studio and pulled out a bag of clay. The dogs had run all their energy out and slept side by side on a rug in the laundry room off the studio.

Clare took her wire cutter and sliced it through the clay. It made her think of Bets. Could potter's wire cutter be used to strangle someone? she asked herself. It had wooden dowels attached to each end of the wire for gripping. Too thin and not long enough? She would ask Glen. Clare pushed the thoughts away and focused on the task at hand—centering the lump of clay on the wheel—relaxing and releasing tension. She pulled the lump of clay up into a cylindrical shape when the sound of breaking glass and a thud exploded through the cottage. She knocked her clay and it spun off the wheel and landed on the floor. The dogs started barking as they raced up the stairs ahead of her. Clare grabbed a towel to wipe the clay from her hands and met Finn in the foyer.

"What the hell… Pull the dogs back. There's glass all over the floor in the living room. Looks like someone threw a rock through the window."

"You stay back. It could be some crazy photographer thinking they could get you outside for a photo." Clare called the dogs and put them in the den behind closed doors. "There's a note tied to the rock. We shouldn't touch it. I'll call 911."

She placed the calls and came back into the foyer.

"Call Mom and Dad too. Tell them to make sure the gates are closed." Finn paced back and forth before he settled on the bench next to the door. "Clare, I'm at the end of my rope here. Hanging on by a thread."

Clare sat next to him and held him until she heard cars pull in the driveway.

"Stay put for a minute." Clare went into the den and closed the curtains, then told Finn to go in there. Maggie and Ginger jumped on him and licked his face. Dogs have an amazing way to sense emotions. The doorbell rang, setting off a cacophony of barking. Clare opened the front door to find Chief Fleming and Chris Reed.

"What happened?" Fleming strode into the living room and looked at the mess on the floor. "Reed, get some evidence bags pick up the rock, but let's have a look at the note."

"Got them right here, Chief." Chris pulled on a pair of gloves and walked across the room, trying to avoid the glass. He pulled off the string that tied the note to the rock and placed it in a bag, then flattened the note and placed it in a separate bag—finally, the rock went into a bag.

Fleming took the bag with the note, and Clare peeked over his shoulder. It was written in block letters. 'LEAVE HIM ALONE OR YOU WILL END UP LIKE THIS!!!!!' There was a crude drawing of a body outline with a red stain in the center of it. The outline had loops depicting long, curly hair around the head. "Clearly this is intended for you. Are you seeing someone?"

"Not really." Clare shrugged.

"Clare, this is not a difficult question. Either you are seeing someone or you're not."

Clare thought, he looked…what? Jealous, angry, frustrated. "Maybe it's you little friend, Rocky. She doesn't seem to like me. I see a correlation here. Rocky—rock. She certainly seems capable of it. Horrible little woman.

"That's preposterous. She's my mother-in-law." He stormed out. "Reed! Let's go."

Clare shot a surprised look at Chris, who nodded his head. He whispered on his way out the door. "We just found out."

Clare watched them through the open door for a few moments. They seemed to be looking for footprints or some other evidence. She went into the den. "Did you hear what he said? That little fireplug produced Fleming's gorgeous, leggy wife? Will wonders never cease?"

Finn shook his head and blew out a breath.

"You sit tight, and I'll bring you a cup of Gran's Irish tea and put in a funny movie." She picked out my *Big Fat Greek Wedding* and slid it into the DVD player.

Clare swept the bits of glass up and vacuumed the area rug. Cold air whipped through the broken window, and she went in search of something to cover the hole until she could get someone over to repair it. Ten minutes later, equipped with a small square of plywood and some heavy-duty tape, she had the chilly air blocked. She placed a call to the local window repair shop that promised someone would be out within the hour. She explained she had special glass squares on hand. It was hard to find the antiquity-looking glass. Gran had stored extras in case of an accident.

Finn seemed to be relaxed and calmed down when she peeked in the den. The dogs followed her to the kitchen.

"No wonder Ms. Rockman was so worried," Clare said to Maggie and Ginger once she was in the kitchen. "She must have sensed that cheat, Fleming, wanted to start an affair with me. But she didn't have to be so nasty. Of course, Rocky's daughter is totally bat poop crazy, and maybe the fireplug is too." The dogs stared at her. "Thanks for listening, my sweeties. Ginger, how do you feel about apples? Maggie loves them."

"Who are you talking to?" Sophie asked as she breezed through the kitchen door. Buck was right behind her.

"The dogs." Clare reached into her fruit bowl and handed Maggie her favorite treat—an apple. Then she held one out to Ginger. Clare could sense the wheels turning in her doggie mind. 'Is this a ball or something to eat?' She seemed to decide on the latter and followed Maggie's lead.

Buck and Sophie chuckled.

"So, what's up, puddle duck?" Sophie asked. "Is Finn here, and did I see a broken front window pane?"

Clare told them everything that happened up to and including the rock being thrown through the window. "I can't imagine what Rocky would have against Eve and Bets, though."

"Buck and I have been doing some background research on Gage Brinker and Rene Bertrand. Looks like the pretty boy, Rene, hasn't had a gig in the last year."

Finn walked into the kitchen. "Too temperamental. He pitches tantrums, and has a list of demands. He's not famous enough to get away with it, nor does he have a cadre of fans. He brings too much trouble to a set. Good-looking guys and gals are a dime a dozen. Gage hasn't written a hit in the last three years. As they say in my business, you're only as good as your last hit." Finn held his hand out to Buck. "Finn Harrigan." He leveled a questioning look at Buck.

"Buck Carlson." He shook Finn's hand. "Nice to meet you. And yes, I'm a journalist, and I hope for an exclusive when all of this is over."

"Buck's been a really big help to us. Would you like another cup of tea, Finn?" Clare put the tea kettle on. "So Gage had to be counting on his association with Eve to get back on top?"

"Yes, please, on the tea, but I can get it. You don't have to wait on me." Clare flicked her hand at him. "Thanks, Clare. I watched the movie you plugged in with Gran shortly before she died. I felt like she was sitting next to me today, laughing. It lifted my spirits." Clare set his tea on the table and smiled. She was glad he was feeling better, but she still felt shaky from the rock.

"Has Clare kept you up to date on everything that's happened,

Finn?" Sophie looked up from where she had her head stuck in the refrigerator.

"I don't think I know everything that's happened. Maybe it's better that way. Pete told me some and Clare a little." Finn stood. "I don't know about any of you, but I'm hungry. Clearly, I can see Sophie is foraging around for something to eat." He pulled the marinating skirt steak, cheese, and vegetables out of the refrigerator and started slicing and grating. "I can't see Gage or Rene as killers. Rene probably wields a mean flyswatter, but hitting someone with a club or a bat? Nah."

"What about Gage?"

"The outside belies the inside. I've seen real nasty anger flash up in him a few times, when he slips out of his jolly Santa Claus *façade*. So, yeah. He might be able to wallop someone."

"Bets' apartment manager, Mr. Springer, described a couple of men who we're a hundred percent sure are Gage and Rene. They were talking to her one evening. He felt they were being threatening to her. They told her to get what they wanted and there would be more money in it. Springer said she looked frightened. So, he made his presence known, and they left."

"What the hell… Eve's laptop is probably what they were after. Ironic, really. Here she is telling me she how much she cares for me. Me of all people—an Oscar winner in the category of Lotharios. I was actually thinking maybe, maybe I do have it in me to be with one woman—Bets. What the hell…"

"That's why the laptop wasn't found in your car. She must have taken it and given it to them." Clare set the table with the Mexican placemats and napkins she had purchased at the Bazaar del Mundo in San Diego a few years earlier. The colors were lively and matched the terra cotta dinnerware she made in colors of cobalt blue, sunny gold, persimmon, and hunter green. One of the great things about being a potter was, if you wanted a new set of dishes, you made them.

The doorbell rang. "I'm guessing it's the window repairman," Clare said.

"Let me take care of this. I'm not much help with lunch, but this I can handle," Buck said as he stood and walked to the foyer. Clare told him where the glass panes were stored in the basement.

Within thirty minutes, they had rice, refried beans, and sizzling fajitas on the table and the window was replaced. Sophie filled Mexican bubbled glass goblets with wine.

"What started with Finn and me having lunch at the pub when The Evening Star burst in, has devastated our world, and that of so many others. It seems an eternity ago.

Sophie nodded. "Finn, what did Pete say about you taking Cole, and going up to my place in Sequim?"

"As long as it's still all right with you, Sophie. Pete said it was fine as long as we keep the authorities informed of where I'm at. He talked to a friend who's handling the case in the DA's office. I have to check in with the cop shop up there," he said with a wry smile. "Not sure why. They must think I'll run the border into Canada."

Sophie, who had just taken a bite of a fajita-filled flour tortilla that dripped sour cream, she nodded and smiled her assent.

"We need to get Cole and Mia over here and all of you up to Sequim. It won't be easy. Pete's kids are really attached to both of them," Clare said.

"I'll take them all. Between Mia and I, we can handle them. It'll be fun. What the hell… I need some fun. Give Dana and Pete a chance to get moved back in their house. After all the trouble, I've caused them…"

Was this her self-centered younger brother talking? "I'll bet Mia can help with the homeschooling if she's game," Clare said. "She told me she taught school for a while."

"My neighbors, Brian and Penny, love kids. They have a passel of grown kids of their own that are always around with their kids. Even in November we have plenty of sunny days so, you should be able to get the kids outside for some fun," Sophie said. "Brian and Penny foster children too."

"Why do they call Sequim a little bit of sunshine?" Buck asked, as he loaded another tortilla and piled more beans and rice onto his plate. The man could pack away the food.

"It's something called the Olympic Rain Shadow. The mountains create a kind of shield that protects the zone from a lot of the rain that blows through. We get our share of wet weather, but a whole lot less than the rest of the area," Sophie said between bites of beans and rice. "Delicious, Finn. Thanks."

Finn went upstairs to pack while Clare called Pete to get the timing of the trip to Sequim. Buck and Sophie cleaned the kitchen.

Buck stretched and yawned. "I'm gonna head back to the hotel. You ready to leave, Sophie? I'll drop you off at your dad's."

"Clare, do you want me to stay?"

"I'm still feeling apprehensive from the rock being thrown through the window, but Bev will come here when she's finished at the pub. Finn isn't leaving until early tomorrow morning. I'll set the alarm."

Buck helped Sophie on with her coat. "I'm going to do some research to find out more information on the fellas in Seabeck and our mystery man. He's staying at the hotel. Maybe I can spot him and strike up a conversation. I'd also like to see if I can find anything on the Woodman's marriage or an adoption of Bets and her brother."

"I'll second that, and do some research too. Where's Libby when we need her? She's so good at this." Sophie picked up her purse.

"And you two aren't? I'll call Lib and see if she can come over tomorrow morning. She might bring us something delectable for breakfast. She and Tom were here for dinner with the boys the night Finn came home."

"I like you gals. You eat all the time, and you eat really well. But who's Libby?"

"There are five of us who have been friends since we were kids. Clare and Bev go back to the diaper and bottle days. The girlfriends—me, Clare, Bev, Libby, Gina, who lives in Seattle, and I told you about Addie."

"Yeah…yeah…you did." Buck frowned and shook his head. "You folks have really been to hell and back these last months. I'm happy to help you all in any way I can."

Clare hugged him and planted a kiss on his cheek. "Thank you." The street fighter and hardened old reporter blushed.

Chapter 22

The next morning Pete picked up Finn with a gaggle of little ones and they were off to Sequim without a hitch. Clare and Bev went to Bibi's to load up on pastries for breakfast. Libby promised to bring her fluffy egg strata.

Clare was squeezing oranges for juice when Libby came through the door, followed by Sophie and Buck, who helped her carry the dishes. "Gosh, Lib, I've missed you."

"I feel the same. I think I finally have everything ready for the Christmas Pageant. I know a lot can go wrong between now and show time, though. I brought a breakfast casserole and rice pudding."

"Food. I'm starved. Where's Tom?" Clare asked.

"He going to take our little guys to a birthday party, then home to his newspaper and ESPN. Our three big guys will be home from college tonight and chaos will reign."

Bev piled the pastries onto a plate, and said to Buck, "Libby and Tom had their three older boys when the rest of us gals did, then popped two more when we were done."

Buck smiled. "Big families are nice." Feeling more and more comfortable in Clare's kitchen, he poured himself a cup of coffee and pitched in to help Bev set the table in the dining room. Libby, Clare, and Sophie brought the food in, and they settled around the table. The view out to Amelia Bay was shrouded in a soft mist. Bev had opened the french doors to the living room, and the crackling fire added a welcoming warmth to the room.

"Sophie and I did a little research on Burl Woodman and The Evening Star. I dug pretty deep into the property records. Woodman owns that compound lock, stock, and barrel. *Everything's* in his name. I couldn't find any records of a name change on him."

"What about marriage licenses, birth certificates, that type of thing?" Clare asked.

"There aren't many men named Burl Woodman in the entire country. Most were either too old or too young, and only one lived in Washington State. That's our man."

"Buck and I went over the information when I picked him up this morning," Sophie said. "There was a marriage license issued to a Brenda Hadley Sikes and Burl Carl Woodman fifteen years ago. He was born in Spokane and married before, but his first wife died. That was about the time he started The Evening Star."

"Brenda lied to us, Clare. She told she us wasn't legally married to him, and that it was a sham of a marriage," Bev said, helping herself to seconds on the strata.

"We knew she was lying, but not about that."

"Does this Woodman fella have any family—brothers, sisters? Is there a will?" Libby asked. "If not, his wife, Brenda, would inherit the compound. Did you delve into adoption records?"

"We didn't get that far," Sophie said. "Glen told us Woodman died of natural causes?"

"Oh, good grief. There are so many questions we need to find answers to. "Clare, is your computer in the den?" Libby was remembering her successful investigations of a few months ago.

Clare nodded at Libby and filled bowls with rice pudding. She handed one to each of them as they filed off to the den.

***

"Leave them to their research. Let's clean up and take the dogs for a walk to town," Clare said. They pulled on their colorful Wellies, which were lined with sheepskin to keep their tootsies warm, and hooded Anoraks to ward off the damp chill. Clare's Wellies were blue with roses on them and Bev's had, of course, galloping horses.

The mist had lifted leaving behind evergreen trees covered in droplets of water that glistened when rays of sunlight occasionally found their way through the clouds. Clare looked over a bridge covering a creek, its water meandered along on its way to the bay. "These banks are covered in fiddlehead ferns in early spring. How do you cook them, Bev?"

"I steam them in butter and garlic, and sometimes I throw in some bacon, then hit it all with a splash of wine."

"My mouth is watering, and my tummy is begging for fiddlehead ferns."

"For goodness sakes, Clare, you just ate!"

"That was well over an hour ago. We're walking, we're walking. I'm building an appetite," Clare said, as she climbed a slight incline up to Main Street. At the top, Clare stopped. "Those two guys getting out of the black truck and going into the pub are Gage and Rene. The couple from Seabeck. Let's hurry and see if we can get a table with, or near them."

The number of media had dwindled slightly, and there were a few tables available. But Clare knew it was still too big a story to ignore. Two murders and the leader of a local cult found dead who, by the way, happens to be the father of one of the victims. Throw Finn into the mix, and it was sensational, tabloid heaven.

The pub was decked out in autumn finery. Jugs, Clare had thrown on her wheel, graced every table. They burst with purple, gold and white mums. Little orange berries and fall leaves peeked through the petals. The fireplace crackled and spread warmth throughout the room.

Bev took the dogs back to the office and returned as Maria walked up to her and Clare with menus in hand. She had just seated Gage and Rene. "Hi, sweetie, could you seat us at that table over there?" Clare asked, indicating one next to the couple. It was a table for four, and Clare hoped she could persuade the men to join her and Bev.

Maria led them over and turned to Gage and said. "I'll be right back with your coffee. How about you ladies?"

"I'll grab a couple of beers for us," Bev said, getting up and walking back toward the bar with Maria.

Clare smiled at Gage and said, "Hello, Gage, Rene. My mother, Grace Harrigan, and I came to your house looking for information about my nephew, Cole. Eve's son."

"Of course, of course. Lovely to see you again." Gage mouth split into a grin that highlighted his rosy cheeks.

Rene looks decidedly uncomfortable, Clare thought. If you're the stinker that ran me off the road…I hope you're squirming right now. "Do you get to Amelia Bay often?" She turned to Rene and smiled.

He returned it with a vapid smile. Today he was wearing a sweatshirt that read, 'Don't even think about it, I'm gay.' He certainly liked to get his point across. Maybe the poor guy got hit on by too many girls. He was a handsome fella.

"As often as we can. It's such a charming little town. Picture perfect, really. Ah, here comes our coffee. Nice chatting with you," Gage said and focused on his menu, then looked at the waitress. "I don't see colcannon here. It's a one of the tastiest dishes you serve. We love coming here for just that reason. Too bad."

"I'm sorry, sir. That's not on the specials menu every day."

Clare grinned at Bev like the Cheshire Cat, as she placed their beers on the table. She had him. "Excuse me, Gage, but even if it's not on the menu, there's usually a pot of it in the kitchen. Colcannon is a family favorite. In fact, Maria, why don't you bring Bev and me a couple of bowls too. Have Ollie slice some nice pieces of Irish sweet bread to go with it, please."

"Sure, that's easy. Be right back."

"Oh, and, Maria, no check for them. It's on the house."

"No, no, we couldn't accept."

"*Of course* you can. I'm Bev Hawkins. Why don't you two join us?" She got up and picked up their coffee cups and whipped the napkins off their laps. Gage and Rene exchanged flabbergasted looks and Rene shrugged. They moved like arthritic turtles, but knew they could not turn down Bev and Clare's hospitality.

"You must still be devastated over Eve's death. I know our

family is suffering because of her death." Clare directed her question to Gage. She meant what she said about the family's suffering, but waited for Gage's duplicitous response.

Bev placed their napkins back in their laps with a flourish once they were seated.

"I couldn't be more upset. I adored and respected Eve. Rene and I both are simply devastated. Aren't we, Pet?"

"We most certainly are." Rene's sour look belied his words.

"What movies have you written?" Bev asked, as she refilled their coffee cups with the carafe she brought back with the beers.

"*Mooning Miami* was quite a hit. *Campus Frolics* and who could forget, *Heat on the Mexican Riviera*? That was a spring break movie." Gage grinned and nodded, reliving the memory of his glory days.

Bev sucked in her lower lip—perplexed— then said, "I don't think I've seen those, but I don't have much of a chance to get out to the movies."

"They're geared for a much…*younger* audience." Clare wanted to wipe the smirk off Rene's face. Even a person of incredible good looks can look ugly when their true character shows itself. Looks only get a person so far in life. Humph, I've known people one might consider unattractive shine with inner beauty, she thought.

The servers, Lily and Maria, brought their meals to the table. Four bowls of potatoes and steamed cabbage mashed together with chunks of ham and chopped scallions—colcannon. "Ollie said you love his honey butter, Clare. This is regular butter, but the other bowl is whipped honey butter," Lily said, as she placed a basket of the warm sweet Irish bread on the table. "Anything else you need, give one of us a wave." They all murmured their thanks. Clare really liked these two new waitresses and hoped they stayed on, along with Lynn who would soon be healed.

"Tell me, Gage, how are you going to finish the script you're working on with Eve not here to help you? Do you have another writer lined up?" Clare asked, as she spread honey butter on her slice of bread.

"It's completed. Her input was minor. Eve was really only adding a few bits of dialog."

"I must have misunderstood you when my mother and I visited your home. I thought you told us that without Eve's work you didn't know how you would finish. That everything was on her laptop."

"No, I do not recall saying that at all."

"Really…?"

"Yes, *really*. Gage is a brilliant writer. Eve was a hack trying to ride his coattails." Rene clutched his stomach. "Gage, we need to leave. The food is not agreeing with me." They both stood. "Neither is the company. You ambushed us!" He threw his napkin on the table.

"Now, Pet. These ladies are just being…inquisitive, but we have no answers for them." The jolly Santa smile creased his face. "Sorry we have to leave, but Rene has a tender tummy. Thank you for lunch."

Bev, who had remained silent said, "Two things before you leave…did you know Clare was run off the road by a black truck after she left your place last week? She could have been killed."

"Oh, you poor dear thing. How terrifying." He cast a sidelong glance at Rene.

"And the second thing, Eve's laptop is missing. The police don't have it, and it isn't in Finn's car where she left it. A car that Bets, the murdered waitress, had been driving. Puzzling, don't you think?"

They turned away from the table, and Gage whispered something to Rene that Clare couldn't hear, but Rene's response carried as he said through clenched teeth, "I told you I hit a deer."

"Looks like Tonto and the Lone Ranger ride again. You shot the silver bullet, Bev."

"I do have a license to carry."

***

Sheets of paper were stacked on the kitchen table when Bev, Clare, and the dogs arrived back at the cottage. Sophie and Buck were hovering over Clare's computer in her den.

"You guys have been busy," Clare said, looking at the piles of papers.

"That Libby's great at unearthing information. She hopped on the computer and before we could finish our rice pudding, papers started to fly out of the printer," Buck said with a laugh. "I'd love to have her as a research assistant."

"I was duly impressed too. I think of her as mommy extraordinaire. I wasn't around to see her in action a few months ago. Buck and I were sorry to see her leave. But I guess we won't see much of her the rest of the week with all of her boys at home." Sophie stood and stretched her arms over her head. "Did you enjoy your walk?"

"It was interesting to say the least. Should we compare notes?" Clare asked.

"Could it wait until morning? I'm plumb tuckered out, and sure could go for a good meal, followed by a good night's sleep." Buck yawned. "Thank you for everything. Lots of good food and good company around here."

"You're welcome. My door is always open for you, Buck."

"I need to get going too. My dad's expecting me. I've been trying to spoil him a bit, and he's thoroughly enjoying it. I have to admit I'm enjoying our time together."

After Sophie and Buck left, Clare and Bev changed into pajamas, curled up with glasses of wine, and settled in to watch a movie. "I like feeling normal," Bev said.

Chapter 23

"I've been ignoring you both and not giving proper attention to your big day. I love the idea of having the rehearsal dinner here by the way. Creating more happy memories in the cottage. How many people do you think we'll have?" Clare asked, Caroline and Mac.

"I would think around thirty-five to forty with all our families and the wedding party—their dates." Caroline bit the corner of her lip. "Is that too many?"

"Of course not. We'll have twenty-five here for Thanksgiving, and that's a sit-down dinner. This'll be buffet style—catered by the pub." Clare walked into the living room. "We'll move some of the furniture down to the basement and set up tables in the living room and den."

"I gave Ollie the menu of what you wanted. He told me—no problem. Since my colors are traditional Christmas, the reception will be white tablecloths with red and green napkins. For the rehearsal dinner, I'd like to reverse it with red tablecloths and white napkins." Caroline cast her eyes around the room.

"It'll be perfect." Clare hugged Caroline. "Just imagine, the house decked out in its Christmas finery. Twinkling lights and candles."

"Mom." Mac called from the kitchen. "Now that I look at this kitchen, the thought comes to mind that it's kind of small. Gran never had any big dinners here. We always had family gatherings at the farm or at your and dad's place—our place now." He smiled at Caroline. "Do you plan to change enlarge the kitchen?"

"I'm glad you asked, son. It's great for one or two people as it is, but I have plans. The deck is rickety, and I want to have it torn down and build an extension out from the kitchen. More like a greenhouse that I can furnish it with wicker and lots of plants. Underneath will be a covered patio."

"Clare, that sounds perfect. As I said the other day, I'm going to love having you for my mother-in-law."

"Thank you, sweetie. Although I can be a little sassy at times."

"I like sassy. Now for the flowers. What do you think?"

Mac groaned and headed to the television in the den. "I'll leave the flowers to you ladies."

After Mac and Caroline left, Clay came in. The dogs raced to him, vying for attention. "I knew you were in good hands yesterday. That's why I didn't come by to be your protector. I also had the rehearsal for the play I'm in. Is Bev here?"

"Yes. She'll be right down. What's the name of the play?"

"*A Christmas Carol*. I'm The Ghost of Christmas Past. There's some good local actors in this. We even have a fella from Hollywood playing Tiny Tim's father, Bob Cratchit."

Clare's ears perked up. "Hmm…what's his name?"

"I'm not sure, the director refers to us by our character's names. Calls me *the past*. The Cratchit fella is a tall, good-looking guy. Why do you ask?" Clare raised her eyebrows and cocked her head. Clay had a confused look, then it dawned on him. "Oh…oh…it could be the fella the apartment manager, Springer, told us about. The couple you and your mother visited in Seabeck. Yes! The more I think about, it he sat in the theater in the afternoon with a man who looked like Santa Claus, but Rene didn't have to read any lines during our rehearsal yesterday."

"Hi, Clay." Bev smiled. She looked darling in jeans, cowboy boots, and a soft pink sweater. "What are you two talking about?"

"Gage and Rene. It seems Rene is in the play with Clay." Clare went on to explain to Clay the interaction she and Bev had with them in the pub earlier.

"He hit a deer, huh?"

Sophie and Buck came through the door. "Sorry we're late, but we had some calls from a couple of research people who managed to dig up some good information on the Woodman clan. We called them yesterday, and they came through this morning. Have you guys been up to anything interesting?"

Bev explained the story of their lunch at the pub, and Clay filled them in on his fellow actor. Clare poured coffee for everyone. She sliced big servings of sour-cream coffee cake and drizzled each piece with raspberry sauce.

"I'll go first," Sophie said. "Brenda lied to you two. Not a surprise, as you thought she was lying. She and Woodman were married fifteen years ago. His first wife—along with his parents—died in a house fire in Coeur d'Alene, Idaho, about sixteen years ago. The cops thought it was suspicious but never charged anyone. He didn't have any siblings. He walked away with a bucket of cash from insurance."

"Hmm…I wonder if he started the fire? I wouldn't put it past him. Sad story."

"Woodman did adopt Elizabeth, or Bets, and her brother, Jonathon. She was seven at the time and her brother was a year old," Buck said.

"What was Brenda's first husband's name? And was there a record of their divorce?" Clay asked, as he took a sip of coffee and offered up his plate, hopeful for another slice of cake.

Bev smiled and sliced him another piece. "Clare, this cake is delicious, did you bake it?" Bev asked.

"No, I bought it at Skate's Market along with the sauce. I haven't had much time to bake lately."

Clay smiled his thanks.

"Back to the subject at hand. There is a record of their divorce and his remarriage. His name is Brad Sikes, and he lives in Coeur d'Alene with his new wife, Bedelia. They have four children. Coeur d'Alene is where he and Brenda were married," Buck said.

"Looks like Sikes didn't run out on his new wife. That is…if Brenda wasn't lying about him abandoning her and their children. Maybe she took off and left him. Bets must have inherited her lying gene from her mother." Clare leaned against the counter and sipped her coffee. "Brenda really laid it on us. Said she thought the compound was a utopia, and on and on."

"The Woodmans disappeared for a couple years and then surfaced about thirteen years ago. There's a record of him buying the land by the Hood Canal and setting up shop with a band of followers."

"I wonder where he was for those missing years. Do you have Sikes' personal information?" Bev asked.

"You mean phone number and address? Yes, it's right here."

Clare picked up the paper. "I think a phone call to Mr. Sikes might answer a few questions."

Clare busied herself making a fresh pot of coffee, then picked up the cake plates and crumbled napkins. She paused halfway to the sink and said, "If I'm understanding all this information correctly, Brenda…legally owns The Evening Star compound. Brenda and her son, Jonathon. Unless Woodman had a will, leaving it to another party."

***

"Let's figure out what we are going to do to bring the person or persons who murdered these women to justice. And hopefully, we can bring the breezy, light-hearted Finn back to some degree," Clare said to Bev and Clay, after Sophie and Buck had left.

"The idea that Gage and Rene appeared to be forcing Bets to give them something… Eve's laptop? Puts them at the top of my list." Clay took his cup to the sink and rinsed it out before putting it in the dishwasher. "I have a couple of things I need to get done. I won't be gone longer than an hour or so."

"No worries, we'll be safe. I want to call Spokane and see if I can ferret out some information about what happened all those years ago. It might not have any bearing on what is happening now, but…"

Clare watched out the dining room window as Clay drove up the road. Bev walked in and sat in the window seat.

"I, and others, have noticed a…closeness developing between you and Clay. He's still reeling from Addie's death. I don't want you…"

"Stop right there. I know he's still hurting. We all are. I want to show him support and bring him some comfort. That's all. In different circumstances, I would be attracted to Clay—even if he doesn't sport cowboy boots and dance the Texas two-step in tight jeans. He's very kind." Bev smiled.

Clare laughed and hugged her friend. "Is it hard for you—living in Addie's old house–I mean?"

"No, not at all. You and the girlfriends took what each of you wanted. I gave the rest of the furniture away. Some went to my kids and some to Mac and Caroline. Those two have a big house to fill. I've put my own shabby chic, cowgirl stamp on the place."

Clare looked at her friend. "You've been busy lately, and you look worn out. Go cuddle up in the den and maybe read for a bit. I'll call this Sikes fella. You've got dark circles under your eyes and it looks like you can barely keep them open."

Clare peeked in the den ten minutes later. Bev was stretched out on the sofa. Her breathing was soft and steady. Clare knew she was sleeping peacefully. She covered her with an afghan, picked up the phone receiver, then tiptoed out of the room.

This would not be an easy call to make, she thought, as she dialed.

A cheerful voice answered. "Hello, Sikes' residence, Bee speaking."

"Hello, Mrs. Sikes? Uh…mm…my name is Clare Harrigan, and I'm calling from Amelia Bay on the Puget Sound. Is Mr. Sikes available?"

"No, I'm Mrs. Sikes. Brad's at a church meeting. May I help you?"

Clare sighed. "Was Mr. Sikes married before? If so, this would be concerning his…uh…first wife."

Mrs. Sikes was quiet for a few moments. "Yes, he was, to a lady named Brenda. They had two children together. I'm not getting a very good feeling about your call. I sense bad news. So out with it, dear, and please call me Bee."

"I'm sorry to be the bearer of bad news. His daughter…Bets…Elizabeth, has died. She was…murdered."

She was quiet for a several moments. "Was it at the hands of that dreadful man? I told Brad not to allow the adoption to go through. I didn't like him from the start, but oh, by golly, he put on a good show, that Burl Woodman. Didn't he just! Told us it would allow him and Brenda to create a solid family, and we could see the children anytime we wanted to."

"I don't have an answer to your question as to who her killer could be. But Woodman is dead as well."

"Aha…I wouldn't put it past that bubble head, Brenda, to have something to do with this. My Brad's going to be crushed. I told him to bring those babies to me. I would have raised them and loved them like my own, Ms… I'm sorry. What did you say your…?" Tears choked Bee's voice.

Clare gave Bee a moment to compose herself, then said, "Clare, Clare Harrigan, and please call me Clare. So, he signed the adoption papers, and what happened then?"

"They disappeared. There was that dreadful fire when Woodman's family died. Suspicious if you ask me. I'm sure Brenda was out catting around with him before she walked out on Brad. What could we do when they took off? Nothing. Nothing! Where is she now?"

"Actually I don't know. She left right after Bets was…found."

"Oh, dear. I can't believe this, but I know it is true. Can I have Brad call you?"

"Yes, of course. I'm so sorry. Let me give you my number and that of the local police department. Your husband can call them or me, if I can help in any way. Also, I would hope I can call you if I have any questions."

"Certainly. Thank you so much for calling. It must have been difficult to make a phone call like this." Bee took a few deep breaths. "Maybe we can bring Elizabeth home and bury her here."

***

Clare needed to clear her head after the emotional phone call. She locked up the house, set the alarm, and left note for Bev and Clay after she changed into running clothes and harnessed the dogs. She knew they wouldn't be happy she took off alone, but she was confident the dogs would protect her. This would be something new—running with two dogs. Ginger was up for the new experience and jogged along with her and Maggie. After two miles, they ended their run in front of Bibi's Beans. Clare pulled open the door. The dogs needed a drink and so did she.

Bibi stood behind the counter, as Clare walked up to her. "Hi Bibi. I'd love a vanilla bean frappuccino, please."

Bibi took one look at her and waved her over to the corner booth. "With whipped cream?" Clare raised her eyebrows. "Of course, I needn't have asked."

Bibi came over with a tray laden with water bowls for the dogs, Clare's drink, and a plate of mini muffins. She placed the water bowls on the floor and put down two treats.

"The treats are peanut butter. I've been making them for my furry friends." Bibi's enchanting French accent soothed Clare. She slid into the booth across from her. "Who's this charming new pup?" Ginger placed her head on Bibi's lap and looked up with brown eyes flecked with gold.

"This is Bev's new dog, Ginger. She more or less rescued her."

Bibi patted her head. "It's quiet here for now, Brady can handle anyone who comes in." As if on cue, he came over, and placed a cup of coffee in front of Bibi. He looked like he wanted to say something, but she thanked him in a kind, but dismissive way. He left—disappointed. "My fella's such a gossip. The nattering class of Amelia Bay flock in here to bend his ear, and he theirs."

"Well…I…uh." Clare was at a loss for words and sipped her refreshing frappuccino.

Bibi waved Clare's stammering away. "I know what he is like, but he is a kind and caring husband. You have whipped cream on your nose." She sipped her coffee and laughed. "Every now and then, though, amid all the chatter and innuendos, a piece of interesting information comes his way."

Clare smiled and grabbed a napkin. "If this is something pertaining to Finn's situation, I'm all ears."

"Mr. Fulbright came in yesterday. The family's house overlooks Pete's place."

"Oh?" Clare remembered it was the Fulbright's deck Bev did her reconnaissance on the morning the bloody clothes were found. She kept quiet about it—waiting to hear what Bibi had to tell her.

"The Fulbright family had one of those o-dark-thirty flights and were getting ready to leave for SeaTac. Mr. Fulbright heard some noise and saw the motion light come on. He stepped out on his deck to see what was going on. There was a dented old car parked in the driveway by the back door. Pete's cars are pristine. So, it caught his attention. He knew Finn was staying there while Pete and Dana were in Europe."

"Did he call out or say anything?" Clare asked.

"No. He saw Bets walk out of Pete's house. Said he knew her from the pub—all the men who went to the pub knew her. She was gifted with a unique beauty. Anyway, he had noticed her on previous occasions coming and going with Finn. I'm quite sure he envied Finn a little. But I digress. She came out and opened the passenger door to the car, then went back inside and turned off the light. As if…" Bibi held her hands up and shrugged.

"As if she didn't want anyone to see what was going on."

"But the dome light in the car was on, so he could see a little. A man—who at the time he thought was Finn—came out hunched over and holding his arm to his chest."

"I hope he told the police? This would've been good to know before Finn was arrested. It doesn't clear him of all wrongdoing, but it seems this would help his case a bit."

Bibi looked up and customers formed a line at the counter. "I've got to go. But to finish, Bets helped the man into the car and closed the door. Then she went back inside the house and carried out a paper bag, which she tossed in the trash. She hopped in the car, and they drove away."

Clare stood and helped Bibi load the tray. She picked up the water bowls and reached for her purse.

"It's on the house, Clare." Clare protested, but Bibi held up her hand. "I heard what happened with you being run off the road. Be careful, my friend."

"Thank you…for everything."

Clare took a shorter route home and was met at the door by two angry people, Bev and Clay. She tried to look contrite. It didn't seem to budge them. "I was careful, and I had the dogs."

Chapter 24

After Clare told them the happenings in the early morning hours of the day Bets disappeared, they decided to eat dinner at Harrigan's Irish Pub. Clare walked up to the bar and asked Jack if her parents were in the office.

"No. Pug's in the office, and Fiona is in the kitchen. I think someone, maybe you, could rescue Ollie. She wants to help with the cooking. They have different styles and different recipes. She's full of advice for the poor man on how to make all his dishes more *Irish*."

Clare chuckled and pushed through the doors to the kitchen. A look of desperation on Ollie's face told all. "Aunt Fio." Clare opened her arms. "Come have dinner with me and Bev. I'd love you to meet our friend Clay."

"Oh, darlin', that's sweet and kind of you, but I'm busy helping Ollie." Fiona gave her a quick hug, then turned her attention back to the prep area. Ollie bit his lower lip, and his eyes pleaded with Clare.

"I won't take no for an answer. Please." Clare untied Fiona's apron and brushed some flour off her shoulders. Pieces of cabbage clung to her sleeves and what looked like bread dough appeared to be stuck in her hair. Ollie expelled a deep breath. He smiled his thanks as Clare guided her into the office. What has she been into? Clare asked herself.

"I'd like to freshen up before we join the others. How about you?"

Fiona looked at Clare over the top of her half-glasses and said, "You're very diplomatic, Clare." She smiled and headed into the bathroom off the office.

Clare planted a kiss on Pug's cheek and snagged one of his Hershey bites. "Aunt Fio is going to have dinner with me, Bev, and Clay. So, you're on your own unless you'd like to join us?"

"Thanks, but no. I want to have everything tidy when your dad comes in tomorrow. The two of us didn't get much done when you dropped him off. He tired pretty quick, and I took him home." Pug grinned. "Thanks for rescuing Ollie. My old girl's driving the poor man dotty."

Fiona came into the room. "I'll pretend I didn't hear that, my love." She had removed the food particles that had been clinging to her and brushed her hair. The bun, while still slightly off-kilter, was free of bread dough. She walked over to Pug and kissed him on the forehead. God, how Clare loved this woman.

Clay graciously stood and held the chair for Fiona. "What a splendid gentleman you are!"

After they had placed their orders with Lily, Fiona said, "I don't understand that man. I have tried to help Ollie—you understand, my dearests—to improve his dishes."

"Aunt Fio, you are a brilliant cook." Bev reached across the table and patted her hand. "You make the most tantalizing deserts, and no one can say your sandwiches aren't scrumptious! My mouth waters just thinking about them."

Clare glanced at Clay and bit back a smile. Bev was laying it on thick, and from the look on Fiona's face, it seemed to be working. Although Clare didn't quite know how this might discourage her from her proffered, albeit unsolicited, help to Ollie.

"Good now, you see there. Darlin' Bev understands." Fiona preened at Bev's glowing compliments. "Now, if I could just get that sow-headed Italian to understand!" Fiona rested her chin on her hands and pursed her rosy, Clara Bow lips.

"His mother is Italian, but his Irish father owned a

restaurant in Dublin," Clare said. "Customers come in the pub and expect their favorite meals to taste the same."

"Humph. I suppose, but..."

"Aunt Fio, I'm thinking perhaps we can add some of your scrumptious recipes to the Daily Specials Menu. Your pear, bacon, and cheddar sandwich is the stuff foodie's dreams are made of."

Clare looked at Clay and he grinned. If Bev tries to come up with any more adjectives, she'll need a thesaurus, Clare thought.

Fiona reached over and patted Clay's hand. "I make a lovely cherry sauce to drizzle on it. It is divine." She smiled and said, "I know I've been a pest to Ollie. I'll apologize, and just so you young ladies understand...I also know when I'm being finessed. But with such charming guile."

They laughed. Clare had been so involved with the matter at hand, she didn't notice the Fleming family was waiting to be seated. His dazzling wife, a young man, she assumed was their son, and...the Fireplug. Her eyes scanned the dining room for an empty table. The only one available was right next to them. What hutzpah for them to come in the pub for dinner after all the anguish Fleming and his mother-in-law had caused her and her family, she thought.

Rocky Rockford—AKA Fireplug—glared at Clare. Fleming's smile was smug and his wife smiled demurely as she gracefully allowed Fleming to hold out her chair.

Clare leaned her head toward Clay, who was sitting to her right and whispered, "Clay, hold my hand and look at me like I'm the love of your life." He nodded and smiled knowingly, then reached over and took her hand in both of his. He lifted it and kissed the tips of her fingers. Clare reached over and caressed his cheek. Fleming's face blazed with intensity. The Fireplug's mouth gapped like a large mouth-bass ready to take bite of a wiggling nightcrawler dangling in front of its eyes.

"What's going on?" Aunt Fio asked Bev.

Bev was biting her lips to keep from laughing. She got control of herself and murmured in Fiona's ear so she could understand and enjoy the moment.

The dinners arrived, and they turned their attention to the food. Every now and then, when Fleming looked over, Clay would feed Clare a piece of his steak, and she would offer him a bite of something from her plate. She picked up a roll, buttered it, and handed it to Clay then looked down shyly. They finished their meal and got up to leave.

Clare heard Fleming excuse himself to use the facilities. He caught up to Clare in the bar area. "You could have taken up with a younger, better-looking guy." He had a disgusted look on his face.

"He has two things going for him that you might find difficult to grasped. A—he is single and B—when in doubt, refer to A."

Fleming glared, spun on his heels, and moved in the direction of the restrooms. Rocky had watched the scene unfold and read the rage on his face. She looked at Clare with a satisfied smile and nodded. She looked pretty darn cute when she smiled, Clare thought, as she nodded back to her. Fleming stopped halfway and squared his shoulders, then turned back to his table. His wife appeared to be oblivious to the entire performance.

Clare pushed through the door leading to the kitchen and found Bev, Fiona, and Clay holding their sides. Tears were rolling down Fiona's cherub cheeks. They replayed the moments with renewed laughter.

Chapter 25

Clare was getting ready for bed when the phone rang. She grabbed it before it could wake Bev. Only bad news came via phone after ten at night, she thought.

"Clare, this is Bee Sikes, you know, from Corte d'Alene, Idaho."

"Yes. Is everything okay?" She clutched the phone between her neck and her chin, as she pulled on her jammies, then sat on the chaise in her bedroom. "How can I help you? What's up?"

"My husband, Brad, told me he saw Brenda and a young man, who he believes to be his son, today." Bee paused for a moment. "Now, mind you, he hasn't seen them in years, even though Brenda and that…that man, Woodman promised, we could see them. Let them know their brothers and sisters. Grrr…I get so angry just thinking about them! I may not be the beauty *she* is, but—"

"Bee, where did he see them, and what were they doing?"

"Oh, yes. Well…they were coming out of a bank. Then they went over to a Mexican restaurant. He followed them over, discreetly, of course. He was in his car, so he parked and waited for them to leave."

"Was he able to follow them when they left?" Clare twisted her hair around her finger and tried to make sense of them being there. Bev stumbled into her room. Clare held up hand.

"Yes, they drove to a motel just outside of town. Brad knows the manager, so he popped in after they were in their room. He asked him how long they were staying." Bee sounded smug with her husband's detective skills.

"And…?"

"Just tonight. And oh, oh, I almost forgot. They left the bank carrying a heavy, extremely heavy, leather valise." Clare smiled. She hadn't heard that word in many years. "So heavy they both held the handles and struggled with it."

"This is all very interesting. I need to think about it. But it's after ten. When did all this happen?"

"This afternoon. Brad had to get back to work, and he didn't have your number. The kids and I have been gone all day. He ate dinner out, and then checked for their van again."

"What is the name of the motel they're staying at?" Clare wrote down all the information. "What does Brad intend to do?"

"I don't know. He's on his way home right now. I had to talk him down off-the-ledge or he would have gone barreling in there. We need to think this through."

"You're right. Give me a few minutes to think too. We need a plan." Clare hung up the phone and told the gist of the conversation to Bev.

"What do you think was in the heavy bag they carried from the bank?"

"I don't know, but I think we need to find out. It's a five-hour drive, plus ferry time adds another hour at least." Clare rooted in her nightstand drawer for a ferry schedule. "If we can catch the 11:35 ferry…we should get to Corte d'Alene around five or six tomorrow morning."

"I'm glad I had a nap this afternoon." Bev rubbed her eyes. "I'll call Clay. I know he'll want to come with us."

"We can't take the chance they'll slip away from us and head for goodness knows where. I'm going to call Bee and let her know our plans so her husband doesn't go over to the motel and spook them into taking off."

"This is a have-to-do thing, but keep in mind there will be at least twenty-five people here this week for Thanksgiving. Is there a turkey on the horizon?"

"Yes, Bev. I ordered two eighteen-pound organic turkeys from Skate's Market a couple of weeks ago. But that's all we have. The gobblers and the linens we talked about earlier and…never mind all this. Go, go. Call Clay, and get dressed. We have a long drive ahead of us to discuss Thanksgiving provisions."

Clare called Bee and told her their plans. She put the Sikes' number in her cell phone and gave her cell number to Bee. Then she called Pug and asked him to pick up Maggie and Ginger for the night. When Clay pulled in the driveway, Clare and Bev hopped in his truck—Idaho bound.

Chapter 26

Bee called, as they pulled into Corte d'Alene—tired and hungry—at a little after five a.m. She told Clare that Brad would meet them at a local diner then gave them directions. He left his car parked across from the motel with their sons in it on stakeout duty. She had packed munchies for the boys to keep them happy. The youngsters loved the covert drama of it all. They would call if they noticed any movement at Brenda and Jonathon's motel. By the time they found the eatery, it was just opening, and Brad was waiting for them outside. He was a big man with a bush of dark hair and eyes. Well over six feet tall and at least two hundred and fifty pounds, he was an imposing figure of a man.

"This is driving me insane," Brad said once the introductions were done. "I've worried about my two kids and regretted my decision all these years. To know I'll never see Elizabeth again… There are no words to express my torment and anger. We tried to find them a couple of times, but no luck. Bee and I don't have a lot of money to spend on private detectives and the like."

Clare looked down and noticed a gun strapped to Brad's hip. Idaho was an open carry state. She knew without a doubt Bev had a gun in her purse, but she didn't know this man or what he may, or may not, be capable of.

"I will not allow that woman to take my son away from me again!"

Clay patted him on the shoulder. "Let's take it slow and easy, Brad."

A waitress seated them and poured piping-hot coffee all around. "Brad, your usual?"

"Just coffee for me, Janie. My stomach is churning right now." Brad's eyes looked wild as his fingers played a staccato beat on the table.

Clare ordered two eggs over medium with hash browns, extra biscuits, and bacon. Bev and Clay ordered the same.

"Bring me a bowl of oatmeal with brown sugar too, if you have it."

"Yep, we serve oatmeal. I'll have it all out in a few." She scooped up the menus.

Bev and Clay gave Clare a look. "What? I'm starving, and it was a long drive. And bring this man a bowl too," she said, with a sidelong look at Brad. "You have to eat something hearty, and oatmeal is comfort food. Please try."

"Is she always this pushy?" Clay and Bev nodded. "You're as bad as Bee. Okay, you're right. I'll try a bowl." Brad smiled.

"Yep. She's pushy, and she eats like a trucker." Bev grinned.

The light-hearted conversation seemed to sooth Brad a little. She didn't want him to go off half-cocked and get violent with Brenda or…pull his gun.

"Once we finish eating, we should head over to the motel. Bev and Clare know Brenda, and they should be the ones to talk to her first," Clay said.

Brad drew back and said, "I know that bitch too, and…well, what if she has a gun and goes after them?"

"I have a gun too." Bev patted his hand.

"A cute little lady like you has a gun? Of course, an awful lot of cute little ladies around here have them. Don't know why I'm surprised. I guess it's because you're so…soft and pretty."

"I have a lot of guns, and I know how to use them. But we won't have to. Brenda's pretty docile, and she's feeling wounded emotionally right now, I'm sure."

The waitress brought their meals, and they ate in steady silence for several minutes. Even Brad polished off his oatmeal in short order, then cast a hungry eye on the plates of biscuits. Clay smiled and plucked a couple off his plate, then passed them to him. He knew better than to take one from Clare.

***

Clare knocked on the door of the motel room. A gawkish teenage boy with strawberry-blond hair opened the door. Freckles were sprinkled across his cheeks and nose. They popped out against his pale face. A thin layer of perspiration glistened on his forehead. He was the image of Bets. He had yet to mature into his gangly frame. Tears sprung to her eyes. He left the security latch in place. "How can I help you, ma'am?"

Clare blinked away the tears before they could fall and asked, "Could we please speak to your mother—to Brenda?" She looked at the boy, with what she hoped was a reassuring smile. His arm looked red and swollen around the bandage that was wrapped around his forearm.

He smiled tentatively and said, "My mother is in the shower. Who shall I tell her is asking for her?"

"What's going on, Jonathan?"

"It's Clare and Bev from Amelia Bay. We'd like to talk to you."

"Son, go take your shower now. We have to get going. Go on now. These are nice ladies."

He hesitated, and after a moment, he turned away. Clare heard the bathroom door close as Brenda slipped off the security lock.

"Well, I don't want to talk to you. I have no idea how you knew I was here. Just take off, and leave me alone." Her words come out with a sob.

Bev leaned forward. "It's either talk to us or talk to Brad and the police."

Clare noticed the bathroom door open a crack.

Brenda's shoulders slumped. She leaned against the door jamb and pulled the tie on her robe tighter. Her loss of weight was obvious—her emotional pain palpable. "I don't understand. How did you find me? I tried to be careful. I should have left here right away, but I had to rest. I guess somehow Brad saw me. Jonathan doesn't know his birth father is alive. He thinks he walked out on us, and I told him and Elizabeth their father was dead."

The bathroom door crashed back against the wall, and the boy charged into the room. "What? Where is he? Where's my father? You allowed that evil man to abuse us all these years? For what? It's your fault my sister ran away! You lied to us."

"No, sweetie, no." Brenda sank down onto the bed and buried her face in her hands.

"It's your fault Betsy is dead! My God, that man stabbed me! I could have died if it hadn't been for..."

The yelling carried outside. Clare had left the door ajar, and Brad Sikes' imposing body filled the opening. His eyes blazed, as he looked at Brenda, then softened as he held his arms out. "Come here, Jonathan. Come here, Son." The boy stood stock-still for several moments. No one else moved a muscle. Only the boy's eyes moved back and forth between his parents. He sobbed, and went to his father, then collapsed into his arms. Brad half-carried the weakened boy out the door. Bee stood outside with her children, Brad's children—Jonathan's new family. They gathered around the boy. Bee murmured to him, "You're safe now. You are loved."

Chapter 27

Clay dropped Clare and Bev off in the afternoon. Clare wasn't sure how he managed to drive most of the way home. She and Bev relieved him for about a half an hour each, and they slept the rest of the time. They all slept in the truck on the ferry ride from Seattle to Bainbridge Island.

Bev filled the coffee pot and rummaged in the refrigerator for something to eat. They had driven straight through without stopping to eat. "How about scrambled eggs and toast? I found some fruit to make a salad." Bev whipped the eggs and sliced apples, pears, and pulled some grapes off the stems. She topped the fruit with some berry yogurt. Nothing too inspiring but filling and comforting.

"Perfect! If you can handle this, Bev, I'll shower, and after we eat, I'll clean up while you shower. Unless you want to head to the showers first."

"Nah, you go. But we have to knuckle down this afternoon and get Thanksgiving dinner together."

Clare grabbed a piece of pear and went upstairs. She didn't linger in the shower as long as she would have liked. She slipped into a cozy pink sweatshirt and a pair of gray leggings. They felt so soft and smooth against her skin. When Clare walked into the kitchen, Bev had the table set and the plates warming in the oven. Piles of scrambled eggs with melting cheddar cheese on top greeted her. Bev had added some mild green chilies and scallions to the eggs for a burst of flavor.

"You didn't tell me what happened when you called the station." Bev scooped up a forkful of the fluffy eggs.

"I spoke to Rocky. She seems to like me now, by the way, after the little show we put forth at the pub. They'll call the police in Corte 'd'Alene and are bringing Brenda back here to face charges—if any are filed. They can't charge her with kidnapping because according to Bee, she had full custody of Bets and Jonathan."

"I'm still gobsmacked over what was in that bag. I have never seen so much gold in one place, Clare!"

"Woodman was such a rip-off artist. He sold all the possessions his followers had to turned over to him when they became members of his cult. Then used the money to buy gold that he stashed away in safety deposit boxes."

"I didn't hear why he went all the way over to a bank in Idaho. I think I actually fell asleep on my feet for a few minutes," Bev said.

"Clay was propping you up, then he led you to the truck, and you were out like a light when your head hit the back seat." Clare munched on a piece of toast slathered in butter and jelly. "They had the boxes for years. He put some jewelry from his family in them years ago, and let Brenda sign on as someone who would be allowed to access them. She said he kept the keys hidden from her all these years, but she found them in the van."

"My memory is hazy, what did she say about the incident that caused his death?" Bev asked.

"Brenda claims they were in the van together, and he was punching her. He stopped the van, and she jumped out. When Woodman came at her, she shoved him and took off."

"Self-defense, Clare."

"Yes, according to her story. After a while, she stopped talking and asked for a lawyer. Brad and his family had already left. I called Bee while I was upstairs. They took Jonathan to see their family doctor. That poor kid. He didn't look well to me. She told me the wound was infected." Clare pictured the boy's ashen face and the way he held his arm. "I wanted to ask Brenda about the laptop and few other questions, but didn't have the opportunity."

"This doesn't solve the mystery of who killed Bets and Eve, though."

"I know, but it's turkey time. Go shower, Bev." Clare gathered the plates and loaded the dishwasher.

Pete tapped on the door and opened it. Clare was knocked over by two high-spirited dogs. She let them lick her face, and she nuzzled their silky coats. "I guess they missed me! Thanks for bringing them over."

"I think I may have the answer to whose blood was found at your house," Clare said, once she disentangled herself. She handed the dogs a few apple and pear slices. "It was Bets' brother, Jonathan. Woodman stabbed him."

Clare relayed the story to of the happenings of the morning. Was it only this morning?

"This may be just what I need to get all the charges dropped. Although Fleming told me yesterday, he still believes Finn aided and abetted in a crime. He's out to get him."

"Probably the little show I put on at the pub last night won't help." Clare grimaced. "At the time, it seemed like a good idea." She told him what she and Clay had done.

Pete's shoulders shook, and laughter rolled up from deep inside him. Something this up-tight fella rarely did. It warmed Clare's heart to see him laugh. "Ah…you are one sassy lady, and I'm glad you're my sister. Don't worry, I'll make sure the facts win out at the end of the day. Now I'm going to head over to the station, and see what I can find out. A bag of gold… Wow!"

After Pete left, Clare called the pub to see if the linens were there for Thanksgiving dinner. Pug answered and asked if she wanted him to bring them over.

"No, we'll head over. I want to pick up the plates, and I need to swing by the farm to get the silverware. Love you, Uncle Pug. Bye."

Next Clare let her mother know she was coming for the silver. She had dropped Gran's silver off a couple of weeks ago. Her mother had volunteered to polish it. A job Clare was thrilled to let her do.

Bev walked into the kitchen with her skin aglow, and her hair a cloud of soft, downy curls framing her face. She had followed Clare's lead and dressed for comfort and for work. Both were wearing leggings, sneakers, and sweatshirts.

"I'll feed the dogs and we can get going." Clare said.

They left the dogs at home and headed out. After picking up the silver, the plates, and linens, they went to the florist for the flowers Bev had ordered. Then over to Skates Market for the turkeys and all the fixings to make the meal great. Skate wandered through the store and wished his customer a happy Thanksgiving. Clare loved the roly-poly man with his curly salt and pepper hair and twinkling blue eyes.

As they were leaving the store, Clare stopped in her tracks, creating a chain reaction. Bev ran into her, and the bag boy ran into Bev almost knocking her down. She waved the boy's apologies away, "It was completely my fault. I'm sorry. Bev, are you all right? She handed the boy the key fob to Pete's Land Cruiser, indicating to him which vehicle it was. He pushed the cart over to the tailgate.

"I'm fine. What are you looking at?"

Clare nodded her head toward two men and a woman getting out of their car. "If I'm not mistaken, those men are True Bergman and his father. I don't know who the woman is, though."

They were dressed in street clothes—no flowing robes. Bev stared at them for a few moments. "I think you're right."

"Excuse me, Mr. Bergman," she said, as they approached. "Clare Harrigan and Bev Hawkins. We visited you at the compound a few days ago. Could we have a word?"

The men's faces froze in fear, then a wary look flashed in their eyes. Their bodies went rigid in a defensive posture. Hmm, Clare asked herself, what do they have to fear from me and Bev? She stepped in front of them, blocking the door. The woman smiled. She looked angelic, but far too young to be Bergman's wife—maybe his daughter.

"It's so sad about Bets, I mean Elizabeth. Who could have murdered a beautiful young woman like her?"

The young girl gasped. "You lied to me. That's why you…"

"Hush, Becca." Bergman grabbed the girl by the arm and

pushed past them. "Step aside."

Becca shook him off and turned to them—eyes blazing. She mouthed the words with boldness, "I know something." Bergman turned and grabbed her again and jerked her into the store.

The bag boy returned the key, and Bev reached in her purse and handed him a tip, then wished him a happy Thanksgiving. "Wow! Thank you, ma'am, and happy Thanksgiving, but we aren't supposed to accept tips."

Bev winked at him. "I won't tell if you don't." He handed the money back and shook his head.

"There goes an honest kid. Now, what was that all about with that gal, Becca?" Bev asked. "I'd love to know what she meant. How do we find her and get her alone without the tyrant watching over her?"

"I'm going to go back inside. Maybe I can catch her alone."

Bev rolled her eyes. "I'll wait for you out here. Give me the key. I have the latest Maisie Dobbs book by Jacqueline Winspear in my purse. I'll read, but hurry up, we have tons of work."

Clare spotted the group at the deli counter and slipped up an aisle to the left. She peered around the corner and caught Becca's eye. She turned to the men and said something, then headed over to the far side of the counter in the direction of the restrooms. True followed her and waited at one of the tables next to the deli area. When she came out, she frowned at him.

"I'm going to pick up a few things. I think I can manage on my own!" She pointed in the direction of his father. "Go."

She's got moxie, Clare thought. She walked with Becca down the aisle as she idly picked up a few things. "I can't talk now. Meet me at the pedestrian gate of the compound. It's ten or fifteen feet to the right of the main gate. Hard to see from the road."

"I'll be there, but with friends. They won't let me go anywhere on my own these days."

"I know the feeling." Another frown appeared on her face. "I adored Sister Elizabeth and her brother. If he or True caused… Never mind. Please meet me tonight, and I will tell you what little I know." Becca placed her items in one of the wicker baskets stacked here and there throughout the store for people who thought they were only going to pick up a couple things and ended up with an armload. She picked up the basket. "I have to go now."

When Clare got back outside she found Bev sound asleep. She entered the security code and tried to enter as quietly as possible. Bev never woke up until Clare pulled in the driveway and touched her shoulder. Sophie and Buck followed right behind them and hopped out of the car and started helping them unload.

"Okay, let's rock and roll." Buck rubbed his hands together. "I haven't had a Thanksgiving dinner in a warm, family home in more years than I care to remember. Thanks again for inviting me."

Clare smiled and gave him a quick hug. "I could use some help bringing the extra leaves for the table up from the storage room downstairs. Bev, will you please show him where they are?"

Within a couple of hours, the tables were set—the dining room table for the adults and the round coffee table for the little guys—the wine was chilling, and the brine for the turkeys was simmering on the stove. It filled the cottage with the mouthwatering scent of apple juice, brown sugar, soy sauce, fresh ginger, and spices. The turkeys would marinate in the brine, once it cooled, until Thanksgiving morning. Clare would then stuff the cavities with chunks of lemons, oranges, and onions before roasting them in the oven.

"Mom and Aunt Fio are baking up a storm, Libby is bringing the dressing and a sweet potato casserole. Bev, you're on the hook for a corn soufflé and rolls. One of us will handle the mashed potatoes and cranberries here in the morning. I'll set up a relish tray with pickles, olives, and such."

"Count on me to do the potatoes, Clare," Buck said.

"And my dad and I are bringing the obligatory green bean casserole," Sophie said.

"I've got some great cheese spreads, fruit, condiments, and crackers for munchies. And some special treats for the munchkins. I bought some ready-to-assemble gingerbread houses for them to decorate with all the candies, frosting, and do dahs required." Clare sighed. "It's takes an army to get everything ready, a couple of days to prepare the food, and less than an hour to eat. But oh, how we all love the leftovers." Clare said.

"What about me?" Clay asked, as he walked through the

door.

Bev smiled. "You can stand around and look pretty, but when it's time to clean up…"

"I'm your man for the clean-up crew!"

"Thank you all, but Bev and I are running on empty and need sleep. Bev, Clay, and I have a late-night rendezvous tonight."

Clay raised his eyebrows. "Whatever and whenever you need me..."

Clare had held off telling them about the midnight drive to Idaho, and the encounter with the Bergmans at Skate's Market. She told them briefly and left Clay to fill in the details on the trip.

With legs that felt like lead, Clare climbed the stairs and fell on her bed.

Chapter 28

"Clare, wake up. It's eight o'clock, and we'll have to leave in an hour or so. I brought you a jolt of caffeine and a sandwich. You can eat while you get ready."

She yawned and rolled over. "I am starved. Hopefully, we can be home and back in bed by midnight."

The ride out to the compound was uneventful, and they found the gate with no problem. Becca was waiting for them next to the open gate. She wore her white robes. Clay and Bev stood off to the side, and Becca glanced at them before turning her attention to Clare.

"Where is Mr. Bergman?" Clare asked.

"He's sound asleep. I generally read for a couple of hours and sometimes take a walk around the compound. I love how quiet it is at night. Sometimes I check on the animals. It's my peaceful time of the day."

"Is Mr. Bergman going to step up and become the new leader now that Woodman is dead? I guess Brenda will own all of this, that is, if she isn't found guilty of a crime as far as Woodman's death is concerned."

"Sister Brenda is an...odd person. I know she and the children were abused by that man. Other men living here are the same.

Children and women run away all the time. There are those in the surrounding area that help them."

Clare thought of Sophie and the help she had given to the young woman she found battered, frightened, and hungry.

"My family, and I won't stay here. We had planned to leave at some point, but all assets must be turned over to The Evening Star whenever a person enters the community." Becca's voice was gentle. There didn't seem to be any anger or bitterness in this woman. "We really have very little."

The case filled with gold popped into Clare's mind. Would it be divided among the followers of The Evening Star? It seemed the fair and right thing to do. But life is not always fair, and people do not always do the right thing.

"What did your father lie to you about?"

Becca chuckled. "He's not my father. He's my husband. I came with nothing at all and was welcomed as a child of God."

Welcomed as a child of God, or as a captivating, nubile young woman? Clare thought. She tried not to allow the surprise she felt show on her face and to keep the shock out of her voice. She was unable to do so. "Oh…you look so young…I thought..."

"I'm twenty-two. Younger than his son, True. I ran away from a bad foster family situation and stumbled into The Evening Star community. He saved me…or so I thought."

"You fell in love with your rescuer?"

"In a way, yes. He has never mistreated me. I do care for him, but in love…no." She paused for a moment. "I have seen him lose his temper, though, which is why I decided to tell you what I know."

Clare witnessed him turn beet red and lose his temper as well the day she, Bev, and Clay had visited the compound. He was a man capable of violence. "And what do you know?" she asked.

"He went to see Sister Elizabeth, or Bets as you call her, the night she died. He said she was fine and staying secretly in her apartment with Sister Brenda. He didn't tell me she was *murdered*! He came home all covered in leaves and told me he had a flat tire and fell into the weeds and brush along the roadside. There were scratches on him too." Becca picked up a fallen leaf and twirled the stem with her fingers. She released the leaf and watched it flutter to the ground. "One more thing," she said, "True was with him that night." She dropped her head, but not before Clare saw pain flash across her face.

Becca turned to leave, but Clare caught her arm. "Before you go, what about the young girl, Leah?"

Becca closed her eyes and bit her lips. When she opened them, fear was evident in her eyes. "Be very careful of her. I considered Brother Woodman to be a wicked man. That was one of the reasons I wanted to leave. Make no mistake, there are many good people here, but there is evil. Leah Foster's a woman who decides what she wants and goes after it."

Clare, Bev, and Clay watched Becca until her swirling robes vanished into the darkness before closing the gate with a soft click and climbing back into Clay's truck. They rode along in silence until they reached Amelia Bay.

"That puts another wrinkle in the cloth we've been weaving. But the question that always comes back to me is why someone would kill two unrelated women. What links them?"

"Bev, I keep going back to the laptop. There's the connection between Bets and Eve. Gage and Rene play into all of this in some way too," Clare said.

"What Becca has just told us is very damning against the Bergman men and frightening about Leah, but it doesn't condemn them. Her husband could very well have been telling her the truth," Clay said, as he turned into the driveway of the cottage. "I'll see you ladies safely inside and head home. I'm beat, and I know you both must be too."

"I, for one, am going to watch our backsides where this Leah chick is concerned." Bev patted her purse and grinned.

Chapter 29

Clare dug around in her closet to find denim shirt she had forgotten about until now. Her mother had embroidered autumn leaves cascading over one shoulder and scattered down the back of the shirt. It was even ironed! She put it on over a pair of black leggings and padded down the stairs barefooted. The scent of cinnamon and pumpkin drifted throughout the house.

"Libby! I'm so glad to see you." Clare gave her friend a hug. "What's cookin'?"

"Pumpkin pancakes with my homemade maple syrup. I made them for my family this morning and started thinking how much I've missed seeing you and Bev. So, here I am, if only for an hour or so."

"Where's Bev?" Clare asked, as she piled the pancakes onto her plate.

Libby poured cups of coffee for herself and Clare, then sat down.

"Clay came by and took her over to her house to get some clothes. If you two don't stop getting involved in these terrible murder investigations, you'll both have to start having armed guards posted outside your houses."

"What happened to me being run off the road was a fluke. Nothing else has happened. Someone trying to get in the house…sure, but break-ins happen every day, and the rock through the window…a reporter trying to get Finn to come outside." Clare scooped up a forkful of pancakes. "A series of coincidences. That's all. These pancakes are scrumptious."

"Okay, but I think you're wrong." Libby looked skeptical but changed the subject since she knew she wouldn't win this round. "When are Finn and the little ones coming back from Sequim?"

"This afternoon. Finn will be staying at the farm with Cole. He wants to keep out of sight. Even though the evidence against him is falling apart, the media and Fleming are still gunning for him. Fleming thinks he may have been an accomplice in a crime, Lib. What that crime might be…who knows?" Clare brought Libby up-to-date on all that had happened since they last spoke.

"Something happened in Pete's kitchen that night. From what you say, we now believe Johnathon came to Bev after being stabbed by Woodman. I can understand Fleming's thought process, although I don't agree with it. Please be careful, Clare."

Bev and Clay returned and Libby left. The rest of the day was a whirlwind of activity. Bev placed beautiful arching branches of pyracantha down the center of the table, and nestled votive candle holders, and small vases filled with snowy white mums among the branches. Clare tied sage leaves, sprigs wheat, and stems of berries with thin chocolate brown ribbon to put at each place setting. Clare showed Clay how to fold the napkins to create a pocket for miniature bouquets to be tucked into.

"This napkin folding employs my architectural skills."

"We'll slip these chocolate turkeys on a stick in the kid's napkins." Clare set them on the table where Clay was working. "We still need to set up a coffee station. Then we'll head down to my studio and assemble all the gingerbread houses for the kibbles and bits to decorate after dinner. It's a mess I prefer to keep in an area I can hose down."

Clay walked through the house at the end of the day. "You ladies have outdone yourselves! Everything is beautiful. Thanks for letting me be a part of it."

"Let's eat some dinner, I'm starved. Who's up for franks and beans!"

Chapter 30

Thanksgiving Morning

Thanksgiving morning dawned with overcast skies and a gentle mist swirled through the air. Clare took the turkeys out of the refrigerator in her studio, where they had been soaking up all the wonderful flavors and moisture from the brine. She rinsed the plump birds in her laundry room sink, patted them dry, and covered them loosely. They could rest on the drainboard for a while.

She looked at her potter's wheel with longing. "I will get back to it soon. My fingers are itching to dig into some clay. I have a special order to complete too. Tonight, after everyone goes home, I'll spend a couple of hours down here," she said to Maggie and Ginger. "Before we put these beauties in the oven, I think we should go for a run." Ginger seemed to debate the run with glances between Clare and the birds. "Oh no, you don't, young lady. Get that crazy idea out of your cute little head." Clare firmly closed the door to the laundry room and put the harnesses on the dogs.

Most of the trees had dropped their leafy jewels—their faded glory nestled at their base. The spectacular beauty of

Washington was a feast for all the senses. The rise of the mountains, the frothy capped waves washed against the sand, streams rushed to the bay, and the crisp tang of autumn filled Clare's soul.

Clare and the dogs jogged along the water close to the bank, where the sand was firm and not littered with small rocks and oyster shells. She ran for about fifteen minutes until she reached Bev's house, where she ran up the bank and around the front of the house. She decided to run along the road toward her cottage as clouds began to shed and raindrops fell on her. Out of nowhere, an engine roared to life behind her. In her peripheral vision, she a saw a blur coming at her—fast! She pulled the leads of the dogs toward the bank, then let them go as she skidded and lost her footing. She rolled to a bruising stop on the rocks. The sound of the engine roared away and faded in the distance. The dogs stood at the water's edge and looked back at Clare. She called them to her. They jumped on her and licked her face. She pressed her hands firmly along their bodies to check for injuries—nothing, no whimpers. They both appeared fine.

"Dammit! Libby's always right." Clare stretched her limbs and stood. Everything seemed to be in good working order. She brushed the leaves and dirt off her fanny. There was some mud on her leggings that wouldn't brush off. "Not a word or woof about this, ladies." Clare gave silent thanks they weren't killed. She picked a few leaves out of Maggie and Ginger's feathery coats and ran her fingers through her own hair. With slow, steady steps they walked home along the beach. Time enough to let everyone know after we count our blessings today…maybe.

Bev was in the kitchen when Clare arrived home and the turkeys were sitting on the counter. She had cut up lemons, oranges, and onions to stuff inside them and was rubbing mayonnaise on the skin.

"What happened to you? You're covered in mud. *And* again, you went out alone." Bev sighed.

"We stayed on the beach. I knew I'd be safe there, but I slipped and fell." Bev seemed to buy her story. "Give me a few minutes to clean up, and I'll come help."

"Wait a minute." Ut oh. Clare froze. "I found several cases of wine downstairs. They're amazing!"

Clare breathed a sigh of relief and smiled. "I stumbled across a company that makes custom labels on the internet. I had special Thanksgiving labels made with a photo of my cottage to commemorate my first Thanksgiving here. Each of the adults, who are going to be here today can take a bottle home as a hostess gift. I bought extra so, there'll plenty to enjoy with dinner, and it's really good wine."

"A very nice gesture, Clare." Bev turned her attention back to the meal preparations. "Go ahead and shower, then after dinner when everyone is gone you can tell me what *really* happened on your run today."

Clare rolled her eyes. Busted! She trudged up the steps.

***

The heady smells of Thanksgiving filled the cottage. In a flurry, family and friends piled in bearing pies, cakes, and casseroles, they lined the kitchen counters and the pine buffet in Clare's dining room. Clare's parents, Uncle Pug, and Aunt Fio had come from Saint Amelia's Church, where they had served Thanksgiving dinner to seniors and those who were alone or in need of fellowship and friendship. The pub was closed. Jack arrived and tooted the horn. Clare peeked out the window, and there sat her Jeep. It looked shiny and almost new. Jack had spent the morning and early afternoon delivering meals to the homebound.

Clare met him at the door. "Thanks for bringing my Jeep back."

"I'm going to have to hang onto it for a little while longer, if you don't mind. I haven't mentioned this to anyone, mainly because I'm embarrassed. My truck was stolen."

"Oh, my gosh. When did it happen?"

"Do you remember the day I ran into you at the police station? I was dropping off the flyers for the Christmas shindig at the Community Center." Clare nodded. "Like a damn fool, I left the keys in it, and it was gone when I came out. Geez, I knew I'd only be in the station for few minutes."

"From the police station parking lot? That takes hutzpah!"

"Let's keep it quiet for now. I don't need a bunch of ribbing from your dad and Pug. I told them my truck was in the shop."

"Your secret is safe with me. Does Bev know?" He shook his head. She hugged him. She liked having a secret with Jack. "Okay. Go on in the den, and I'll bring you a drink. There's a football game on. They're cheering and jeering in there every few minutes. Sounds like a good game."

The doorbell rang just as Clare walked out of the den after she delivered Jack his drink. She opened the door to a man with an enormous bouquet of flowers held in front of his face. He laid the flowers on a table next to the door, wrapped both his arms around her, and dipped her before he planted a kiss on her lips.

She laughed and said, "You are one crazy fool, Glen Wynter!"

He did his Groucho Marx's bit with his eyebrows. "Yeah, but you really like me, don't cha?"

"I'm warming to you." She grinned. "Not hot—just warm." He pulled her up and with a little bow he presented her with the bouquet. Clare turned to find her parents standing side-by-side with astonished expressions on their faces, which they replaced with swift smiles. "Mom, Dad, you…uh…remember Glen Wynter? Pete's friend, and the fella who pulled me out of the muck."

"Of course." Without skipping a beat, Mike stepped forward, held out his hand, and clapped him on the back. "Welcome. Happy Thanksgiving. You're that famous author. I've read a number of your books. Excellent and exciting! Love all that spy stuff." Mike ushered him into the den. His walking cast clumped along on the wood floor.

Clare faced her mother. Grace walked over to her and took the flowers. "Let me put these in some water, dear." She kissed Clare on the cheek and whispered, "Pete says he's a very nice man, and Lord love a duck, I'd like you to have a nice man in your life."

At that moment, Libby, ever the CEO of the girlfriends, called all-hands-on-deck for the last-minute rush to get everything on the table.

Every person settled around the table held a special place in Clare's heart. Love washed over her, and she blinked back tears of joy at seeing Finn relaxed and Cole comfortable with his new family and friends.

Mike took his place at head of the table. "Tragedy shattered our family and friends this year, but we've picked ourselves up.

We're especially grateful for the people seated around this table today. We welcome the newest member of our family, Cole. And we are so thankful Finn is with us today. Pug, will you join me in our traditional Irish blessing? Pug stood, and they bowed their heads.

"May this food restore our strength, giving new energy to tired limbs, new thoughts to weary minds. May this drink restore our souls, giving new vision to dry spirits, new warmth to cold hearts. And once refreshed, may we give new pleasure to You, who gives us all. Praise God, from whom all blessings flow. In the name of the Father, and of the Son, and of the Holy Spirit. Amen."

Pug picked up his wine glass and said, "To those who have prepared this feast, thank you! Let's eat. Glasses clinked, delicious wine was poured, and dishes passed from hand to hand around the table.

Chapter 31

After everyone had left, the last of the pots and pans washed, and the dishwasher hummed, Bev turned to Clare. "Okay. What happened this morning?"

Clare told her about her near miss or near hit, as it should be called.

"And you didn't see who or what?" Bev gathered a pile of kitchen towels and table linens and placed them in a laundry basket. "Promise me you will not go out alone again."

"I absolutely promise. I could have been hurt or killed, I suppose, and I put the dogs at risk too." Clare wiped some gravy drips off a cabinet. "It was misty when I left here and patches of fog swirled around, then it started to rain. It was just a blur."

Bev gave Clare a hug. "I've locked up and set the alarm. I'm beat. How about you?"

"I have to do some work on my pottery. I have a few pieces of special orders that are in the damp room and need to be trimmed. If I wait too long they'll dry out, and I may not be able to save them. I'll only be a little while."

Clare picked up the laundry basket and headed down the stairs to her studio. Maggie trotted along behind her, and Ginger followed Bev upstairs. She went into the laundry room and put the basket on top of the washing machine. She changed into a pair of overalls and a T-shirt.

"I'll deal with the laundry tomorrow," she said to Maggie, who had curled up on the rug in front of the washer and dryer. She reached down and rubbed her head.

Clare lined up her tools, then brought out a large pasta bowl and eight individual bowls to be trimmed. Her client wanted them for her book club's no-more-turkey night—let's eat pasta and pizza get together in the upcoming week.

A low growl emanated from deep inside of Maggie. "What up, Mags?" Maggie ran across the room and threw herself against the doors, causing the alarm to go off. Clare looked at the doors and screamed. A person swathed in all black, who wore an evil-looking clown mask, had a baseball bat poised over his head. Again, no motion lights came on. The terrifying figure turned, ran toward the beach, and melted into the darkness. Bev and Ginger pounded down the stairs. Clare looked down at the floor. Broken pieces of clay lay scattered around her feet. With tears streaming down her face, Clare dropped to the floor and tried to gather the chunks.

"What the hell happened?" Bev pulled her to her feet. "Leave that. I'll get it later."

Clare collapsed against Bev—wracked with sobs and panic-stricken. "What is going on? What did I do? Who hates me this much? Someone…tried to break…" Clare pointed to the doors.

Bev led her to a bench and pushed her down. Then she punched in the code to stop the alarm. The phone rang, and she grabbed it. It was the security company.

"Someone tried to break in, but they're gone. Yes, we're fine. No, please don't send the police. I can give you the code wo…" Bev nodded—resigned. "Fine. I understand. Thanks."

She got a warm cloth and sat down next to Clare, then wiped her face with it. Clare took the cloth and buried her face in it. After a several minutes, the sound of tires crunched on the driveway. Bev walked to the doors and began to open them.

"Don't leave me alone." Clare jumped up and clung to Bev. Don't go out there, you might get hurt!"

"I'm not going to get hurt. The police just pulled in. Man, that was fast! I'll just wave them back here." Bev leaned around the side of the cottage and motioned for them to come to backyard. Pug and Mike pulled in shortly after them. The security company would have called them as well. The room filled with Chief Fleming, Chris Reed, Pug and Mike. Everyone started talking at once.

Bev held up her hand. "Stop! Quiet! I'm taking Clare upstairs to get her something hot and soothing to drink. She can't tell us anything until she calms down."

"Someone tried to break in the french doors," Bev said, looking at Chris.

He stooped down and started looking at the doors.

"I have to question her first." Chief Fleming stepped forward. "What happened?"

Bev ignored him and started for the stairs. Fleming grabbed her arm and tried to stop her. Pug walked over to him and said, "Let her go." He towered over Fleming. He was a formidable figure. His nickname came from the several undefeated, years he spent in the boxing ring—pugilist. "Look at her. You're welcome to come up with us, but be quiet until she collects herself."

Pug helped Mike, who clomped up the steps with his cast. The police brought up the rear. Pug stirred the embers in the living room fireplace and added a couple of logs to get it going again, while Bev helped Clare into a chair, and Mike wrapped an afghan around her. Her teeth chattered. Clare watched Bev as she went into the kitchen and poured a cup of coffee from the pot still resting on the counter. She warmed it in the microwave, then poured a healthy splash of brandy into the cup. Looked at it and added another splash.

The doorbell rang when Bev walked back into the living room. She handed the cup to Mike. He could smell the booze and nodded his approval to Bev. Clare wrapped her hands around the mug as Mike handed it to her. She took a sip and felt warmth spread through her. She took a couple more sips before she tried to place the cup on the table next to her chair. The coffee sloshed, and Mike took the cup from her hands. Pete and Jack rushed through the door when Bev opened it.

"What happened? Mom called me and Jack after the alarm company called."

"I'll put on another pot of coffee," Bev said, as she went back into the kitchen. She set up a tray with enough mugs for everyone. Clare watched her through the open doorways. Fear was still present in her eyes. Bev seemed to be her talisman at the moment.

Bev set the tray of cups on the coffee table and went back to fetch the fresh brewed coffee. "Help yourselves." She walked over to Clare and shooed Mike away. She took Clare's hand in both of hers. "Before you tell everyone what happened tonight, I'm going to tell them what happened this morning."

Clare nodded. She leaned her head on the back of the chair and closed her eyes.

Bev told them what had happened on Clare's run that morning. "Are you ready to tell us what happened tonight now?"

Clare told her story. Occasionally, she paused to wipe tears from her eyes with a hankie Mike gave her.

"How tall was this alleged person?" Fleming asked, his voice laced with skepticism.

Bev glared at him. Pug stood and leveled a stern look his way. Fleming lifted his mug and took a sip of coffee to hide his smirk.

"I don't know how tall he was. I just saw this mask. It was like something out of a horror movie. White with blood dripping from the eyes and mouth." She broke down and started to cry again. Once she had control of herself, she said, "He was all dressed in black and ran when Maggie charged the door."

With a condescending smirk, Fleming said, "Clare, we do know you can…let's say…conjure up stories to get attention. It *is* a crime to make a false report to the police. I'm willing to overlook…"

Pug moved toward him, along with the other men. Bev stood and placed her hand on Pug's chest and waved the rest of them back. In a low, menacing voice that built to a crescendo, she said, "Get the hell out of this house. Now! Right now! You're egotistical bastard!"

Fleming sputtered. "You'll…you'll regret this." He tripped as he backed toward the door. Chris caught his arm to steady him, then shook his head. He looked at Clare with sympathy on his sweet face before he closed the door behind them.

Chapter 32

Clare looked around her room, and felt confused. The whole horrible night flooded back. Everyone had finally left at 10:30 last night, and she fell into bed. It was certainly a Thanksgiving she would never forget. She rolled over and looked at the clock on the bedside table and sat bolt upright.

"Ten o'clock! Holy Mother of God, how could I sleep so long?" She grabbed her head—the brandy. "It relaxed me and helped me sleep, but oh, I'm paying for it now."

Grace opened the door. "Are you talking to yourself? Get up and shower, darling. You'll feel better," she said, as she opened the shutters that kept the room dark. "There's a party going on downstairs. Libby's cooking brunch for everyone. Glen, Sophie…well, let's just say the gang's all here. Glen is such a nice young man."

Clare groaned. "I'm not sure I'm up for a party." She slid out of bed and padded across the hardwood floor to the bathroom. She turned on the shower and looked at herself in the mirror. Racoon eyes looked back at her. She grabbed a couple of aspirin.

"How are you feeling this morning?" Her mother asked when Clare came out to get her robe. She was making the bed. Clare walked over to help her.

"Slightly hungover. You're right, once I shower and the aspirin kicks in, I'll be fine. I'm still scared and confused about why this is happening…again. If there is ever another murder in Amelia Bay that involves anyone we know, we're all getting on a plane and heading to Tahiti until it's solved."

Grace walked over to Clare and wrapped her arms around her. Clare buried her head in her mother's shoulder and breathed in her comforting scent.

"I was thinking the same thing, Clare. Lord love a duck! Here we were two months ago, someone trying to kill you *and* Bev. Both of you hiding out. A terrible time, and now this." Grace stepped back and looked Clare in the eyes. "Promise me you will be more careful, young lady. I'm frightened too."

She felt safe for the moment, but this was not a bruise her mother could kiss and make go away. "I absolutely promise. But this time, it's just me. Why? Bev and Clay have been poking around with me." Clare opened the closet door and grabbed her robe. As she walked into the steamy bathroom, she shook her head and looked back. "Why me? I'm sure about one thing, Mom, I'm not leaving my home today." She closed the door and twisted her hair into a knot on top of her head.

After a twenty-minute shower, Clare felt energized. She found Maggie cuddled on the down-filled chaise when she came out of the bathroom. She sat down next to her, and leaned over to nuzzle her face in Maggie's silky fur. "No more tears. What do you think, should I get one of those ballcaps that reads *No Fear*? We have a wedding to pull together, and I can't allow someone to continue to terrorize me and you. You were my hero last night. You scared away the bad guy. Thank you." Maggie turned her golden eyes to her, then licked Clare's nose. She was rewarded with more cuddles and a kiss on the top of her head.

Thanksgiving kicked off the beginning of Christmas for Clare. She searched in her closet for her red turtleneck sweater and a pair of jeans. Then plucked the cute little Santa pin out of her jewelry box that Dilly had given her last year. She added a little blush and some under eye concealer to chase away the circles from last night's crying jag, and she was ready to go. "Come on, girl, let's go greet the troops.

Libby pulled a cookie sheet out of the oven with two fruit galettes on it and placed them next to the two that were already on racks cooling. She reached out her arms to Clare with tears in her eyes.

"Stop. Maggie and I just had a conversation about this, no tears and no fears. Now, what are you cooking?"

"Ah…and what was Maggie's opinion on no fear, no tears?"

"She agrees with me." Clare broke off a piece of the golden-brown crust and moved away before Libby had a chance to shoo her hand. "Come on, Lib, I'm starved. I had a shock last night."

"Go sit down, and I'll serve you." Libby wrapped her arms around Clare.

"How can I help? You and Bev are here cooking up a storm and entertaining. I feel like a slug in my own home."

"But a cute slug." Libby smiled and poured two cups of coffee. She set one cup on the table in front of Clare, then sliced a piece of one of the cooled galettes which she topped with a dollop of whipped cream.

"Maggie and I are always in total agreement." She took a bite of the galette. "Lib, this could win a blue ribbon at the county fair. What's in it?"

"Apples, pears, and cranberries, along with all the sugary, spicy stuff. Everyone's in the den watching the pre-game shows for college football." Libby leaned against the counter. "Clare, I get it, no fears, no tears, but I'm scared for you."

"Honestly…me too. I have to stay strong. Mac and Carolyn are getting married soon, and I do *not* want this to mar their happiness. I'm thankful Finn is out of jail and things are looking up for him. Dad's leg is healing. Lots of things in the good column. Still far too many things to be sorrowful about—Eve and Bets. My heart breaks when I think of Cole growing up without his mother."

Libby nodded. "We'll do what we can to keep the little fella happy, but no one can ever replace his mother. At least he has his dad, and Mia seems to adore him." She sighed. "Let's perk up. Still hungry? There are some mashed-potato puffs, sausage, and scrambled eggs in the oven that I've been keeping warm for you."

"Always hungry. Bless your heart. I'll have another slice of the galette too."

Grace and Bev walked into the kitchen as Libby pulled the plate out of the oven.

Grace walked over and hugged her daughter. "I see your fright of yesterday didn't spoil your appetite, darling. Have you two come up with any ideas of what *is* going on?"

"Mom, I don't know. The only common denominator is Finn. Both Bets and Eve were connected to him."

"I believe Eve's laptop plays into this somehow, Mrs. H." Bev poured herself and Grace each a cup of coffee and sat down. "Rene and Gage wanted it, and from what we surmise, Bets stole it from the back of Finn's car."

"Maybe there are two people involved in the killings. But, I guess you if really think about it, both were bashed over the head. The blow to the head killed poor Eve, but Bets was strangled as well as bashed. Vicious. Could have been a copy-cat killing where Bets was concerned. You know with the addition of the strangling. That makes it different." Grace said, as she leaned against the counter. "My money's on those two fellas, Gage and Rene, though."

Libby topped off Clare's mug. "The person in the scary clown mask who terrorized Clare last night had a ball bat. Again, it comes back to Finn and the women in his life. His sister, the mother of his child, and a woman he was involved."

The four women were silent for a few minutes when Bev asked, "What about the stalker woman?"

Grace shook her head. "I'm afraid not. I asked Pete about her. He still has the private detective keeping tabs on her in Los Angeles. It seems she's found a new love who she's scooting around town with, and he's moved in with her."

"Here's a thought, Bets could have killed Eve to get her hands on the laptop," Clare said. "That opens up all kinds of possibilities. Then there are the Bergman men, Josiah and True. I don't think for one minute those are their real names. Although his wife, Becca, seemed to think Josiah was gentle. I saw him lose it, and if it hadn't been for his son calming him…"

"What about the girl, Leah? She's clearly in love with True, and her jealousy was a little over the top. She's obsessed with True Bergman." Bev sliced a piece of the galette and heaped it with whipped cream. "True was seething about Finn and Bets' relationship."

"You're right, Bev. Becca told you, me, and Clay that True

and Josiah visited her apartment the night she died."

"Lord love a duck! I don't know what to think. I need some time to reflect and digest all this information. Clare, I would like you to come home with your father and me."

"Mom, you have enough on your hands with Finn, Cole, and Mia. Let's not forget Uncle Pug and Aunt Fio, plus Pete and Dana's crew." Clare knelt in front of her mother and clasped both her hands. "I made a commitment to a client, and I smashed her bowls last night. I have just enough time to get them made and through two firing processes before she needs them. I'll be cautious, but I will not live in fear."

Sophie, who had been hanging out in the den watching the game, walked into the kitchen. "I have to head out now. Buck's with my dad, and I promised them I would be home. Those two are bonding." She looked at Clare. "Are you going to be okay? I know you've got your pistol packin' mama with you, but…"

"We'll be fine," Bev said. "Clay is going to stay here too."

"I've done what I can to help with Finn, but I've been MIA for a lot of what's been going on." Sophie smiled. "The reason is, I've been offered a plum job here. No more traveling for me. Well, only occasionally."

"Ah ha, so that's the distinguished fella we've seen you talking to," Clare said.

A round of congratulations broke out, and Sophie held up her hands to quiet them. "First things first. We have to get the blond bombshell elected mayor after we make sure Finn is completely exonerated."

Libby headed home to get her big guys ready to go back to college and her little guys ready for school on Monday. Clare's parents followed her out the door. Clare pressed Clay and Glen into bringing up her boxes of Christmas decorations from the storeroom.

In her studio, she pulled out some clay and weighed an eight-pound piece and eight two-pound pieces. She started with the large pasta bowl. Throwing these types of bowls can be tricky. She knew if she wasn't careful, she would end up with a plate if gravity had its way with the clay. Clare pressed her arms against her body to center the piece, then began to pull the sides up. As always, she relaxed as the slippery clay took shape and went from a lump of clay to a bowl. Once all the bowels were in the damp room and everything was wiped down and washed, Clare hopped in the shower in the bathroom she had installed in her laundry room. She pulled a pair of gray sweatpants and a soft, pink T-shirt out of laundry basket. Satisfied with herself, she went upstairs.

Glen met her in the kitchen. "I got a phone call from my editor, and I have to go home. I need to get on the computer and go over his comments on my new book. It's due at the publisher by the end of next week."

"You've been a great help to me today. Thanks for hauling up the boxes and putting up my outside lights."

"How about I fix a plate for you? Just pop in the microwave and *déjà vu*, it's Thanksgiving all over again. You can munch and work. I'll add a couple of pieces of pie."

"Thank you, I accept. The lights aren't finished yet. Clay says he'll finish them. *And* he and Bev will be here for you tonight." Glen placed his hands on Clare's shoulders. "I want our relationship to go somewhere—somewhere good. I care for you—a lot." He looked at her with hope-filled eyes.

"I like you, Glen, and I want to see this, whatever this is, maybe develop into something more. But you have to understand, I'm new at dating. I haven't *dated* since college."

He placed his hands on her cheeks and tilted her face up, then kissed her forehead. "Please, call me if you need anything or if something frightens you. I'll be here, and to hell with my editor and publisher."

***

Clare sat in her dining room window seat sipping a glass of wine. Headlights rounded the corner, and she recognized Bev's new Escalade pull into the driveway. Bev hopped out and waved to her, then sprinted up the stairs to the deck. She had gone home for some clean clothes. Clay, who had been stringing lights, spoke to Bev then took off in his truck.

Clare smiled as Ginger jumped out of the car behind her and bounded off toward the beach. "I'm going to throw the ball to run some energy out of her," Bev called from the kitchen door, as she dropped her purse and bag on the floor. "Clay's going to the big box store for more strands of twinkle lights. They'll be able to see your cottage from the Space Station before he's finished."

Maggie raised her head at the sound of Bev's voice then, stretched, and curled into a doggy donut—nose to tail—and promptly fell back asleep. Soon enough, Ginger would roust her from her cozy spot next to the fireplace, Clare thought, as she walked into the kitchen. She gently closed the door between the kitchen and dining room. Maggie was used to hanging out with Mitzie, her parents' old, deaf poodle mix. The lively Ginger wore her out, but she seemed to love being with her.

Leftover turkey and cranberry sandwiches for an easy dinner for them, along with slices of pumpkin pie topped with a dollop of whipped cream—perfect. Leftovers are one of the great joys of Thanksgiving, Clare thought.

Clare pulled everything out of the refrigerator and put it on the counter. She smiled and hummed as she thought of Glen. Ginger's barking drew her to the window. She could see her in the brilliant light the moon cast across the water and into the backyard—no Bev. She pushed open the door and stepped onto the deck. A wind swirled and sucked the door shut behind her with a bang. Out of nowhere, a deranged-looking woman charged up the steps and stood in the far corner of the deck with a baseball bat in her hands. Short, dark hair framed her face. The porch light reflected off her brilliant blue eyes—wild eyes laser-focused on Clare.

"Who are you, and what do you want?" Clare thought she looked familiar. She put her hands up, trying to calm the woman. "Wait a minute, you're one of the waitresses from the pub. Maria, your name is Maria." Instead of the long blond tresses she appeared to have when working in the pub, her hair was now coal black and spikey. Hadn't her eyes been brown? Clare asked herself as she stepped back toward the door. She slid her hand across the small of her back and rested it on the doorknob. Clare tried to smile, but knew she probably looked as demented as this woman. Where was Bev? she asked herself. Had this woman hurt her or worse? "You remember me, Maria? From the pub?" She slowly turned the doorknob and pushed back against it.

"Stay where you are! You may be Finn's wife, but he is mine! With you and those other women out of the way, he will be mine!"

"Finn's wife?" Clare was stunned. "I'm not… Whatever gave

you that idea? He's…" She could hear Maggie's wild scratching and barking at the door leading from the living room to the kitchen. A door she had closed. Clare twisted the doorknob and shoved the back door open in a swift movement. She spun into the kitchen and tried to shut the door. But not fast enough. The baseball bat slammed down on her arm. She screamed and fell to the floor. Pain shot through her arm and gripped her shoulder.

Maria raised the bat over her head when a man's voice cried out. "Maria Elena! Stop!" His footsteps pounded up the stairs, and then the crack of splintering wood rang out through the night air as the deck railing gave way. A grunt was followed by a crashing noise—then silence. He had distracted the mad woman for a moment.

The commotion was all the time Clare needed. Her good arm landed within reach of Bev's purse. She edged toward the purse and reached for the gun burrowed inside. She gripped the cold, but welcoming, touch of smooth steel and released the safety the way Bev had shown her. She pulled it out and levelled it at the woman she knew as Maria. Everything felt like it was happening in slow motion. The gun didn't seem to faze the her at all. It was as though she didn't see it. As the bat was coming down on her, Clare fired one explosive shot.

***

Jake Fleming stood next to the gurney as the EMTs helped Clare onto it. The other two ambulances had left with sirens blaring. Clare grimaced with pain as she was wrapped in a blanket by the attendants. They propped her up to a sitting position to relieve the pressure on her arm.

"My friend, is she going to be all right?" she asked, through chattering teeth. The warmth of the blanket could not stop the trembling that racked her body.

"I don't have any information on either of the ladies. One had a gunshot wound, and the other, I believe, a serious head injury. The man who fell off the deck was treated here for minor scrapes, but refused an ambulance. He landed in one of your bushes, and the fall knocked the wind out of him. I'm not sure if the bush survived, though."

The medic held up a hypodermic needle. Clare shoved his hand away. "No, not until I get to the hospital and find out what happened to my friend." Clare winced at the word *serious* where Bev was concerned. Her eyes beseeched them. "The one with the head wound—how is she?"

The EMTs looked at her and shook their heads. "No idea, ma'am. We'll know more when we get you to the hospital. The docs and nurses will be able to answer your questions."

Fleming walked alongside the gurney. He was joined by the mystery man from the pub. His limp was more pronounced as he tried to keep up with the gurney. His suit jacket was ripped and covered in dirt.

"Who are you?" Clare asked.

"I'm John E. Taylor of JET Investigations. I was hired by Maria Elena's family to track her down. I didn't recognize her with the blond wig and contact lenses. She's an actress, and she sure knows how to disguise herself." His round chestnut face softened when he said, "I wish I'd gotten here sooner to prevent this tragedy."

"Yeah, me too. But my brother has a private detective watching her in Los Angeles. How can she be in two places at once?"

"That's not Maria in LA. That woman is Angela, her identical twin. The family hoped Maria would turn up at her house down there so, her twin has been staying there. But everything pointed to her being here—in Washington. She's…she's always had some…problems…issues to deal with. A beautiful woman, but very troubled. I've known the girls since they were youngsters. Two women from the same egg, and one is normal and the other one…nuts."

"How could she think Finn was my husband?"

"As I said, she's troubled. Maria doesn't like to stay on her meds. She creates her own fantasy world and lives in it. I'm sorry about all this. Hope your friend pulls through. Maria Elena's family has had her in several mental hospitals over the years. The family's very wealthy. When she told them to start planning a wedding, they knew she was off her meds and hired me to find her."

Taylor turned to Fleming and said, "Look, if you don't

need me, I want to get over to the hospital. I'll swing by the station in the morning to make a full statement." Fleming nodded and Taylor walked away. His gait gave credence to his battered and bruised body.

"When my men and I are finished here, we'll lock up. I'm sorry you had to go through this," Fleming said.

"You're always telling me you're sorry about something. If you had believed my brothers, none of this would have happened." Clare was pissed. There wasn't another word strong enough to convey her mood at the moment.

Fleming had a sardonic smile on his face. "Your friend may have shown you how to release the safety and fire a weapon, but not how to shoot straight. That gal you shot should survive."

"I am thankful I don't have to live the rest of my life knowing I killed someone. How did Bev seem when she was taken to the hospital?"

"You never know with head injuries like that. I'm being honest when I tell you there could be brain damage or bleeding on the brain. It was a blunt force trauma with the same bat that most probably killed Everest Johannsson and knocked Bets Woodman out, I would imagine. We'll know for sure when we get it tested."

Clare squeezed her eyes closed, and still the tears leaked out the sides and soaked the edges of the blanket she was wrapped in. Please, please, please, God, let her live, she prayed.

"I've been thinking, perhaps I can buy you dinner sometime, and we can start over again."

"You. Are. A. Pig! You can't start something over that never started in the first place. You're a married man!"

"True, but she's left town for a while."

"Get out of my sight and stay the hell out of my life. I never want to see you again. Take care of your wife, you idiot. Believe me when I say, I would crawl over hot coals and broken glass to escape you."

"Excuse me, sir. You're upsetting my patient. She needs calm and a hospital." The attendant, who had overhead the entire conversation, unceremoniously pushed Fleming aside and lifted Clare into the ambulance. Once he and Clare were inside the ambulance, he said, "Ya know, there's a saying where I come from in Texas, if ya shoot a guy like him…a good defense is…he needed killin'."

Clare heard tires skidding to a stop and Glen's voice. "What the hell is going on? Clare, where's Clare?" Panic filled his voice. "I saw the ambulance when I was driving home and turned around."

"She's in the ambulance. Who are you?" Fleming asked.

"Is she going to be all right?" Glen turned to the EMT standing by the open door.

"I repeat, who are you?" Fleming grabbed his arm.

"Take your hands off me. I'm…I'm…her fiancé." He wrenched his arm away, causing Fleming to slip on the wet grass and fall back. He landed squarely in a muddy puddle. Chris and the other officers turned away and snickered. They knew the chief could count on one hand the number of days he had left in Amelia Bay.

Fiancé? What is he talking about? Clare asked herself.

Chapter 33

Saturday December 8th

The late afternoon clouds shrouded the final fleeting moments of daylight. Snowflakes drifted gently to the ground and blanketed the world in soft brilliance. Crowds of people filed out of the church and formed lines along each side of the path—waiting, crying. The heavy, oak doors to Saint Amelia Church opened. Cheers and applause greeted the bride and groom as they passed through the doors. Caroline, looking like a princess in a fairytale, had opted for a long, white cape with a fur-trimmed hood instead of a veil. Mac sported a goofy grin. Bev stood next to Clare, her bandaged head covered by a fluffy hat. Clare, with her arm still in a sling, stood next to Glen. Finn held his son, Cole, who tried to catch snowflakes on his tongue. Mac and Caroline glided along the path, swirling the featherlight snow into clouds all around them and those who wished them happiness.

The entire group of family and friends made their way to the pub. It had been transformed. The tables were decked out with crisp white tablecloths and Christmas red and green napkins. Centerpieces of red roses, sprigs of pine, and white orchids graced every table. Twinkle lights and candles sparkled throughout the room and the bride and groom seemed to float across the floor. Soon everyone began to join them on the floor.

Glen walked up to Clare and held out his arms. She stepped

forward and let him encircle her—awkward, with her arm in a sling.

"In all the hoopla, since that terrible night I keep meaning to ask you something, Mr. Wynter. Just exactly when did you propose marriage to me? Did I say yes? And, if so, where's the ring?"

He sighed and rolled his eyes. "I had to say something to get that damn fool, Fleming, to let me go. Plus, it worked like magic getting information in the emergency room before any family showed up. I'll bet you didn't know I'm Bev's brother. That worked pretty good too!"

Chapter 34

A Sunday afternoon
Tea, Wine, and Munchies

The girlfriends gathered around the fieldstone fireplace in Clare's living room. The warmth from the cozy fire surrounded them. Sipping wine, they munched on the sinfully delicious goodies Gina Vitali brought from her tea shop in Seattle's Pioneer Square. The Christmas tree sparkled in the living room of the cottage. Clare had nestled all the ornaments her children made over the years among the branches along with her gran's ornaments she found tucked away in a box. Tiny lights flickered in the garland draped across the mantle, and the heavenly scent of pine drifted through the air.

"I'm so relieved the wretchedness and uncertainties of last month are behind us," Libby said. "How's Finn doing?"

"He and Cole are back in Los Angeles. Mia went with them. She's a stabilizing force for both of them. There are a lot of loose ends to tie up with Eve's estate," Clare said. "I believe this has been an eye-opening experience for Finn. Fatherhood has changed him for the better."

"What about the dastardly duo from Seabeck?" Sophie asked, as she topped off everyone's wine glass.

"Thankfully, Chief Bradshaw is back, if only for a little while until a suitable replacement can be found. The city council promised to dig deep with the vetting process of the new candidates. According to the chief, Gage has been charged with grand theft and aiding and abetting a criminal in the commission of a crime—Bets' crime. Also, accepting stolen merchandise and illegally soliciting that merchandise from her. She hid out at his place until her mother picked her up and took her to the apartment. Maria watched Bets' place and waited for her chance," Clare said. "Rene claims he knew nothing about it, and Gage is backing him up."

"Yeah, right, like I believe that. It should be a felony. Not only the value of the laptop, but the intellectual property that was on the computer." Sophie took a sip of wine.

"Why did Bets steal the laptop?" Libby asked.

"Mrs. Woodman told the police she wanted money to help them get away from Woodman. Finn said, if she'd been upfront with him, he would have helped."

"What's going to happen to Mrs. Woodman?" Gina asked, coming back from the kitchen with another tray of goodies.

"Stop. I'm going to gain five pounds by just looking at this stuff." Sophie reached for a cream puff. "Okay, maybe one more."

"Right now, she's out of jail. The court let her go on her own recognizance. They know she attacked Woodman in self-defense. But…they aren't sure if he had a heart attack because she pushed him, or if he would have had one anyway." Clare stood up and put another log on the fire. "Remember the woman who shot her husband and he died of a heart attack? They gave her parole for a couple of years. There wasn't any weapon used in Brenda's case—she just shoved him and didn't stick around to help."

"True. She did leave the scene. He might have lived if she hadn't shoved him down the bank and left him for dead," Sophie said, as she twirled the wine in her glass. "She claims he was already dead. As he's the only other witness… I hope probation is all she gets, if that. She's lost a daughter who, although misguided, had only tried to help her family. She'll inherit the compound, and has committed to return the money to those still living there. That goes a long way to redeem her."

"Brenda told us a pack of lies about how she came to be living at the compound. And she did it with such ease," Bev said. "Told us she was never married to Woodman. Humph!"

"She's did relinquish custody of Jonathan to his father. The oddest thing we found out is Sophie's neighbor, Brian, had the boy with him. It seems he and his wife were known by some at The Evening Star as a safe place to run to. Bets dropped him off there before she went to stay with Gage and Rene," Clare said. "He'd driven Bets' junker over to Pete's the night the poor kid was stabbed."

"I'm surprised I never knew that Brian and his wife took in the runaways from The Evening Star," Sophie said. "I always thought they were *all* foster kids or their grandchildren."

"I can understand. You're on the road so much of the time. I'm confused—a perennial state for me, I'm afraid. But how did Eve's body end up behind your garage, Clare?" Gina asked.

"I asked Chief Bradshaw about that. Maria was staying at the hotel in Silverdale when she first arrived. So was Eve. She saw Eve with Finn one day and decided to befriend her. Maria asked her for a ride to see Finn's, sister—me. I wasn't home, so they walked down to look at the bay. Maria already had the ball bat hidden there."

"The clues were there…if we had just paid attention." Bev sipped her wine. "Who found the passport? Maria. Who called you Mrs. Harrigan, Clare? Maria. Then we find out she's the one who stole my dad's truck to run you off the road. *And* tried to run you down Thanksgiving morning. She broke into an empty summer cottage and was living there. She kept Dad's truck hidden in the garage. The summer cottage is only about a quarter of mile down the road from here."

"Bets' car was never in the shop, as she told Finn. She wanted to borrow the car Finn was driving to get the laptop."

"I don't know why she planted the passport," Sophie said.

"In her warped mind, she thought she was punishing Finn. Once she killed off all the women in his life, they'd ride off into the sunset," Bev said.

"One more thing, if I had thought about it," Clare said. "The song, *Maria Elena*. Finn told me his stalker's name was Elena. That's an unusual and beautiful name. I don't know if it's much of a clue, but…"

"What a crazy, topsy-turvy world it has been for us these last several months. I want to be normal again," Libby said, as she refilled each wine glass. "To Bev, the next mayor of Amelia Bay."

Everyone laughed and all started talking at once.

Clare's thoughts wandered, as she gazed around her cottage at the twinkling lights and the decorations. What would the new year bring to her, her family, her friends, and her town…Amelia Bay?

Until next time.

"Every saint has a past, and every sinner has a future."
Oscar Wilde

About the author

Kathleen Joyce is happily married to a delightful man for more years then she ever thought possible in her twenties. She is a mother and grandmother of perfect children, and one slightly neurotic dog. Her life has been filled with travel along smooth and sometimes bumpy roads. Those roads have taken her to all four corners of this great country during her husband's naval career. Her experiences and travel have given her rich fodder for her books. She draws on the wonderful friends she has known and a few that are as neurotic as her dog. When she isn't writing, she loves digging in the dirt, reading, pottery, and sewing. She owned a home furnishings store and worked for twenty-plus years as an interior decorator. She lived in the middle of an avocado grove in California. She does make a scrumptious guacamole. Laughing! Laughing and lunch with friends is important to her.

Follow Clare Harrigan Mysteries on Facebook
Kathleen Joyce, Author, Clare Harrigan Mysteries

Coming in the fall of 2018

Harrigan III

Chapter One

A Wednesday Morning in December 2008

One year later

Clare pulled into the snow-covered parking lot of City Hall thankful she wore her boots. Bev's SUV was parked next to the building. "Ginger and Maggie, you wait in the car for a few minutes. I'll get Bev, and we'll go over to Bibi's for breakfast. I don't know why she texted us to meet her here." She tousled the silky coats of the good-natured pups. "Ginger, you're going to be so happy to have Bev home." Clare still couldn't get used to the idea that her Marilyn Monroe-esque friend had actually won the special election, and was now mayor of their charming community, that was nestled along the banks of Puget Sound. It had been a peaceful year since all the terrible happenings of the previous fall and winter.

She stomped the snow off her boots before she entered the private back door that led to Bev's office. "Welcome home Madam Mayor, and what was so all-fired important you had to text me and…What's the matter?" The horrified look on Bev's face struck fear in her gut. "What's that smell?"

Clare looked around. She and Bev both spoke at the same time. "Blood." The acrid smell came from blood splattered on Bev's desk, the walls, and dried in a pool that had seeped onto the floor around the body of, what appeared to be, a young man. A small Christmas tree that had been sitting on the credenza behind Bev's desk had been knocked to the floor. Broken shards of ornaments were scattered in the bloody puddle. The desk chair was overturned, and a knife with blood crusted on the handle was sticking out of a slashed chair. The victim was wearing a pair of faded jeans, cowboy boots, and a navy blazer. His lank, blond hair partially covered his tanned face.

"Who is he?" Bev shrugged her shoulders and shook her head.

"Have you called the police?"

She nodded.

Clare took Bev by the arm and guided her outside and away from the gruesome scene in the office. They both gulped the crisp, fresh air for a few moments, then Clare put her arm around her friend's shoulder and pulled her close to try to stop her shivering.

Sirens from two police cruisers, an ambulance, and fire truck shattered the quiet of the Sunday morning. The new Chief of Police of Amelia Bay hopped out of his squad car and approached them. Charlie Briggs had replaced the outgoing Chief Bradshaw. The interim man, Acting Chief Fleming, had been less than qualified to say the least, and had been booted out. Bev, her city council, and Bradshaw had hit a grand-slam homerun with the new chief. Briggs and his wife and three children had turned out to be wonderful additions to their little community.

He swiftly walked to the door, looked inside, then turned to the women. "Mayor, Clare. What happened here?"

Bev began to speak. "I don't know. We…I flew in on the red-eye from Hawaii. We arrived this morning. I had Clay…Clay Fuller drop me off at my house. I needed a wa…warm coat and boots. I…I drove over here because I wanted pick up my messages and some reports. You know to…to be ready to go tomorrow morning."

"Did either of you touch anything?" They both shook their heads. "What about your boots?" They looked at their boots and shrugged. "Clare what are you doing here?"

"Bev texted me. I was on my way to meet her for breakfast at Bibi's and bring her dog, Ginger, to her."

"Who's the victim? Do either of you know him?"

"From what I could see of his face, I have no idea." Clare turned to Bev.

"I didn't recognize him either, Charlie."

Ginger and Maggie were both barking and poking their noses out a window Clare had left partially rolled down.

"Okay, thank you. I'd like both of you to go sit in the Jeep with the dogs while my men, and I check things out." He called to one of Clare's favorite people. "Officer Reed, show the ladies to the Ms. Harrigan's vehicle and bag their boots, please. We'll need them for footprint evidence, Mayor. I'm sorry to inconvenience you."

"We'll be fine, chief. It isn't a problem."

The coroner pulled up just as Chris escorted them to the Jeep. Once they were in the Jeep, they slipped off their boots and Chris put them in evidence bags.

"Clare, this *canno*t be happening again!" Bev wrapped her arms around Ginger and buried her face in doggy hair. Ginger sensed her human's sadness and licked Bev's cheek. "I've missed you, my sweet girl." She was rewarded with another lick on the nose when she leaned back. Bev sat cross-legged in the back seat and Ginger laid her head in her lap.

Clare started the Jeep and blasted the heater. Maggie's watchful eyes scrutinized her. "It's okay, girl" She given up being surprised by how intuitive dogs can be, and reached over to reassure the girl with a scratch behind her ears. Maggie settled down and curled into a doggie donut in the passenger seat. "I don't know about you, but I'm starving."

"Of course you are."

Chris Reed tapped on Clare's window. She rolled it down. "The chief says you can both go home, and he'll be by to talk to you later. We'll be here for quite a while. Uh…sorry about your boots."

"Not a problem, thanks. We'll be at my place." Clare reached through the window and touched Chris' shoulder. He had been her daughter-in-law's partner in solving crime until Carolyn took leave to have her baby—Clare's first grandchild. "We'll be at my cottage."

"One more thing, Mayor, the chief wanted me to ask if you had to use your key to get in this morning."

"Yes, on both locks. The deadbolt and the one on the knob."

Clare drove home and pulled up as close as she could to the walk-out basement that housed her potter's studio. The cottage was built into the side of hill that sloped down to Amelia Bay. "It's lovely living in my gran's old home, but having an attached garage on days like this would be nice." The dogs bolted out of the Jeep and romped through the snow while Clare and Bev gingerly ran to the door in their stocking feet.

They peeled off their coats and wet socks. "I'd like a shower. All night on a plane…and just try to wash away the…" Bev balled up her hands, and her eyes filled with tears. The shivering overtook her again. Clare wrapped her in a hug, and they both wept.

The dogs scratched at the doors. They bounded in and shook snow all over the room as they raced around in circles. Clare grabbed some towels from her laundry room and smiled at their antics.

"Do you have any dry clothes in the laundry room?"

"Yep. There's some sweats and shirts stacked on the shelf." Clare had installed a shower in her laundry room to clean up after she worked on her pottery or came in from the garden.

"I'll start some breakfast. Pancakes?"

Bev nodded and went in to shower. Clare closed the french doors that led in from the yard and set the alarm before she headed upstairs to the kitchen.

Bacon sizzled in a pan and Clare ladled batter on the griddle of her new stainless steel Wolf range. Bev walked in and poured herself a cup of coffee. She wandered out to the greenhouse addition that replaced the rickety old deck.

"I feel like I'm still in Hawaii surrounded by all these tropical plants." She sat at the wicker table tucked in the corner and looked out to the bay. "Here we are in your new beautiful kitchen. It's as if that terrible scene we saw this morning never happened...but it did."

Clare carried plates heaped with food to the table. "I understand how you feel. I wish I knew who that young man was, and how he got in your office."

Bev looked away quickly, then reached for the butter and started slathering it on her pancakes.

"Bev Hawkins! You know who he is! You lied to Charlie."

Bev sucked in her lips and looked at Clare with her luminous brown opened eyes wide. Her lips popped out, and she said, "Not exactly. Not really."

Made in the USA
San Bernardino, CA
12 June 2018